JAMIE C★LLINS

THE Secrets & Stilettos SERIES

★

POP! Flash!

BOOKS BY
JAMIE COLLINS

★ ★ ★

To Michelle, my Bunny sister. True friendship never goes out of style. Cheers, gorgeous!
 ~ Mimi

PROLOGUE
★ ★ ★

GLOBAL STUDIOS / NEW YORK CITY
SEPTEMBER 4, 2015

AT EXACTLY FOUR THIRTY, A representative from the network phoned to announce that the photo session for the new daytime talk show *The Gab* would have to be postponed. The contact informed that Casey Singer, the youngest and most capricious of the cast members, was missing. Deemed a flight risk, she had last been seen just after signing onto the show at a gambol the evening prior, at film director Zeke Buchanan's premiere. There had been no word since. She hadn't shown up for makeup or wardrobe. Needless to say, corporate was furious.

The jittery junior editor for *High Style* magazine slammed her electronic tablet shut, fuming. "Goddamn prima donna! What does she think she's pulling? This will be my ass!" she ranted. "*My* ass!"

The pretty photographer she'd hired nimbly fussed with her camera settings, hoping to catch a few candid shots prior to the official shoot.

Kathryn walked into the studio already bracing herself.

Seeing the photographer, an immediate pang registered, causing a sudden pain tinged with gladness to sear through her body in all directions, though nothing registered on her stoic face. Instead, she took in a deep breath and stood still and silent, doing her best to ignore the fact that her heart felt as if it had just been stabbed with the business end of a stiletto.

CHAPTER 1

★ ★ ★

BATON ROUGE, LOUISIANA
JULY 1967

EVANGELINE DEL RAY SCREAMED BLOODY murder with each contraction that ripped through her abdomen, clutching so fast to the bedpost that her brown knuckles turned sheet-white. She had been drifting in and out of consciousness for nearly an hour.

She bore down, digging her ragged fingernails into Mercy's flesh.

"Hol' on, honey . . . jest a'lil bit longer, chile. Ain't no time for pushing, not jes' yet!"

Mercy was Evangeline's mother, and her one and only hope at the moment, as Ms. Eunice, the town midwife who had been summoned nearly half an hour earlier, had yet to arrive. Mercy was frantic, attempting to hold off nature by pushing back the baby's head, which was quickly crowning between her daughter's legs.

"Mama, help me! Please . . . get it out! Get it out!"

Evangeline dripped with sweat in the midday heat. At only seven months along, she was about to give premature birth at the tender age of sixteen. She plunged with all her strength at the searing pain that threatened to tear her body in half. She had to do it. She *had* to push. Convulsing grotesquely, she wailed in excruciating agony, bore down, and then, all at once, collapsed back onto the pillow limp and still as the bloody, blue fetus—now freed from its confinement—slid from her lifeless body.

"Evangeline!" Mercy shrieked, standing stupefied at the foot of the bed, staring at the mass of tissue and flesh. Moving quickly, she severed the cord with a paring knife and then bundled the infant tightly like a mummy. Emptying a nearby dresser drawer, she placed the child in it, certain that it was dead—and so deserved to be for what it had done.

Lowering herself atop the blood-soaked feather bed, she pulled Evangeline's body to her bosom, praying feverishly over her, moaning and rocking, begging for God to wake her little girl.

But it was too late. Evangeline was already gone.

Ms. Eunice burst through the door of the dim shanty house, alight with the full measure of noontide daylight mixed with the heavy lull of death's pallor. She was followed by Evangeline's little sister, Tully, who was five, and Charleen Del Ray, the girl's auntie. The two ran to Evangeline's bedside.

"Sweet Jesus! Lord, Ms. Mercy!" the midwife shrieked. "What happened?"

The woman had collapsed onto the corpse, her body racked with deep, silent sobs, relentlessly taken to beating her breast as tears spilled from her disbelieving eyes. She clutched Evangeline's limp hand to her face and cried, "Our Father who art in heaven . . ."

Tully tugged at her sister's nightgown with mounting distress. "Evangeline? Wake up! Evangeline!"

Ms. Eunice, who had driven all the way from Kenner, and who had assisted in well over thirty births in East Baton Rouge Parish alone, had never witnessed such a scene. She had to pry the hysterical little girl from the body, along with her mother, in order to assess the situation.

Mercy continued to wail to the heavens " . . . gives us this day, Lo'd our daily bread, as we forgive thems who trespass against us."

Ms. Eunice quickly surveyed the room . . . the blood-stained sheets, the fleshy cord trailing from Evangeline's body. "Where is it? Ms. Mercy? Where's the baby? She done birth'd that chil'd only minutes ago!" She seized the woman and shook her willowy frame like a birch reed. "What'n in God's good name have'n you done with it? Tell me!"

Mercy motioned weakly to the bureau with a defeated, blank gaze.

"My soul! You *didn't!*"

Searching frantically, she slammed the drawers open and shut, one by one, terrified of what she would find. There, in the third to the last, lay a newborn, facedown, in a tangle of blood-soaked rags. It was still and not breathing.

Lowering the baby to the floor, the midwife went to work, ripping open the wrappings. Charleen gasped, and everyone stopped their praying. Then she shot Mercy an incredulous look. Together, they all watched as Ms. Eunice blew frantically into the baby's mouth, pressing down over its little chest with two fingers over and over again, delivering short, quick thrusts until, gradually, its skin turned warm and strangely pink in color. With a rattle in its throat, it drew in a lungful of air, then choked and gasped before releasing a resounding cry.

Mercy buried her face in her hands, weeping all the harder. Not for sadness. Not lest of all, for joy. She would not so much as look at the creature, tiny, frail, and new, much to Ms. Eunice's disbelief. She had guessed by appearances the infant's father to be white. The child's skin and hair were too fair for negro heritage. It was a mulatto.

"It's a girl! An' she's perfect," Ms. Eunice said. "Evangeline has done given yern a gran-baby. Ms. Mercy, look! She's beautiful, she is!"

Mercy turned her gaze and backed away, returning to Evangeline's bedside. Charleen also turned away, now shielding young Tully's eyes in the folds of her dingy skirt.

Reading their empty hearts, Ms. Eunice scowled. "Heaven help ya'll. This here's yo *family*! Come on, then—take this sweet chile, I says."

Neither woman budged.

Mercy raised her head slowly, long enough to denounce the child as being no family of her own. "Take it to its folk. That no-good trash, calls hisself Buddy Delacorte. He'n done my Evangeline this way. Now he got blood on his hands! And on his family name too." She spat and it was so. Tears streamed down her sallow face, wetting her lips and chin. It was a mother's pained face, the timeworn mask of a life hard-lived that suggested an age far beyond her thirty-five years. "It's his bastard that took the sweet life breath from my baby!" She rose to her feet, her fist cutting circles in the air with a rage that shook her frail body as she sank to her knees. "Take it to him, I says! I'll kill it myself just as soon look at it, so helps me God!"

Ms. Eunice scooped up the swaddled child and evoked Charleen with pleading eyes. "Do you knows where this Buddy Delacorte lives, Miss Del Ray?"

Charleen shook her head despondently, stroking her niece's hair, not lifting her gaze from Evangeline's lifeless face.

"I knows where, Ms. Walker," Tully piped up, straining to see the tiny, wondrous bundle. "Sister's wit Jesus, now?"

"That's right, hon'. That's where she be. Can you please show me where'n this here baby's daddy be?"

The little girl nodded.

Buddy awoke to what sounded like a catfight about to

bust out just outside his bedroom window. He cursed and rolled over forgetfully, discovering that he wasn't alone. A rumpled figure lay next to him. Snoring. The curtains were drawn, but a sliver of bright morning sunlight had crested and broken through.

What day was it? Sunday? Or, was it Monday? He wondered fuzzily if he had to be at work. And exactly who was it he brought home last night? His thoughts were still decidedly pickled from the tequila. *Ahh . . . last night!* It was all coming back to him, slowly.

Hugh's Icehouse on Route Twenty was his favorite watering hole. *A game of shooters in the parking lot, or was it at the bar?* His balls decidedly ached, so he figured that the woman next to him could not possibly be Colette. He'd never have her again stone sober *or* dead-ass drunk. He remembered something of two town women. He had danced with the one from Jefferson. He had offered her a ride. He could barely remember the details, but the pounding in his head begged him to leave well enough alone. He staggered to the john and had a good pee. *Christ! But the air was stifling!* There wasn't a goddamn working fan in the house.

Making his way to the front, he checked the usual spots for his smokes. Nothing on the coffee table, on the counter, or on the window ledge, so he fished a half-decent butt out of the ashtray and steadied his hands to light it. The nicotine felt good mixing with what was left of the whiskey in his system. *Damn! It was hot!* Parting gauze-thin curtains, he peered out the window just off the kitchen panel of the house trailer, and scratched himself liberally. The clear blue sky and blaring Southern sun promised yet another scorching Louisiana summer day. A hell-fire furnace of a day, all right. Just like all the rest.

CHAPTER 2
★ ★ ★

TWO WEEKS AFTER MERCY DEL Ray buried her daughter in a potter's field just outside of the city, a mulatto infant with blue eyes was anonymously delivered to Buddy Delacorte's residence, coincidentally on the morning of his thirty-first birthday.

He could scarcely believe his eyes when he nearly tossed his duffle bag right on top of it—a strange basket placed just so onto the passenger seat of his pickup truck. He never kept the locks down or the windows up, so it would have been easy for someone to slip in during the night or at early dawn to make the delivery.

At first, he thought that it was a litter of pups or kittens that some kind-heart had left because he noticed right away that the basket seemed to be moving as if something was stirring inside. He was stupefied to find, tucked deep into the basket, a newborn— a Negro infant fast asleep in a binding of well-worn sheets.

"What the hell?" He stood, stunned and confused in the early morning sun. The truck was hot and smelled of a mix of oil and tar. A stash of soiled work clothes was baking on the floorboard. You could fry eggs on the fender of the cab. He swatted a june bug that coasted on the steamy air, landing threateningly just inches from the child's face near the edge of the basket. A hundred thoughts raced through his mind. *Who would just up and leave a kid?*

He thrust his hands deep into his dungarees and looked around for any sign of the child's mother. *What kind of crazy person would do this?* he wondered.

Could it have been the boys down at the tonk? Maybe they were playing a prank on him on account of this being his birthday? *That was it! A prank. It was just a joke!* He chuckled nervously and called for them to come out and show their sorry-ass faces.

"Hey, Rankin! You son-of-a-bitch! Gig's up! I ain't no baby's mama—come and get your nigger child, man. She looks just like you, ya ole dog!"

The air remained still. Even the trees stood silent and waiting, begging for a breeze. "C'mon on, guys . . . Kelsco! Tuck! Hey, I'm not shittin' man . . . gig's up!"

Five full minutes passed, and not a soul came out to claim responsibility for the prank. *This has got to be a mistake.* Buddy stiffened. Either that, or something very bad—like a kidnapping. Perhaps, it had been a *botched* kidnapping, and the culprits were just passing off the child because they changed their mind! Or, they had heard that the sheriff was on to them. That was it. He would drive the kid over to the sheriff's office and turn it in. He breathed a sigh of relief, mopping the sweat from his forehead with his grizzly forearm, wondering why on earth anyone would want to kidnap a nigger baby anyway.

Just then, he heard a stirring behind the house trailer. Someone had obviously been creeping around, watching him from a distance.

"Hey! Hey, you there!" he called out to the figure. It was a black woman wearing a cotton turban. She shot out from behind the trailer and padded away on bare feet across the grass embankment, disappearing into the woods, quick as lightning. She didn't stop. She didn't look back.

The child began to scream at the top of its lungs, a pow-erful, blood-curdling wail. Buddy contemplated running after the woman, but thought better of it. He was fighting a feeling of panic that was rising in his gut and up into his throat. *The turban. It seemed so, familiar.*

He opened the passenger door and stared stupidly at the screaming child. It wailed heartily for someone to abate the hunger pangs that racked its little body. Frantically, Buddy searched the basket for supplies. The turban-woman had apparently left next to nothing. The only items to be found left alongside the child were three cotton diapers, a weathered Bible, and a cheap silver bracelet with a sin-gle tin charm in the shape of a horse. Buddy immediately recognized it as belonging to Evangeline Del Ray—the colored girl from the river bend shanties whom he had known. That was it! The woman with the turban was one of them. A river shanty nigger come to bring him some-body's child. But *why?*

A distressing realization suddenly seized him. "Christ, it's not . . ."

He offered the near-empty bottle to the child for suck-ing. He held it steady with one hand and examined the Bible with the other. It, too, was Evangeline's. Tucked just inside the binding was a torn piece of newsprint. It was Evangeline's obituary, dated July 17th, 1967. But more dis-turbingly than this, scrawled crudely in lead on the inside cover of the Bible, a *new* name was recorded just beneath hers. It read: *Kathryn Wanda Delacorte . . . born July seven-teenth, 1967.*

CHAPTER 3
★ ★ ★

"WHAT ARE YA GONNA DO, Delacorte? Ain't ever day a man gets handed his own flesh and blood child in a handbasket!"

Everyone laughed.

Kelso dropped two coins into the jukebox, and soon the smooth-as-silk vocals of Patsy Cline were drifting across the smoky air of Hugh's Icehouse, making Buddy forget about things like birthdays and babies. He couldn't believe his goddamn luck. A hundred lays in a year, and he had to go sticking his dick into the fire. Real fire. He had no business, he had told Tucker earlier in a moment of candor, no business at all, getting involved with the black girl.

"Ain't no matter anyhow," Tucker explained. "How she come to be underage an' knocked-up and all. Hell, ain't no fault of yours they's all whores over there—the whole lot of 'em, prancin' around like they do, learnin' the trade early on from they whore mamas on how's to catch the white boys. Poor river shanty niggers is all they are and all they ever gonna be!"

The group collectively nodded and clicked their beer glasses in agreement.

"Don't take it so hard," Kelsco contended, slapping his

old friend squarely on the back. "Women and childbirth don't always agree. See? What I'm sayin' is, it ain't your fault that she died is all."

"That's right, Delacorte, ain't no way you'll be takin' the rap for puttin' that girl in the grave. Hell no! Jus fo' puttin' her in a *family way*!" Kelsco couldn't resist. They were cut-ups, every last one of them.

Everyone howled. Especially Buddy. But inside he was scared. Real scared. What was he going to do now? There was no way that anyone could *prove* that he was the father of the mulatto child. The state of Louisiana, although not particularly concerned about the plight of poor nigger girls in the Plank Road river shanties, would not take kindly to learning that a respectable citizen like Buddy Delacorte, of the respected lineage of the reputed famed New Orleans Delacortes was responsible. But then again, so what that he found his pleasure in dipping his pen in the ink of poor-stricken river shanty nigger girls who frolicked free and easy in the sun and exchanged sexual favors for two-bit trinkets and loose change?

He decided to take the child over to Colette's for safe-keeping. Having never been a mother in her own right did not factor in when it came to Colette's nurturing abilities. The girl had a knack for fixing what was broke—almost anything, he was fond of saying.

"She lit up like a goddamn Christmas tree when she first saw it," Buddy had bragged to Tucker the next day while dropping the last of the cement casings onto the bed of his pickup. The day was early yet, and already the merciless sun was making its presence known with intensity as it prepared to bake them like cookie dough to the newly laid blacktop that unfurled before them.

Slipping heavy work gloves over his chapped hands in order to handle the boilers, he mixed hot tar for the next two and a half hours before getting his first break.

At a time when jobs in Louisiana were hard to come by, all that Buddy could do was think about getting out. Doing anything else other than tarring endless miles of interstate and hauling gravel. Highway work was grueling, and as far as Buddy was concerned, the thought of moving on and getting out onto the open road was the dream that kept him going. Hell, it was the only thing that got him out of bed at all.

"Nobody's gonna get in the way of what I got in mind to do. Come early fall, I'm doin' it, Tuck," Buddy proclaimed between bites of cold chicken from a tin pail wedged between his dungarees as they sat on the tailgate of his truck. "I'll be rollin' my way crost Virginia no sooner than ya'll can say Sayonara Sam! I'm a gonna drive highway interstates 'stead of pavin' 'em. Dooley got me set up with an outfit out of Sulphur that makes runs up from Detroit City hauling automobiles. A goddamn *legitimate* job!"

"How in the hell did he manage that?"

Buddy spat. "Someone done left or up and died or something I guess. No matter to me, 'cept to say that the job is mine. Alls I gotta do is show up when he calls. Should be early September, I reckon."

Tucker seemed to envy Buddy. Things always managed to work out for him. He had always said that Buddy Delacorte could fall into a pile of horse shit and come out smelling like posies. So it was his pleasure to point out the obvious. "What about the kid? Don't reckon you'll take her wit' you?"

Buddy shook his head, indicating that he didn't guess he would.

CHAPTER 4
★ ★ ★

COLETTE KEPT THE CHILD FOR three days, as promised. Just until the weekend when she had to get back to work. That was the arrangement. It was Friday night, and she would have to be at the restaurant by nine or Hugh would give all her tables over to the other girls. It was the end of the month, and things were tight enough as it was. Buddy showed up at eight forty-five with an open bottle of Thunderbird and a red rose. He was drunk.

"Goddammit, Buddy Delacorte. I done tol' you to be here an hour ago," Colette called from the porch as Buddy stumbled up the steps. He stood on unsteadily legs, arms akimbo, splashing the bourbon all over himself.

"Do ya see how much I—I mean, *we*, need ya, baby?" It wasn't a question that merited an answer, so she just shot him a spiteful glare.

"I don't reckon you need much of anything, Buddy, 'cept what you pour down your throat. And I'll thank you not to bring that liquor into my house or anywhere's near your daughter."

She disappeared behind the screen door, with Buddy following close behind.

Colette placed the child into a makeshift crib fashioned

from a laundry basket and some sheets. She handed Buddy the baby's bottle. "Feed her in about an hour. First, check it, but be careful—not too warm, else you'll burn her, Lord help you. Measure halfway down what she drinks, and then gently burp her upright, like so." She demonstrated on her shoulder with a dishtowel.

He followed Colette into the kitchen. "Water's on the stove. She'll need to be seen by Doc Drummond. It appears that she's got the croup. I suggest that you drive into town first thing on Monday morning—are you getting all of this, Buddy Delacorte?"

He nodded, thinking all the while that Colette never looked more beautiful.

Colette Cadieux and Buddy had been schoolmates ever since the first grade, where he used to pleasure in gluing her pencils together and swiping her books. By the fifth grade, she had grown tall enough to defend herself from his lovesick antics, and was then able to ward him off until high school, when his attentions turned decidedly exciting and she gave herself to him in the gazebo of his mother's garden beneath a summer moon.

Colette was born in New Orleans and never had ventured farther than Central Texas her entire life. She was simple, reliable, and while not particularly glamorous, she possessed an earthy radiance. Plus, she had a heart of gold. She had the type of soul reserved for martyrs and Peace Corps missionaries.

Following high school, Colette went to work in a secretary pool for a downtown department store that sold garden hoses and women's hosiery. She later picked up a waitress job at a local diner and supplemented her part-time salary with steady tips.

Buddy and Colette dated on and off for several years, but eventually had a falling out when Colette pressed him to get married, causing Buddy to run in the opposite direction. It was not until several years later that Buddy feared that he might have made the biggest mistake of his life.

It was Colette who bailed him out. She loaned him the money to pay his bookie and made arrangements with the bill collectors who hounded him mercilessly for extensions on the debts he owed. But that was as far as her generosity went. She had been dating Lenny for nearly a year by then, and marriage was imminent. She was just grateful to know that Buddy had escaped a far worse fate working in illegal dealings. He had since been given a chance to start over, and she was glad that she could be of help. Somehow, it always seemed that he would need her, and knowing that made her feel strangely glad.

He had taken a legitimate job with the state, laying blacktop for minimum wage, and was happy to have it. Things were looking up for Buddy, so it seemed. He needed only to stay straight and sober long enough to focus on a future. He deserved that.

Colette worked part-time at the Roadhouse, where Buddy would often hang out with his work buddies, playing pool for beers, and kickin' up trouble at least once a week. But, fortunately for Buddy, the days of squander and excess were long gone. He was living clean once again and trying to fly straight. She was proud of him. Earlier that spring, Buddy had managed to save enough money to finally pay Colette back in full. Everything was looking bright for Buddy's new and hard-bought future—at least it did until three months later, when little Kathryn showed up on a hazy Louisiana morning and threw another curve ball into Buddy's plans.

Colette was an angel for letting them stay on with her until he could figure out what to do next. She truly was an angel—once his very own angel, but that was a long time ago. Now, she was promised to another, and there wasn't a goddamn thing he could do about it. Lucky for him that she didn't turn him away when he showed up at her door with the baby.

"They say it's mine, and well, considering things as they was, I ain't got a way of proving it ain't any different."

She had taken one look at the infant and knew it to be true. "She's got your eyes, all right. What a precious little one she is."

Colette took to the infant immediately. A phenomenon that Buddy hoped heartily for, though he scarcely understood the why of it. She wasn't entirely cold-hearted, although she had once swore him off forever after he broke her trust in a way that she said could never be forgiven. But that was all water under the bridge now. At least for him.

Luckily, she could find it in her heart to do him this favor. She seemed happy to help. But now there was Lenny—her new beau—and they were going to be happy. She had said that she had earned the right to finally find true happiness, and everything about her new fiancé seemed to confirm that such happiness would be with a man like Lenny. He seemed decent enough. He was Colette's future now.

"Only for a few days," Colette had said. "Lenny's comin' home on Sunday, and so help me God, you'd better be gone by the time he rolls into Louisiana." There was no chance that she could help him out after that. Maybe not ever again.

Buddy was nothing short of indebted. Indebted and undeniably in love with her—still. But that was his problem. Colette was the one and only woman he ever truly loved. She most certainly had the biggest heart Buddy had ever known in a woman, except for his mama.

Colette arranged all the particular things a baby would need for raising and wrote down special notes on index cards about what he should do to keep the baby fed, dry, and clean. She spent his cash and some of her own to buy little T-shirts and new cloth diapers with silver pins, ointments, and powder and bottles.

"This here's where the umbilical cord was cut. Don't worry, it will fall off later and heal up. Keep it clean and dry. Be careful to hold her head when you lift her. She likes to be held close when you are feeding her." The instructions went on forever.

Colette returned home after midnight. Buddy was sitting quietly in the moonlight, on the front porch, smoking and thinking. The notecards she had written were strewn on the coffee table. She tossed a paper sack filled with Hugh's hamburgers and french-fried potatoes she had brought from the restaurant, along with two ice-cold bottles of Pepsi cola. The food smelled heavenly wafting from the bag.

"How is she?"

"Sleeping, *now.*"

Colette smiled. "Did she fuss much?"

Buddy shrugged. "Reckon she knows the difference 'tween women and men. I think she wants her mama."

Colette pulled a greasy hamburger from the sack and took a generous bite. She was famished. "So you picked her up and held her like I showed ya?"

Buddy stared at the paint chipping away from the hand-rail. "Yeah, I did some."

"Ain't ya hungry?"

"Naw."

"Look, don't you go worrying and all now, Buddy. Everything is going to be just fine. I know it. But not the way you think. It never is."

He sat there smoking. He didn't know what to say. He never knew what to say around Colette, so he just said nothing.

This was his one last chance, and he knew it. All he could do was stare off into the blackness, mesmerized by the distant drone of the crickets rising from the swamp grass and the amazing peaceful pull of the moon, calling to him somewhere deep in his soul, *daring* him to run.

"Ya just can't close your eyes and pretend it ain't happening. Not this time."

Was she talking about *them,* or the baby? He wasn't sure. He winced and shuffled through his pockets, extracting a pack of Lucky Strikes. "Want one?" he asked.

She took a cigarette from the crumpled pack.

He struck the match, and she bent forward over the flame. Her honey blonde hair swept across his arm and made him tingle.

"So, now you smoke?" Buddy grinned, kicking his feet out in front of him, reclining back on his elbows. "You never did before."

Colette took a long, satisfying drag, letting the smoke tickle the back of her throat before releasing it in a slow stream. The gesture made her seem strangely free. He envied her.

He closed his eyes and tossed his head back and regarded the stars in the black Southern sky. He was still young at heart, wasn't he? Full of a hell fire that no woman could ever really understand or ever hope to tame. Even she had to know this well. After all, she had loved him, once.

The peaceful glow of the bayou moon threatened to make him reveal more than just minor regrets and confessions. He thought better than to give in to his desire to kiss her right then and there and to take what was not his anymore. For one brief moment, he thought that maybe he could. Memories were stirring up fast, but her cool indifference told him otherwise. He had decided it was better to leave the past buried in the graveyards of the past, once and for all. Things *had* changed. But could he roll with the punches this time?

"I reckon' I'll be gettin' off to bed, then," Colette said. She took her time standing up, first stepping out of her sandals, and then unfastening the first three buttons on her blouse. He sensed that she felt him staring, as her cheeks flushed. He looked away.

She paused and then gathered up the leftover food into the sack and quickly slid behind the screen door, back into the house. An eternity passed and at long last, she sighed.

"Well, ain't ya comin'?" she finally said, holding open the screen door. She had decided to give in, after all, one last time to lay bare her heart without regard to reason. One last time, she would remind him of what he had lost. He would have the rest of his life to remember, and hundreds of miles between them at last. *One last night.* Then, he would be gone before daybreak, well before she would awake to regret it. This time, it would be him who would keep his promise.

CHAPTER 5

★ ★ ★

BATON ROUGE, LOUISIANA
1955

JUST FOUR MONTHS AFTER HIS discharge from the army, Buddy had hooked up with an ex-con named Vernon Tarot, in the spring of 1955. Vern had a chronic nervous condition that made his left eye twitch from time to time, which made him appear to be just edgy enough to be considered cool. He was also an incorrigible flirt, a real Casanova of sorts with the ladies. He carried a thick bankroll at all times and flashed fifties and hundreds under everyone's nose like they were going out of style.

Buddy had met Vern on a barstool at the Roadhouse, where Vern was a regular. It eventually became a Thursday night ritual of whiskey, hound dogging, and a little friendly pool hustling with anyone foolish enough to take them on.

Eventually, Buddy drew up the nerve to ask his new friend the obvious question. "Where ya gettin' all this cabbage you're always doling out? You got a printing press or something?"

Vern had counted out the wad of crisp fifties on the bar. He was hoping that Buddy would trust him enough by then to consider working for him on the side. Most guys like Buddy were always on the make for scoring the fast cash, and Delacorte was drooling like a Blue Tick at a biscuit bake off. Sure, he could cut him into a little piece of the action. He trusted the guy. There was something in Buddy's manner that Vern felt he could trust. There was something behind those old-soul eyes and rugged jaw. He had a good sense for guys like that.

Vern had been nefarious for his less-than-reputable associations, and if ever there'd ever been good action to be had in town, he was certainly the man to find it. Surely Buddy knew this. Vern was a dealer and a pusher, and he was certain that Buddy would be interested in learning from the best. They all were.

"You earn that doin' county work?" Buddy had asked, baiting him.

"Naw," Vern said, removing a toothpick to spit. "From the kind of work that won't sweat your back, if'n ya know what I mean." Vern twitched. He leaned forward with a cheek full of chew and watched it hit its mark on the sticky wood floor, leaving a trail of brown liquid in his scraggly goatee.

Buddy nodded, indicating that he wanted to know more.

"It's not fo' jus anyone. I mean, not ever Joe kin do this kind of thing . . . takes a crazy *som*-bitch like me." His laugh rattled loosely in his chest, causing him to gasp and choke momentarily before catching his breath. Vern was not exactly the picture of perfect health. He was an anemic one hundred twenty pounds, was well over six feet, and was built like a scarecrow. He had deep-pocked skin, an ugly scar on his right cheek, and was missing an incisor on the left of his crooked, shit-eating grin. Vernon Tarot was not in the least an attractive specimen, but there were always women who didn't seem to care and were happy to help him spend his money just the same. Vern could be found most every Saturday night on the Quarter, escorted by New Orleans's choicest hookers, one on each bony arm—*the genuine articles,* he would say—swarming all over him like honey bees.

Vern's one good eye was bloodshot, and by anyone's guess, it was obvious that he was somehow managing on "artificial means" and whiskey. His hair was a dirty brown, long on his neck, and plastered slick behind his ears. Affixed to his Levis was an enormous belt buckle with an emblem of an eagle that matched the tattoo on his left forearm. He and his reptile cowboy boots had seen better days, for sure. He looked like a fifty-year-old rodeo clown. Truth being, he was only thirty-seven.

"I heard you done hard time in Leavenworth. That true?" Buddy had asked.

Vern bit the filter off a Camel, lit it, and sucked the poison deep into his corroded lungs.

"Yep. Did ten-in-five at Alcatraz too. Not many folks know it, he bragged.

Buddy had tried to sound matter-of-fact. "What was it like?"

Vern snorted and looked away at the two hookers at the end of the bar, who were falling all over two out-of-towners who were drunk as loons.

The barkeep placed a bottle of Jack Daniels and two small shot glasses on the bar in front of them. They each helped themselves.

"If'n I tole, you wouldn't believe me. Alcatraz makes Leavenworth look like a fuckin' amusement park. But don't you worry none, cause if'n ya ever get caught, it ain't likely that they put you there, being that it would be a first offense and all." He further interrogated his prospect, "You like adventure? Travel? Intrigue? Well, we got all that by the shitload . . . only no fuckin' medical plan. Gotta go to Louisiana Steel for that!" Vern snorted. "So be real with me, Bud, you want *in*?"

Buddy stiffened and reached for another shot and the

relief of the whiskey's potion. He did not correct Vern for calling him, Bud. Not when he was on the verge of cutting him in on some action. He simply nodded and threw back a quick double, sealing the loose but binding agreement the two had just exchanged. The deal was closed. It was as simple as that.

By the summer's end, Buddy had been working for Vernon Tarot as a full-time runner. Buddy was too smart to get caught, too quick, and too damn lucky for that. Except for forgetting that it was a real bad luck that got him into his current unfavorable predicament in the first place. What he needed was cash—a lot of it. And he needed it fast. He had lost every dime he had in two months' time in a run of lost bets. You name it, Buddy played it: dice, cards, ponies, baseball, semi-pro fights—he loved the fights most of all, *too much*. That was why he was currently hiding out from his bookie, Crazy Jimmie, who did not take kindly to IOUs and who was presently threatening to have one of his goons work him over for the overdue loans Buddy had owed for eighteen months running. Jimmie wanted every cent back. Interest was mounting, and his patience running short. He would settle for payment any way he could get it, even if it was paid in broken bones.

At only nineteen, Buddy was already several thousand dollars in debt without a prayer, and with a growing gambling habit that threatened to render him penniless by the time he reached twenty-one.

Buddy did "runs" for Vern, mainly transporting parcels over the state line into Memphis and on up to Chicago over the next several months. He never asked questions, and he never refused the work when he would get a late-night call to meet a contact south of the train tracks for the exchange of a map and several small tightly bound paper parcels, which he was instructed to stuff discreetly into his boxers. Then, he would drive all night northward into Mississippi to make the drop-off, and return to the city by dawn. He sometimes did this six to ten times a month.

Once, when Buddy's old pickup truck died cold just before a big run, Vern and he stole a car from a church parking lot in Bridge City by hot-wiring the starter beneath the dashboard, and they were back in business sooner than you could say, Amen! It was a Century convertible. Buddy switched out the plates and repainted the body, hanging a set of large dice and a strand of Mardi Gras beads from the rearview mirror to christen his new ride, believing himself to be living the good life in high style.

On occasion, Vern would require Buddy to be on hand to serve as a lookout on one of his quick trips to Arkansas or Texas. All he had to do was sit waiting in the dark behind the wheel, at the ready to transport Vern and his accomplices from the scene of a swift and flawless "lift." Vern robbed people, and he was good at it. Always by night, mostly homes and businesses of wealthy folks Vern said were deserving of being relieved of their excess affluence.

It did not take long before Buddy was heading for bigger trouble, as he was gambling more frequently and for much higher stakes. He began experimenting with the drugs that he and Vern moved across state lines. Amphetamines mostly used by over-the-road truckers and student athletes, as well as a new "truth drug" called LSD sold mostly to the biker set. He started experimenting first with sundry narcotics and marijuana, and eventually, graduated to cocaine. His newfound habit soon rendered him dependent, requiring him to use the majority of the side money he would make just to support his addiction.

Buddy had soon became Vern's biggest customer, and eventually worked solely for the dope, which ultimately began robbing him little by little of the pathetic life he was living.

Forced to take a job at the refinery by day, Buddy ran drugs for Vern at night, sometimes three to four times per week. He stayed wired on coke and barbiturates which, enabled him to continue on his erratic schedule at first, functioning on little to no sleep most of the time. This cycle continued for four months, until Buddy's dependence on the drugs and his mounting gambling debts and spending plunged him deeper into the decline. He was eventually let go from the refinery, to nobody's surprise. Not least of all his.

To make matters worse, when Buddy could no longer count on the frequent runs to Missouri or Arkansas to make the deals, he had taken to stealing from the parcels, helping himself to the stuff, claiming that the suppliers were short-changing their end buyers anyway. Of course, Vern had been aware that Buddy was stealing from him, but cared little, as long as he made his cut. After all, he was not the only patsy Vern had driving over the state lines for him. Most all of his runners were strung out on the stuff.

When the runs became fewer, it became imperative for Buddy to find a way to make some quick cash. That's when he convinced Vern to school him in the fine art of armed robbery. Armed robbery was serious business and required greater skill and attention, as there was always the risk of being caught or making a mistake. Buddy was careful never to get sloppy, because for him, prison time was not an option. Vern taught him all he needed to know about how to take care of himself while taking care of the job. The first time Buddy held a revolver was exhilarating; the first time he used it to make a man do whatever he said for fear of his very life, he was hooked on the rush.

Buddy felt invincible at the command of a trigger that would make people jump when he directed, hand over their possessions, shit their pants, beg him for their life. "It is better than sex," Buddy testified, stroking the barrel of a Smith & Wesson on loan from Vern's arsenal. The beauty proved to be an unfailing perpetual hard-on, which Buddy enjoyed waving around.

Together, they held up a filling station just outside of Jackson, hooting and hollering all the way back to Louisiana, high on speed, with a sack full of US currency, tossing an armload of moon pie wrappers in their wake, which soon became their trademark. From that point on, they took to referring to themselves as the "Moon Pie Mongrels of Mississippi." It was crazy-easy to dupe unsuspecting country folk who bowed to the business end of a .44 Magnum shoved in their face. They were two kings of the road, all right; kings on a highway leading straight to hell.

CHAPTER 6

★ ★ ★

1958

VERN HAD FINALLY HAD ENOUGH of the stinking swampland sauna of the South and eventually decided to up and move to Colorado in 1958. He had heard of an opportunity in Boulder with an outfit that printed counterfeit bank bonds. He had considered letting Buddy in on it, but then thought better of it. The kid was hocked up on a fast lane to destruction, and he saw no need for dragging his junkie ass with him.

Before leaving, as a favor of sorts, Vern decided to let Buddy in on one last take he was planning on pulling down by introducing him to a guy who could set them up with a quick job that would pay big. Vern figured that maybe it would help Buddy to settle his debts, or to straight out disappear. Whichever didn't matter to him either way. Loyalty was loose as pig shit when it came to survival. All he knew was that he needed the extra body, and Buddy was his man.

Vern had arranged for them to meet up at a small lodge out off Highway 10 on the way to Beaumont, just a few miles outside of town. It was called Hugh's Icehouse and it was famous for Texas-style slaw burgers.

"Who's this guy I gotta see? What's he got going down?" Buddy drawled into a crackling phone line in a booth on the corner west of the general store.

"Don't be stupid. No questions. Just be there like I said— and make damn sure you're alone."

Buddy was anxious. He was not at all happy to have recently learned that Vern was bailing on him. He had heard it through the honkytonk grape vine. He had needs, and it would be important to do whatever was necessary to keep the leather-head goons from Crazy Jimmie's outfit at bay for as long as possible. If he could, he would consider leaving town as well, going with Vern—if he would have him. The gambling debts were nearly paid by now, and Buddy could, for the first time in years, see the light at the end of the tunnel. Just a few more jobs and he could walk away form it all a free man and move on with his life. Make a real run at a normal life. Maybe then he could get clean again and settle down—set things right with his family. Certainly this one job could be all he would need. He could only hope.

At Hugh's Icehouse, Vern had motioned Buddy over to an empty booth, and the two slid in on either side of the well-worn Formica. A gorgeous brunette with eyes like Natalie Wood floated into view, balancing a load of dirty glasses and half-empty beer bottles on a tray like a pro. An orange apron encircled her narrow waist, accentuating curvy hips and a full bosom protruding prominently beneath a low-cut blouse. Hugh liked to keep all his waitresses in uniform. It made the right impression.

Buddy gaped, watching her pass by.

Vern was his jittery self, clasping and wringing his hands atop the table like he had no idea what to do with them. His left eye was twitching up a storm. Just talking about the Loretto family, as he was about to do, unnerved him.

The attractive waitress approached their table and bent forward, issuing them each a cocktail napkin and a smile. Her fingernails were short and neat, but painted fire-engine red, same as her lips.

"Hi. Will ya'll be want'n dinner, or are you just drinkin' tonight?"

Buddy smiled his best shit-eatin' grin, as he liked to call it, and moved closer on the edge of the booth to better see her nametag. It read, Misty.

"Why, thank you, kindly there. I reckon' we'll jus' be having a couple of cold Schlitzes and two of them hamburgers folks is always braggin' about."

His eyes beheld her breasts, now in full view.

She caught him in the act and seemed amused with the character that fancied himself to be James Dean or some such sort. "What's your name, cowboy?" she asked, coolly staring both he and Vern down as she waited.

"I'm Buddy, ma'am. Pleased as pie to make your acquaintance. This here's my friend, Vern."

He loved the ones with style, and she was a looker, all right. However, the dangling dance hall earrings and glitzy wrist full of dime-store bracelets seemed overkill. It made her look like Merry Christmas and Happy Birthday all wrapped up into one. No matter, he was already imagining the things he would like to do with a woman like her.

"Well, hello there, Buddy and friend Vern." The girl shot them a little laugh. Then, she slinked from view, leaving a trail of cheap fragrance in her wake. Buddy decided that she smelled of rose blossoms and honeysuckle combined. His eyes followed her irreverently clear across to the opposite side of the room.

"Oh, me! But that one's a looker!"

Vern was annoyed. "Hey, Romeo. You ain't never seen a broad before?"

Buddy ignored the implication. "Hey—ya think she'd go out with me?"

"I think ya oughtta quit lettin' your dick do your thinkin' fo' you, that's what I think. No names, man—ever. Rule number one. You best listen carefully to what I come here to tell you—unless you're more interested in scorin' bikini burger than gettin' in on a real deal. Plenty of time for gettin' your fair share of *that* later—it's entirely up to you, son."

"Yeah, sure. I'm interested." Buddy ran a shaky hand through his tussled pompadour with a single sweep, arranging it to perfection. "What'd ya got?"

"This guy, Otto Serrate," Vern began, spewing the facts in staccato rhythm, keeping his juddering voice to the lowest of tones, making Buddy lean forward to hear him. "I know him from the pen back in Leavenworth. We served time together. I saved the bastard's life once, a favor you don't easily forget. We were taking a small grocery in Montgomery, and right in the middle of things, the store owner's wife comes barreling out of the back of the store a hollerin' and a hissin' hell fire right before she shoots Otto with a hunting rifle—right in the goddamn leg, missin' his freakin' knob by a hair. It was me who saw to it he got medical attention, see? Only not at the county clinic or nothin'. He told me to take him instead to an *I-talian* doc up in Jackson, who fixed him up. No problems. No questions. I was happy to do it, for Christ sakes—we were once cell mates."

Vern leaned forward. He was fidgeting around so much that Buddy didn't know which eye to follow. "Turns out, Otto's got ties to several connections in the Loretto family—get me? Don't ask me how. Said if I ever needed anything at all . . . *anything*, to call—jus' like that and it would be goddamn done. He's runnin' a ring out of a restaurant in Miami these days. I hear Otto's lookin' for a couple of discreet boys to help him out on a job down here. I'm in for sure, but now I come to hear that he needs a couple more cowboys, so naturally, I thought of you."

Buddy nodded.

"If you should decide to do it, think carefully. These guys are fuckin' big league. Do you hear? They don't fuck around, and they don't do anyone favors, like yours truly." He sat back as if spent by the exertion of his own words, and stared Buddy down. "Otto will see you. I can make the arrangements. The rest would be up to you."

Buddy extended his hand, and he and Vern shook on it. What choice did he have? "Yeah," Buddy blurted. "I'm in."

Vern grabbed a napkin and wrote down an address for a motel and bar located in South Miami, and shoved it across the table. "This here's where you need to go to meet him. You're doin' this one alone," Vern announced, rising up on his lanky scarecrow legs. "Don't ask me any more questions. Forget you know me."

Then he just walked off and left Buddy there in the booth. It was the last time Buddy would see Vernon Tarot until the day the deal would go down.

The attractive waitress returned with their order and the check. She also delivered a small, folded slip of paper with the order of beer and burgers. The note was marked with a lipstick imprint on the outside. Inside, her phone number was inked with a tiny heart over the "*i*" in Misty.

Buddy stared at the note for a moment. Cheap and easy was a dime a dozen, but nothing compared to the real thing. Not in the least. Nevertheless, he shoved the note into his jeans pocket just in case. One never knew, he thought.

The very next day, Buddy was on a plane to Miami.

CHAPTER 7

★ ★ ★

MIAMI. FLORIDA
1958

THE MOTEL WAS A DUMP, as was evidenced by the absence of cars in the poorly maintained parking lot. The ride from the airport had been brief, and he did not make small talk with the driver. Buddy had the cabby drop him off at the corner, just in case anyone might be thinking about ever asking any questions.

The Palmetto Arms sloped decidedly to one side, which made it seem as if it had been once shifted on its foundation by a quake and left that way. The marquee stood silent and dark against the stark blue sky, announcing vacancy. The tired units were all walk-ups with large, hand-painted numbers above the doorways and heavily curtained windows framed on either side with green and white shutters.

Buddy checked in under an assumed name and was handed a key to room number seventeen, which sat back, farthest away from the motel's office. It was sweltering hot. White cement gravel sizzled like coals in the glaring heat.

A blast of stale, musty air hit him hard as he cracked open the door, slipping quietly inside, unnoticed. There was nothing to greet him except for a few black spiders in the bathroom sink and the stench of sweat and urine clinging to the dirty walls and soiled carpeting, along with a contingency of unspoken ghosts from decades of unspoken sins within its thin walls. He had been summoned to wait there in the stink and the squalor in the total and complete obscurity of the run-down roadside motel, where vagabonds and those with lesser virtues found cover for the night.

He fiddled with the portable fan and then stripped down to his briefs, removing the questionable bedspread and flopping down onto the lumpy mattress. The whir of the fan's motor muffled the drone of traffic passing along the nearby interstate just outside the door. It was eleven a.m. He opened a fresh pack of smokes and decided to wait for what would come next.

Otto Serati loved getting head, especially from Mercedes Morales. He often thought that she could suck the chrome clean off a bumper, and probably would, too, if asked. He felt like a king, especially whenever a broad was going down on him. Even with a stubby cock like his, watching women suck on him hungrily was the biggest turn-on imaginable, except for when there were two broads doing the deed both at the same time, taking turns with the royal cock and stirring themselves up into a creamy frenzy. Now *that* was the ultimate!

Otto needed sex, and he needed it frequently. One way or another, if he did not get off at least once a day, he would go crazy. That made life with Otto Serati close to impossible to predict. One learned never to talk about a deal with him until well after ten a.m., after he had his morning feast of eggs and salsa, fried bacon, and burnt toast, right after his morning rub-down by his personal domestic Mercedes, who would "finish him off," so to speak, with superb oral gratification techniques, while her mother, Consuella, cooked up his breakfast and looked the other way. The arrangement worked out well, as both women were assured continued employment in the Serati household so long as Otto was kept happy and the help all minded their own goddamn business.

Mercedes was a feisty little nymph, barely nineteen years old, with a fascination for his impressive gun collection and minuscule cock. A phenomenon that Otto found conveniently to his advantage. Besides, Mercedes' mother, Consuella, was a terrific cook, and more than anything, Otto loved to eat. Everyone knew how hard it was finding decent help among the hordes of Hispanics who pawned their services cheap for passage and freedom.

Otto, being a man of generous tendencies, had even on occasion, promised the Moraleses the possibility of hiring on a second daughter, Estella, who remained back in Cuba. "Maybe in the fall," he would faintly elude, when business would be picking up and he would require the need for three housemaids. *Maybe* was the empty half-promise that kept them eager to stay on for a pauper's wages and a victim's ransom.

He shook and spasmed, making three quick guttural sounds in succession, followed by a deep full-body sigh that signaled to her that the master of "cock kingdom" was finished. She released her hold on his tiny member and scampered off to the bathroom quickly to spit his tawdry load into the sink. She fetched a damp cloth and hurried back into position at the edge of the bed to see if he would require anything further, dabbing at his shriveled genitals, which had retracted to mere nubs beneath his massive gut.

Oddly, Otto had only one testicle, which made the whole package a rather pitiful lot.

Sometimes it was good enough to warrant a second round. She had a real talent for making him horny with her little moves. Most of the time, though, he would just release her, issuing her back to her household duties until the next time he wanted her again. She knew better anyway than to ever refuse.

By noon, Otto Serati was shaved, showered, and dressed to kill—ready for another day of business as usual.

He slipped into his finely appointed Buick Roadmaster, backing it gingerly out of the driveway onto the street. As if on cue, the tinny radio blasted a Sinatra tune as he sped off. Turning off the Florida Turnpike, he decided to take the scenic route past Bal Harbour, feeling the sunshine on his face, and letting his thoughts drift along, carefree, with the wind.

He drove the extra distance to the shore, where he pulled over near the dock. There she was, *The Conquistador*, bobbing majestically on the jeweled water. She was a beauty, all right. From stern to bow, the glistening seventy-five-foot yacht would be yet another testament of his accomplishment and prowess in this world. Making money the old-fashioned way was for peasants. Otto Serati was way too smart and savvy for that. He found ways to make money come to *him*! He was just a few short months away from buying her, and fulfilling his dream of sailing free on the glistening sea.

CHAPTER 8

★ ★ ★

OTTO ENTERED THROUGH THE BACK door of the restaurant, as usual, just off the kitchen, where first thing, he would stop by and have a few words with Mario, the sous chef, and then with Francois, the head chef. It was Francois's kitchen, and he ran it like a tight ship. Otto would next work his way over to the maître de, Armand, to go over the evening's reservations. He was always interested in checking the names, keeping track of how the evening would shape up. He had to be well prepared and careful never to make a dignitary or VIP wait any longer than absolutely necessary for a choice table. Even if it meant that other patrons with legitimate reservations had to wait. People loved to clamor for a table at The Grotto. It was *the* place to be seen.

As the manager, Otto kept a close watch on the comings and goings in both the front and the back of the house. From the day he was given the charge of being sole proprietor of the restaurant, it was for him, truly a day of great honor. It also marked the day his biggest troubles began.

The Grotto had quickly come to be a major source of strife and headache for him—a major hemorrhoid in the proverbial ass. But who could refuse the generosities of Victor Fortunato? His trusted and revered friend of so many years. At the same time, it wasn't so bad, Otto reasoned, because the arrangement afforded him much-needed sustenance to buy into a couple of clubs of his own and a few well-deserved toys, like yachts and fancy sports cars.

As general manger, Otto had been skimming off the books for more than a year. Sure, Victor offered Otto the opportunity to buy the business from him someday, and he would indeed. Only Victor Fortunato had no idea that Otto planned on doing so using funds acquired from his very own coffers. The arrangement worked out so well, in fact, that Otto managed to steal enough to buy into two gentleman's clubs, or *titty-bars*, as the locals aptly referred to them, over the course of just eighteen months. Otto had half ownership of China Dolls, and a third of the action of Club Pink, both located on the city's west side.

Plans were in place for yet a third establishment, a strip club, of which Otto would be sole owner. He intended to have it constructed near the airport, surrounded with marquee lights and huge neon signs that could be seen for miles off the interstate in a sleek art deco design. He planned to call it The Wet Rose, a high-class, two-story Vegas-style gentlemen's club that would sell private memberships to its patrons and feature the hottest, sexiest girls on the Pacific Coast.

Business was booming at The Grotto and Otto was raking in the cash in more ways than one. But, at the rate things were going, his dream of opening his own gold mine was destined to remain as such if he didn't find a way to score some sizable capital—*fast*.

It was an extreme risk continuing to steal from the Fortunatos, and although his cut of the profits from the West side clubs were decent and steady, it was far from enough to fund such an ambitious business venture.

Otto made some calls and hooked up with a former player from the old neighborhood, Michael Gagliardi, who offered a solution to his little problem. Gagliardi informed Otto of a heist about to go down in Texas involving two Cuban exiles who were looking to purchase some automatic weaponry. "They will be needing a contact in the States who deals in the specialized artillery."

Otto was thrilled to help, and even to bring his boss's nephew, Nick Manino, on as well. Manino had been chomping at the bit for a piece of any action. He was up and coming and hungry to make his mark in the family business, having just scored a cool fifty grand on the sale of a dirt lot in Vegas with don't ask, don't tell purposes. Nick was always interested in making a quick buck, and in the process, making his revered father-in-law, Victor, stand up and take notice every chance he got.

As it played out, the Cubans were said to be bringing a large sum of money to the table. It would be a perfect opportunity to first set them up by winning their trust, and then rob them blind before they would even know what hit them. A quick and clean operation—if it was executed correctly and by the right players. Nick would be the perfect front man. A win for everyone involved.

Gagliardi had masterminded the ingenious scam and could scarcely believe his luck. When he heard that his old pal Otto Seratti wanted in, it was a done deal. Just like old times. Otto certainly could deliver the players to make it all happen. He had contacts in the South who could deliver the muscle. Gagliardi wouldn't even need to show up, just collect his share of the take. Life was good.

The timing was perfect. The deal going down just weeks away south of the Mason-Dixon Line was going to be one of the biggest hauls to date. Otto and Nick were charged with assembling the players down South, while Gagliardi made arrangements from the confines of his cushy East Coast headquarters. The meeting was to take place in a farmhouse in Dallas.

Otto had been dreaming of big plans for his new nightclub when he got the call from Vern Tarot, right on cue. He would need a few cowboy-types to add authenticity to the scam, and Vern was the perfect choice for the job, along with two ringers Vern vouched could be trusted. The first was Terry "T-Bird" Crawford, a thirty-year-old parolee from Shreveport who ran deliveries for Vern on occasion, and the other, was Buddy Delacorte, a slick Southern renegade Vern hailed as having sharp Cajun instincts and coyote-quick reflexes in a brawl.

The setup was to go down as follows: Vern would meet up with the Cubans in a Dallas nightclub, where he would wine and dine them on porterhouse, booze, and just enough Texas hospitality and back-of-the-house rounds of twenty-one, to gain their trust. He would introduce them to his business "associates," Buddy and T-Bird, who would be seated at a blackjack table. Once their needs were determined, Vern would agree to arrange a meeting with a local arms dealer, the reputed Nick Manino, under the pretense of selling them the weapons. Vern would then lure them to an abandoned farmhouse just outside of San Antonio, instructing them to bring two and a half million in cash for the buy.

At the site of the exchange, T-Bird and Buddy, posing as buyers themselves, would suddenly draw guns on the exiles and hold them at bay, while Manino and his goons would appear in full force, take the cash, and then execute them, leaving them gagged, bound, and bleeding on the side of the road, where they would be fifty miles from the nearest town.

The plan would be seamless. In turn, Otto Serati would receive a cut of the take after paying off his bosses' son-in law, Vern, and the Bayou boys, netting several hundred thousand dollars himself. Not a bad pittance for playing middleman from the comfort of his desk chair.

CHAPTER 9

★ ★ ★

THE TELEPHONE ERUPTED, STARTLING BUDDY, who had dozed drunkenly in the stagnant heat.

"Hey, kid—it's Vern's *amico*. How was the flight?"

It was the garlic and meatball-drenched voice of Otto Serati drifting across the line. Buddy shook his head to clear the cobwebs, searching the nightstand for his wrist-watch.

"I don't fly so much, but I guess it was all right."

"And the accommodations?"

Buddy snarled, "Sure, real great." *If you're into piss-holes! What was up with this asshole?*

"What time is it anyway, man?" Buddy slurred fuzzily. A solitary bottle of Jack Daniels stood empty on the night-stand. He still could not locate his watch.

"It's time to get to work, hot shot. It's show time. Is the other one there yet?" Otto asked.

"Did who get what?"

"Vern's other runner. Calls him T-Bird. Hell, he should have checked in by now. Should be in room fourteen. Look, why don't you make yourself useful and go over and wake his sorry ass up. He should have contacted you by now."

"Yeah, okay, sure." Buddy was slowly waking up. *So, Vern hired on a second runner?*

Otto fired another directive. "Meet my driver out in front of the motel—the both of you. Eleven fifteen sharp. You'll be filled in on the rundown later. Just be out there and ready *on time*. No dickin' around, *capiche*?"

Before Buddy could respond, the line went dead. He slammed down the receiver.

"Capiche."

CHAPTER 10

★ ★ ★

BUDDY SLIPPED INTO HIS BLUE jeans and a button-down shirt. He splashed cold water on his face and stared intently into the dingy mirror. His reflection was hard and unfamiliar. The stranger he saw staring back at him troubled his very soul. It would be just enough dough, he reasoned, to get him squared away with his bookie and his creditors once and for all. One more job—a simple sting and robbery. No big deal. Just the one more and then he would hang it up.

So what if Otto Serati was a mafia-type thug with a mammoth-size power complex? It's not as if he was planning on massacring anyone. It was a fact that Serati held all the marbles and he, Buddy Delacorte, was lucky to even be asked into the game. His ass would not have been there if Vern didn't think that he had what it took to do the job. He was not proud of his life, or the person he had become. Just the same, it was the only life he had, and the only way he knew to set things right. He thought about Colette. If nothing else, she would be impressed when he'd cleaned up his act. Maybe.

He felt jittery. He was clean out of booze. He wished like hell that he had a joint or something—anything to calm his jumping nerves. He was hoping to be back in Baton Rouge by early the next afternoon, when hopefully, he could score something back down at the Roadhouse.

He sauntered up to the door marked fourteen at exactly eleven o'clock and tried to peer past the gaping curtains. There was movement and laughter inside. The lights were on, and a radio was blaring Jimmy Damon. He rapped on the window. A moment passed, and suddenly, a giant figure appeared in the doorway.

Buddy hedged uncertainly, "You Crawford?"

The giant nodded and spoke in a low, slow, Southern drawl, stroking his bare grizzly chest. "Folks call me T-Bird. You Delacorte?"

"Yep. S'okay to just call me Buddy."

The two shook hands awkwardly. T-Bird was stark naked except for a bed sheet he was wearing around his massive waist, along with a carpet of thick body hair covering his arms and legs.

"Got instructions from Serati. He's sending someone to pick us up. We got to be out in front in fifteen minutes."

"Sure." T-Bird nodded.

The introduction was short but effective. There was an instant unspoken bond. In less than five seconds flat, they each had to instantly and completely trust the other, as they were about to embark on a common mission into the unknown.

Buddy tilted his head and grinned. "Hey, man, excuse me for sayin', but you're a fucking Amazon!" From where he stood, Buddy could make out the figure of a naked woman standing near the bed, quickly getting dressed in plain view.

T-Bird grinned back. "Perfect timing, huh?"

The woman zipped up her skirt, strapped up her sandals, and tied a crocheted bikini top across her bodacious bare breasts that were Florida-bronze and void of any discernible tan lines. She scooped up two bills from the nightstand, bummed one of T-Bird's smokes, and brushed past them, sauntering off toward the road in the dark without so much as a word.

The car arrived on schedule. A burly thug with a head of kinky hair wearing dark glasses—even though it was the dead of night—drove it. He wore a pinkie ring and a good deal of gold around his thick wrists and fleshy neck. He smelled like Copenhagen mixed with BO and bar smoke.

The interior of the limousine was musty and stale from the constant humidity and general overuse. It was a rental, and the driver was nobody. Buddy picked up on that right away.

The car pulled into a gated estate in West Palm Beach, letting them off at the front entrance. A housemaid received them at the door and escorted the two into a small waiting room just off the foyer. "Please to wait here for Mister," she instructed in broken English, leaving them alone in the silence. It was a large and lavishly appointed room with couches and small glass and teakwood end tables with slim, pointed bases.

Two unmarked manila envelopes were set on the coffee table innocuously.

Twenty minutes passed, and the chimes of the desk clock on the far side of the room signaled twelve thirty a.m. Otto appeared unannounced and without apology for making them wait. He lumbered over to the wet bar to fix himself a drink. Buddy and T-Bird stood stupidly at attention.

"Sit . . . sit," Otto directed, pouring out three Scotches, neat. Carrying them over to where the two were seated, he offered one to each off a bamboo serving tray. He folded himself into an oversize leather chair that appeared every bit the king's throne. Otto was at least two hundred eighty pounds stuffed uncomfortably in a poly-blend leisure suit the color of rice pudding. A thick gold chain encircled his enormous neck, and he wore a plain gold band on his swollen right pinkie. His boots were alligator-green and buffed to a pristine shine.

He eyed his court reflectively. "Which one of you is the wise-ass I talked to on the phone earlier?"

Buddy quipped, "That would be me, sir. Wise-ass Buddy Delacorte reporting for duty, sir!" He performed a mock salute and smirked, flaunting his "I-don't-give-a-shit" attitude with aplomb, downing the expensive Scotch, challenging Serati's tolerance for wise guys.

Otto only half-smiled. He found Buddy's theatrics amusing, though not endearing. "Where are you from, boy?" he asked.

"New Orleans, sir. Originally. That's where I was born. Right now I'm keeping a place in Baton Rouge. That's where me and Vern met up."

"I see." Otto lit the tip of a slender brown cigar that looked ridiculous in his pudgy fingers.

T-Bird chimed in. "I'm from Shreveport. Vern's my uncle on my mama's side."

"Is that right?" Otto intoned. *So he was Madeline's boy,* he thought, smiling.

"How did you come to know Vern?" T-Bird asked, trying like hell to decipher the unorthodox connection between his uncle and the would-be gangster, Serati. "I'd never figure you two as being acquaintances, if you pardon my sayin' so."

Otto whooped, sounding a little like a broken engine, setting himself into a cantankerous coughing fit of laughter that lasted a full minute before eventually catching his breath. Buddy and T-Bird waited for Otto to right himself and go on. It required a second shot of Scotch and thirty seconds of throat clearing.

It frightfully occurred to each of them that the tub of lard could have very well just dropped dead right there on the spot from a coronary and the entire deal would be off.

Late the next afternoon, Buddy was back in Louisiana, outfitted and armed for action. He and T-Bird had each been issued a thirty-five-caliber pistol, a road map, directions, and a layout of the San Antonio farmhouse. They were given cash advances and instructed to purchase Western-style clothing from hats to boots, including a dinner jacket for the casino. Also, they were told to brush up on their card playing.

"Big spenders are high rollers," Otto coached. "You don't want to choke at the table and lose credibility, now. And be sure to break in those new boots. Ya don't want 'em spotting you a mile away, wincing' from a goddamn blister on your freakin' tootsies. Pour water in each boot and let 'em sit overnight. That'll loosen them up just fine."

The heist would take place on the fifth of October, just three days after the Cubans were scheduled to arrive in Texas, and exactly one month since T-Bird and Buddy met with Otto Serati.

It would be up to Vern, Buddy, and T-Bird to play their roles to perfection. Everyone was counting on a flawless performance from start to finish, particularly Michael Gagliardi.

CHAPTER 11

BUDDY WAS GROWING PROGRESSIVELY MORE nervous as the day approached. He just wanted the whole thing to be over with. He wished that he could talk to Vern and go over details, but it was out of the question. Vern had moved right away to Dallas to set up residence beforehand, and to begin putting the plan into place. Even Otto was off-limits at this point.

Nick flew out one week prior to join Vern. Buddy and T-Bird were to drive over from Louisiana one day prior to the Cubans' arrival.

The North Star Hotel in Dallas was an architectural wonder and a luxurious testament to the privileged class of the city's elite. Michael Gagliano's family had direct ties with the entire chain, so the set up was secured with a few well-placed phone calls to his cousin Georgie. The decadent hotel housed a 1930s-inspired, art deco nightclub, which posed as a perfect front for the less than reputable recreation of an illegal gambling parlor.

The posh, sprawling casino comprised the full back quarter of the hotel restaurant, complete with gaming tables, including craps, roulette, and blackjack. The club had a live show band, and cabaret entertainers featuring the best local acts in the state. It was an underground haven; a world unto itself, a play den for the coterie of Dallas's rich astute, who gathered to throw dice and rub elbows with millionaires, mobsters, and moguls.

The Cubans spoke little English, so conversation was kept to a minimum. They did, however, understand the universal language of fine wine and fast women, which were served up with abandon. George Gagliano saw to it that his maître d' and personal hostesses catered to their every whim, even going so far as setting up a private poker game for them in the club's back room, as was the plan. There, they met Fort Worth businessmen, "Dale Baxter" and "John Stark," a.k.a. T-Bird Crawford and Buddy Delacorte, along with Texas entrepreneur, "Conrad G. Watson"—Vern Tarot's performance of a lifetime.

Buddy could scarcely believe his old pal when he first saw him. Once a tall, gangly drink of water, Vern had gained fifty pounds and was sporting new digs and a short-cropped full head of hair with a peculiar handlebar mustache waxed to perfection. It was a first-rate transformation that had Buddy and T-Bird disbelieving their own eyes.

They were introduced around the table, and the five played cards for thirty-two hours straight. By the following evening, the Cubans and two businessmen had confided in their new pal, Conrad Watson, who was eager to set them up with a local dealer whom, he said, could be trusted. They eagerly agreed to meet his noted contact, Nick Manino, reputed East-Coast arms and drug dealer, the very next day.

Everything had gone according to plan, or so it seemed. The meeting had been set for ten a.m. in the parlor room of an old abandoned farmhouse awaiting demolition on 17 County Line Road, about fifty miles outside of San

Antonio. Vern had agreed to pick up the Cubans, and escort them to the meeting site. He had acquired a brand-new Ford pickup for the honors.

Buddy, T-Bird, and Nick had arrived earlier that morning to stage the weapons in crates and to make preparations for the Cubans' capture.

The truck was spotted coming up the road, and the three quickly took their places. Buddy was stationed behind the house just off the kitchen, from which he would enter at the appointed time from the back. He would arrive, as planned, shortly after Vern and the buyers got there, making his appearance approximately ten minutes later. T-Bird and Manino would already be in the process of conducting a "buy" of sundry ammo and handguns, strategically left unloaded during the inspection, so that the Cubans could not use them for their own defense during the robbery.

The Cubans entered the house along with their escort, Conrad, and met Manino at the door. Dale Baxter, the larger of the two "Texans", was currently examining a forty-five pistol and pointed it at an open window, flipping the barrel with his thumb. Vern popped open a large trunk on the dusty floor and revealed an impressive collection of brand new revolvers still in their packing crates. The Cubans nodded excitedly moving in for a closer look.

"Eh? What'd I tell you boys? My man Nick here—he's got the goods, eh?" Vern said. "Take your time, gentlemen, please."

Buddy placed his hand on the back door and counted to ten before going in. His hand was trembling. In a frightful instant, he dropped his revolver onto the porch with a thud. He froze.

No one seemed to notice the disturbance. The pistol had fallen through the planked flooring of the porch, so he quickly jumped down and slipped beneath the landing to retrieve it. Just as he did so, a strange tension in the still air bid him to wait. He paused, cautioned at the sound of distant footsteps pounding up the front steps.

In a fraction of a second, an army of five hooded goons with automatic machine guns broke through the front door of the house, quickly apprehending Manino, along with the cash and then delivered a merciless spray of bullets throughout the parlor, splattering every living body onto all four walls, felling Vern, T-Bird, and the Cubans in a mangled heap of limbs and torsos, gruesomely massacring every last one of them.

Buddy heard it all from the tiny crawl space where he crouched in utter fear beneath the porch, listening as the final clink of bullets had ricocheted, bouncing off the brick and cinder posts onto the floor like tiny marbles, dropping down through the wooden slats just above his head. Paralyzed, Buddy could not move a muscle.

Every nerve had gone dead in his legs. Every soul upstairs had been obliterated. He was sure of it. Except for Manino whose screams could be heard as two men dragged him to the car for what would well be a fate far worse than that which they had just delivered in the bloody massacre.

Buddy listened as Manino cursed the wicked, heartless faces of his comrades—his betrayers.

Silencing him first with several blows to the head, they then stuffed him into the truck to be dealt with later. Buddy watched, terrified, in the darkness through the slats of thin wood—the only thing in the world between him, and thanks to the grace of God, the purest evil he had ever witnessed.

Victor Fortunato got the call. Manino had been reportedly marked for sometime by a warring faction led by the Gagliano family, and the sting was the perfect time to collect. It was just considered a bonus by Michael Gagliano.

Manino, as a street-hardened teen, had first worked as a messenger and lookout for the notorious mob Don Salvatore Diamond under Gagliano's direction, eventually graduating to working larger jobs by the age of twenty-one. Later Manino deserted to become a gunman and enforcer for a Sicilian Loan Shark named Pauly Lo Cicero before marrying into Victor Fortunato's family. Diamond and Fortunato were rivals.

In an attempt to silence one of Diamond's informants from fingering his involvement in an East Coast narcotics setup that threatened Diamond's well-established operations, Manino panicked and acted simply on a "hunch" that the suspected informant was about to turn him over to the authorities. So Manino pushed him to his death from a five-story hotel room window after luring him to the location on the pretense of his meeting with a choice high-price hooker as a gift from a friend. The so-called "informant" was none other than Gagliano's then twenty-six-year-old nephew, Tony.

For Michael Gagliano, the payback could not have come at a sweeter price. Manino's body was found one week later, retrieved from Lake Austin one hundred twenty miles from San Antonio. Manino had been badly beaten and tortured. All of his teeth had been knocked out and his jaw was crushed, and several of his fingers had been chopped off with a blunt axe. After his killers tired of carving several meaty portions of his body like a steer, they ended the grisly torture with a shotgun blast to the head.

Victor Fortunato was more than happy to accept Gagliano's gracious offer to help sanitize the family by doing away with his worthless son-in-law, and restoring the family to their rightful place. "That was good work your boys done down there in Texas," Victor breathed hoarsely into the phone, as throat cancer had since reduced his voice to a mere whisper.

Gagliano was honored. "The pleasure, Victor, was all mine. You just say the word if I can ever be of any further assistance."

Victor paused and smiled tightly. Michael Gagliano was a tough and loyal breed. "Now that you mention it, there is a certain proprietor at one of my restaurants that comes to mind—Otto Serati—the bastard's been stealing from me for months!"

CHAPTER 12

★ ★ ★

NEW ORLEANS
1967

ABIGAIL DELACORTE LIVED ON A tree-sheltered little street just off the thoroughfare, nearly a stone's throw away from Tulane University, where Kenswick Delacorte, her deceased husband, now gone fifteen years, once taught linguistics.

Not much about the house ever changed. It was just as Buddy had remembered years before when his grandparents, the Champards, and his grandfather's parents before then, had owned it. The stately plantation had once shone in magnificent splendor, withstanding the press of time and ravages of war. The facade had undergone countless renovations, but nothing would ever serve to change or alter the spirit of the lives that passed through its doors. Abigail had grown up in the home from childhood, as had all her own children as well. All were blessed, especially those fortunate to live within the shelter of Rose Gate Manor's magnificent walls.

The namesake was a loving tribute from its first occupants, Abigail's great-great- grandparents, who named the shining little plantation on the bayou for its floral splendor. It had the most uncommon arbor gardens festooned with wreaths of yellow jasmine and endless hedges of white and cream English roses bordering the magnificent garden gate.

Buddy pulled his truck up just shy of the driveway, where he would not be seen from the house. He pictured the scene inside, Ms. Gretta, tending to the cornbread that had been baked earlier that morning. She would be cutting it into triangles for the supper plates. Had he happened to walk in the back door, Abigail would jump to rustle up some cool ice for the tea that sat steeping on the stove. It was hot, and she'd know he would be thirsty, no doubt. On the table would be a vase of the white roses picked freshly that morning. Abigail never forgot the special touches. No matter how long he stayed away, most everything at the Delacorte house remained constant. Buddy was Abigail's last-born, and he knew that so much about him reminded her of his father, Kenswick, especially his notable blue eyes. He was a Delacorte by design. There was no denying that.

Rose Gate Manor was the house that Abigail had lived in for sixty-five years—her entire life. Kenswick had first won her heart back when he was studying under her father, Waltman See Champard III, an honorable professor of science who lovingly raised his family just as his father and his father's father before him, on the prized historical French soil of the new America, along with the Acadians in the mysterious land of swamp grass and bayou dwellers.

Abigail and her sister, Genevieve, were first-generation Americans born to Rose and Waltman Champard. The twin girls were only twelve minutes apart, regarded by most everyone who knew them as living dolls.

The two were inseparable, joined at the heart their father was fond of saying, yet they were very much different in style and appearance, as different as two people could be.

Waltman loved his girls and never minded much that he had no sons to carry on his family name. He made for them, a life of love and enchantment fit for princesses, as they were so duly regarded.

Waltman Champard was later to become a Louisiana legislator whose father had served in the Civil War as an officer under General Polk. In the early years, Waltman had a professorship and taught the new physics in Tulane's great halls of prestigious higher learning reserved for the rich and privileged aristocracy of New Orleans.

Both of his daughters were reared in fine culture and repose, repute of charm and each blessed with extraordinary beauty and grace. Abigail, the first-born twin, took to matters of one's nature and compassion, as was her mother's inclination, with a keen artistic disposition that drew her to music halls and lofty literary prose of the great poets of the century. Genevieve, quite the opposite, shared a hunger for science, nature, and politics with her father, and concentrated her studies on anatomy and matters of modern medicine. She aspired to be a physician, which seemed dreadfully improper to their dear mother, Rose, who prided herself on instilling every etiquette required of ladies of fine lineage upon her daughters, dating back to her own strict and regimented upbringing in the Carolinas.

The Champards were most proud of their lovely daughters' talents and sharp minds. "Education is the key to success," Waltman would pontificate, while waving his porcelain tobacco pipe.

Tragically, in 1917, Genevieve died at the age of fifteen from the deadly influenza virus. It was the time marked by great sadness as light so extraordinary and bright, had been extinguished from their lives. Soon after, Abigail lapsed into a deep, inexplicable depression that caused her health to decline dramatically and weakened her heart irreversibly, reducing her nearly to the point of utmost fragility. She spent her days confined to her room, reading for countless hours, lost in the fantastic places of great classic novels, until several seasons passed and finally, with them, a peaceful healing began to restore her spirit.

Oftentimes she would speak aloud to Genevieve in her mind, quite certain that her dear sister could actually hear her—and respond, a secret she kept concealed from the rest of the world and never betrayed.

The Delacortes had moved to New Orleans from Raleigh, North Carolina, where Kenswick's father had served as chaplain at West Point and later entered into church duties until his death in 1918. At age seventeen, Kenswick and his mother came to Louisiana to live with his elderly aunt, who also was a widow, and so he enjoyed the affections and attentions of the two doting maternal mavens.

Kenswick Delacorte began visiting Rose Gate at 211 East Fontinelle regularly on Tuesdays and Thursdays starting in the spring semester of 1921 at Tulane. He was a bright and ambitious pupil, and Professor Champard eagerly looked forward to their hour lesson each week, as he viewed Kenswick as more than just a gifted student, but rather as a protégée of sorts. Kenswick was nary a genius, but his ambition to learn and his thirst for knowledge was unlike any the professor had encountered in his tenure.

Professor Champard hoped to groom the Delacorte boy for teaching someday, and perhaps even a professorship, or politics, following in his own humble footsteps as he took to him almost immediately, like a son. However, no one looked more forward to Kenswick's bi-weekly tutoring visits than Abigail. It was the only thing that seemed to lift her spirits, giving purpose to the droll, mundane life she had succumbed to, lamenting her sister's passing and nursing her ailing body. Few of life's pleasures inspired her at that time; limited curiosities intrigued her—except, now, for the boy.

She made it a point to be around the house whenever Kenswick would arrive for his lesson. On occasion, she would greet him at the gate just off the pavement on her way to market, or sit in plain view upon his arrival, on the shady portico swing, reading sonnets in the sunshine, where the entire length of an hour could pass, and find her staring at the same single verse while waiting for him to emerge from the study at the end of his session.

Luckily, Kenswick took notice of her beauty and alluring charms and indeed had every inclination of initiating a dialogue with Abigail, but was regretfully paralyzed with fear each time he encountered her presence. A phenomenon that kept him returning to Professor Champard's lesson reviews for many more months than were actually required of him. What was regarded as insatiable passion for science and discourse was, in truth, a compelling passion for far more carnal desires—those of the heart. All things began and ended with the most beautiful girl Kenswick had ever laid eyes upon, Abigail Champard.

It was good that Abigail and Kenswick had broken through their mutual shyness in the spring of 1922 just in time for weepy moss trees, butterflies, and soft Southern Gulf spring breezes that stirred the yellow jasmine wreaths and the longings of young lovers' hearts long enough for them to fall blissfully in love. They courted from that point forward, stealing their first kiss on the shore of Lake Pontchartrain on a sweltering Louisiana afternoon in July, where Abigail had prepared for him an exquisite picnic lunch of applesauce sandwiches, glazed ham, sweet buttermilk kept cool in a covered metal pail, and large molasses cookies for dessert with swirls of white icing. It was there that he took her hand, proposing marriage, announcing her to be the most beautiful girl in all the world, promising her eyes to be more stunning than cut diamonds and more worthy than starlight to bejewel the night sky below heaven. It was there that he promised his love to her forever.

They married at St. Louis Cathedral nestled in the

French Quarter on an afternoon in May where Abigail wore fresh lilacs in her hair and descended the aisle in an hand sewn dress that trailed majestically to the floor making her feel like a princess. She thought that day and every day thereafter that Kenswick was the most handsome man she had ever seen with his warm coloring, piercing blue eyes, distinguished, regal nose, and finely trimmed moustache—features that might have mistakenly suggested the lineage of a Kentuckian or Virginia-born native rather than the more regular features characterized by his commonplace Carolina ancestry. Abigail, needless to say, reveled in the telling and re-telling of her own special fairy tale at every indulgence.

Buddy was the last of four sons born to Abigail and Kenswick who had lost a newborn girl in the early months of autumn between their first and second sons. Abigail named the baby Marietta Genevieve and laid her to rest at Magnolia, within her beloved sister's tomb. From that day forward, the colorful weeds that grew between the cracks of Marietta's and Genevieve's headstone could never be discouraged from growing, wrapping so in a chain of blossoms one unto the other. When removed with pruning by the groundskeepers, they would only spring to life once more, within a week or two, growing ever stronger with their lovely lavender blossoms. More than once a visitor had sworn to tell of the faint but clearly heard "lullaby of bells" ringing on the wind when there was no wind to be found stirring up the floral vines that serenaded the peaceful souls of Genevieve and her infant niece. This was, of course, no surprise to Abigail. It was, in fact, all the proof she needed, and she took it as a beloved nod from heaven that her dear sister and daughter were watching over the Delacorte family.

Abigail was always pleased when Buddy would just walk

in after being gone for so very long. She would be glad that his world travels had finally brought him home. He would say that he had been working hard, moving from here to there, from town to town. She would not know that all the while he had been living in Louisiana on a rented lot outside of Baton Rouge and taking on highway work where he could find it. It was the best way that Buddy knew to avoid breaking her heart and to evade responsibility to anything or anyone—just the way that he preferred things. He was, after all, a drifter; a contradiction to his namesake and the close-knit family credo of camaraderie that the Delacortes had always stood for. Buddy never complied. He strove to be different than his brothers from the day he was born.

Warren and Franklin were both trial lawyers living just outside of New Orleans. Each was married and had children of their own. Joseph, a third brother, who had ambitions to the priesthood, joined the seminary out of high school, where he started teaching at a boys school in Nebraska, later moving on to a mission in San Antonio. It was Father Joseph who gallantly rendered the heartfelt eulogy at Kenswick's funeral Mass in 1952, honoring the father that he and his brothers only knew as a distant and disapproving man, who, regretfully was never the same after the death of little Marietta. Kenswick had far too much pride for public sorrow and held his emotions inward, particularly in community, with Delacorte dignity, until it wound up killing him with the poison of cancerous erosion at the age of fifty one.

Raymond Eugene Delacorte nicknamed himself "Buddy" for no apparent reason, announcing to the family from the first grade on that he wanted to be referred to as *Buddy*. And so it was. The family complied with his wishes, as he was the youngest and last of the brood. Abigail's birthing days had since ended. Joseph was the only one in the world who ever referred to him as Raymond, or was ever allowed to.

Buddy played the role of the wayward son with aplomb. Unable to compete with the sterling ambitions of his brothers and hard-driven demands of his father and highly ethical mother, he rebelled, and reveled in gaining attentions through acting out and defying authority, much to his family's disapproval. By the time Buddy reached seventeen, he was positively incorrigible. About this time, Abigail had worried that she possibly had managed to fail him somehow, attempting to raise him as a single parent after he suffered the loss of his father. It was a mother's lament. So, in the spring of his eighteenth year, she sent him away.

Not even the U.S. Army could do better in trying to make an upstanding soldier out of him. Buddy was dishonorably discharged after only twelve weeks of duty for striking a fellow bunkmate for mocking his tattoo—a small rebel flag inked on his right bicep. He had called Buddy a goddamn hillbilly queer and smashed a chair across his face, breaking it, along with three of his teeth.

With the assistance of four other comrades from the genteel Southern state of Georgia, Buddy managed to take out the rival quite good. Four former citadel cadets lent a hand in the schooling of the poor Yankee fool, who took twelve brutal blows to his chest and head before collapsing to the floor, where he received multiple boots and fists to his face and kidneys for six merciless minutes, until a bunk officer finally stepped in with a fully engaged fire hose to end the beating.

The unfortunate fellow never spoke or walked again.

From that point forward, they did everything they could to break him, succeeding only in incensing Buddy more. Although he wanted more than anything, to excel at something, to be good at just one thing, it never seemed to happen. Finally, Buddy had decided that if he could not be good at anything in life, he would just simply stop trying. That is why he had stayed away for so many years. Why he was now sitting in front of Rose Gate Manor, his truck still running, and remembering.

He knew one thing for certain. He could not do it. The last thing in the world he wanted was to disrespect his mother, to see the disappointment in her eyes over what he had done. He would not go in. Instead, he pulled the truck slowly away with the infant nestled in the seat beside him and drove into the night. He didn't stop until he reached Saint Martin's Mission in San Antonio—and the only person he could trust to help him do the right thing.

CHAPTER 13

★ ★ ★

SAN ANTONIO, TEXAS
1972

IT WAS MORNING, JUST BEFORE dawn devotions, when Father Joe was called to the girls' quarters expeditiously. It seemed that five-year old Katie had encountered a frightening nightmare and was calling for Father Joseph to comfort her. The nursemaid, Sister Felicity, was beside herself with worry, as she could not seem to assuage the child with regular assurances. As much as she hated to disturb Father from his morning prayers, she simply had no choice and was in tears by the time the young priest bolted into the room in a panic.

"What is it, Sister?"

"It's Katie, Father. She has been crying and calling for you for over an hour. It seems that she has awoke from a dreadful dream. Nothing calms her. She has also been running a fever for two days, and—"

He felt her forehead. "Indeed. She's burning up!"

Katie's flesh was on fire. Sister Felicity called to the other sisters for help. There were so many beds and children on the ward, and hardly enough hands to go around.

"How long has it been since you checked her last?"

The young nun stuttered fretfully. She had never seen Father so angry. He would report her for certain if he found it to be her fault that Katie's condition went unwatched.

"How long, Sister?" His voice boomed to a frightful level that sent a chorus of cries to erupt throughout the nursery corridor.

Two nuns cloaked in white frocks hurried to the scene. One attempted to console the novice nun, who promptly broke down into a fit of tears.

"I-I don't know exactly. I got so busy. I swear that she was sleeping fine just a few minutes ago!"

Monsignor Donnelley was the only other soul who knew that Katie was a Delacorte by birth and that her paternity was that of Father Joseph's despondent brother, who had brought her to Saint Martin's, tragically unable to support the child on his own. Father Joseph had explained to Monsignor that he had agreed to look after little Katie for a short while, just until his brother was able to get back on his feet, find good, steady work, and build a home for him and his daughter. This, of course, was a lie. One that the good father would take to his grave, and would spend the rest of his life repenting for. But what could he do? He had lied when he told the Monsignor that Buddy was unmarried and preferred to keep the birth of the child a secret from his family. That one, Father Joe was certain, would earn him another few decades in purgatory. He was just trying to buy some time, vowing that his brother would definitely come back for the child and do the right thing by God and the Delacorte family. In the meantime, though, he had convinced the Monsignor that it would be prudent to keep the child's identity secrete, to keep up appearances and watch over her there at the orphanage. Monsignor faithfully agreed, and so no adoptions were arranged for the beautiful doe-eyed mulatto child every-one simply called Katie.

While Father Joseph was grateful for Monsignor's gen-erosity, he knew that he could not uphold false promises of Katie's long-lost father's eminent return for much lon-ger. Shortly after Katie's fourth birthday, Father Joe had received a letter, as he did once yearly around the same time. The letter relayed that Buddy had been working in a steel manufacturing plant up North and would soon be driving rigs cross-country for union wages. Things were looking hopeful, but the final letter came just two days after Katie turned five. In it, Buddy simply asked his saintly brother if he thought he could find Katie a good home with a decent family who would love her.

Father Joe replied to the return address given, a post office box in Springfield, Missouri, that Katie did indeed have a loving family and that he would see to it that she knew it. Then, cutting Buddy off from his heart, which would be the nail in the coffin of his brotherly duty, he never spoke to him again. Further, and in doing so, Father Joe feared that it would also most likely put a wedge between him and God for eternity.

The doctor emerged from the examining room, his brow etched with a permanent furrow—the kind he often wore when he delivered bad news. "Who is acting as this child's legal guardian?"

Father Joseph answered, "I am, John. Katie is actually . . . my niece."

The scholarly old man raised a silver brow and then motioned for him to follow. Together, they walked in silence down the dark hallway, the doctor and the priest, past the room where Katie lay comfortably sleeping, while a stone-faced nurse kept watch at the little girl's bedside.

The hospital was a cold, sterile place; not unlike the children's home in many ways. Father Joe was certain that Katie had much preferred the nurses' hats to those of the heavily cloaked sisters whose dresses draped the floor, never showing their arms or legs, and who were strangely bound with thin white ropes and beads around their veiled waists.

Doctor Bionet ushered Father Joe into his office. He was a straight shooter. That is what he liked most about the doctor and expected nothing less in his assessment of Katie's condition.

"Well?" The harried priest remained standing, staring intently at the old doctor as he watched him take his place in a stiff leather swivel chair behind a mammoth oak desk.

Dr. Bionet invited Father Joe to sit as well.

"John. Now, please . . . the *truth*."

The good doctor sighed his disdain for senseless illnesses that invade especially the most unworthy of innocents with their criminal design.

"I'm afraid the tests are conclusive. Katie has juvenile diabetes."

Father Joseph paled, understanding very little about the facts of the disease, but nonetheless, knowing it to be the very worst of all things ever told.

"What exactly does that mean?"

Dr. Bionet removed his spectacles and pinched his angular beak. "Her immune system is deficient in a way that causes her to 'use up' levels of blood sugar too quickly. This, unfortunately, can, if triggered, cause fainting, nausea, and even possible coma if not caught in time. It's very serious, Joe. The child will need special monitoring the rest of her life. Most likely she will not outgrow it. There are frequent blood draws, daily, hourly sometimes. Insulin injections daily. With proper care and attention, though, she can live a full and otherwise normal life."

"There is nothing ordinary about Katie's life," Father Joe said sadly. He was fraught with shock and disbelief. *As if she hadn't endured enough already. It just wasn't fair!*

Dr. Bionet's words were growing hollow as he continued to explain the ramifications and particulars of Katie's affliction, although Katie was not Father Joe's child. He felt what should not be possible, but was—a parent's lament, a father's sorrow.

And in the silence of his room that night, on his knees before God, he prayed for a miracle. He remained there until dawn, asking for an answer that would help him understand to what purpose Katie would have to endure medical tests and prodding needles that poked her seemingly mercilessly to administer insulin and medications into her tiny body. Through it all, Katie remained compliant, learning to cope with her illness with ease and dignity—Delacorte dignity.

Katie was put on a strict diet of special foods and denied the pleasures of simple sugars found in cakes and candies that had been a frequent treat on the trays in the dining hall of the orphanage, replaced by bland fruits and tasteless meals for reasons which Katie could not understand.

It broke Father Joe's heart to deny his little angel the gingerbread cookies at Christmas time, the chocolate marshmallow Easter eggs in spring, and most unfortunately, her very own birthday cakes each passing year. These were often substituted with handsome apple spice loaves baked special by Sister Ursula, who would light them up with candles and pretend that they were the most magnificent little cakes.

Then came the day that Father Joe met with both dread and relief. It had been seven years since Buddy had left little Katie in his care, a gesture that had remarkably brought him joy beyond all measure—as well as unrepentant guilt shrouded in a secret that could no longer be kept silent. Together, he and Katie shared a journey of unfathomable joys and sorrows. Father Joe loved his niece as truly as if she were his very own child and chided himself relentlessly for despising the brother who had abandoned her so many years ago. That would be between Buddy and God someday. Saint Martin's orphanage was the best life the good father could have given her. And while it served to see her through life's rocky and initial beginnings, there was still much more of life to be lived, and she deserved to do it outside the walls of an institution. It was time, Father Joe had concluded. It was time to take Katie home.

CHAPTER 14

★ ★ ★

BATON ROUGE
1974

ABIGAIL RE-READ THE LETTER FOR the tenth time. No matter how many times she read the words, nothing, it seemed, did a thing to dull the excitement.

I'm bringing you a grand surprise. A child, Mother. She's a beautiful child and she is your granddaughter, a treasure from God Almighty. She is Buddy's daughter, and she has his eyes, and Mother, your sweet smile. Her name is Katie. I am sure that this is a shock to you. I would like to discuss arrangements for Katie to live at Rose Gate Manor with you—just for a little while. She has been here, at the orphanage these past seven years, with me, and has received the finest care and love from the dear sisters and myself. Institution is no life for such a fragile creature. She is afflicted with juvenile diabetes. I am hoping that there would be room enough for her light to shine there with you, just until Buddy returns to his responsibilities. He has always been one to leave the difficult tasks to the strong ones. We are the strong ones, aren't we, Mother? God bless you, and see you soon.
~ Joseph.

Abigail pierced her finger again with the sewing needle, managing somehow skillfully not to stain the stitch work. It was a dusty pink pillow sham for the guest room bed she had started for Katie's arrival. What kind of a home could a sixty-five-year-old grandmother give to a sickly child? she wondered. What did Joseph mean by *just for a little while*? She shifted smugly in her chair. She knew Buddy better than them all. He would be back as soon as he was able.

Joseph said that they could teach her how to care for Katie's illness. But she'd let all the servants go for good, and Gretta had not the strength, nor the patience for raising a little one. Those days were well behind. Abigail would be taking it all on herself. While she was elated at the prospect of having a new granddaughter, the reality of raising Katie at this time in her life, was unsettling to say the least. What would Katie be like? Would people be able to discern her mixed heritage? Would it matter? And ultimately, Abigail struggled with the task of truly wondering if she could ever hope to bond with her. It was, after all, quite a shock, and Abigail would surely need some sort of *proof* that Buddy was indeed the girl's father. The myriad of thoughts both troubled and excited her. What did this all mean? Each day that passed brought Joseph's visit ever closer, and Abigail prayed that the good Lord knew what He was doing.

The answer came in a heartbeat when Joseph finally arrived, bounding up the walk with a dark-toned child with coarse hair tamed with two clip bows; clinging to his frock, and smiling. Her beautiful blue eyes shone in the sunlight; the imprint of generations past as if frozen in time within her cherubic face. One hundred years of those striking blue eyes that all but made Abigail gasp with joy. They were her father's eyes—Buddy's eyes—as clear and true as Kenswick's too. It was the Delacorte legacy, all right, shining there in those azure blue orbs that Katie most certainly had. Abigail stretched out her arms, giving the child a grandmother's embrace.

Katie was indeed home.

CHAPTER 15

★ ★ ★

KATIE GREW TO LOVE ROSE Gate Manor and took to Abigail, her paternal grandmother, right from the very first hug. It was strange at first, living in such a large, quiet house with so few people around. Most unlike the comings and goings at all hours of the night she was used to from the orphanage at Saint Martin's. With the exception of Ms. Gretta, who worked only half-day shifts, it was just the two of them.

Katie loved getting lost within the maze of hallways and closet doors that led to mysterious corners of the mansion. Attic eaves, dusty crawl spaces, and dank cellars were all her secret hiding places, where Katie explored happily and contentedly for hours on end, reveling in her newfound freedom.

She had a lovely room of her very own, which Abigail had commissioned a local shop owner to furnish and decorate. There was a frilly canopy bed swagged with pink crepe and lace-trimmed fabric with matching sheets and duvet. The curtains matched perfectly, right down to the tiny gold piping and tassel sashes that accented the cherry wood of her massive four-corner post bed, which her grandmother had called an antique. Her *Meemaw*, as she so affectionately called Abigail, had sewn Katie's name on two dusty pink pillow shams arranged on her princess-style bed.

There were pink and yellow flowers arranged in a vase from the garden on the bureau, along with a tiny just-her-size matching vanity complete with a silver hairbrush, comb, and velvet bows. There was a collection of dolls and books and plush toy animals arranged along several shelves.

And in the center of the room was the grandest surprise—a child-size tea party play set. It was complete with matching pine wood table and chairs, and imported china cups and plates. Abigail had spared no expense and reveled in indulging her granddaughter. Katie was awestruck for days. She had decided that her newfound luck was nothing short of what the sisters of Mercy back at the orphanage called, a holy miracle from God Almighty!

Grandmother Abigail had the finest house Katie had ever seen. She could not have dreamt of a more perfect place to live. It was like walking into the pages of one of her storybook fairy tales that Father Joe would read to her from time to time.

The garden was astonishing, and quite the most magnificent of all with its white and yellow blossoms and magnolia trees dipping gracefully behind the hedges. Her favorite of all were the towering oaks with their strangely flowing mosses that trailed down to the ground that Meemaw called "locks of the Spanish maidens' hair." Living at Rose Gate Manor was truly a wondrous adventure.

Katie loved to work alongside Abigail in the gardens, turning up the soil and planting tiny seeds that were no larger than a speck that would someday turn into squashes, and cabbages, carrots, and bright yellow peppers for Mardi Gras salad.

Abigail's kitchen was filled with the aroma of the finest Southern delicacies compliments of Ms. Gretta. The only thing in the whole world that Ms. Gretta loved to do more than cooking up a storm with her sauces and soufflés was baking scrumptious desserts. Whenever Ms. Gretta would pull down the big black pot from the pantry shelf, Katie knew that incredible delights would soon emerge from the globs of fresh sweet dough she and Ms. Gretta would fry up in the golden oil to crisp perfection.

They would lay the beignets out, still hot and sizzling from the fryer on the cooling rack high atop the kitchen counter, and sprinkle the little pastries with a generous dousing of confectioners sugar. It was pure delight what Ms. Gretta could do in Meemaw's kitchen. She even invented a special batch of Katie's very own pastries—made without sugar, and a special dipping sauce of blackberry currant and carob that was positively scrumptious. The first bite she ever took of the creation named in her honor, "Katie Puffs," was pure heaven.

Katie grew within the grace of a loving home, where generations of Delacortes had presided in the stately shelter of Rose Gate Manor for centuries before her, and came to regard herself, rightfully so, as the luckiest little girl in the entire world.

One fated day when Katie stopped off at Tucker's bayou to try her hand at knocking gnarly toads off their lily pads with the smooth flat side of a pitching stone, was a day that threatened to change everything. It was a day she would never forget.

She started home from school with her good shoes in hand, stopping to attempt to brush the evidence of swamp grass and moss weeds from her tall, lanky legs. Her lace socks were covered to the ankle with burrs and soiled with black dirt clear through the soles.

From the gate, still some distance from the house, she could see the figure of a man standing on the porch talking to her grandmother. Her heart leapt, as she was certain—it was *him*. She recognized his tall, slender build and short cropped auburn hair coming into fuller view as she began running ever faster in her stocking feet toward the porch, calling out at full pitch, "Uncle Joe! Uncle Joe!"

Katie reached the porch steps and stopped cold in her tracks. One of the shoes she was carrying had toppled onto the wet grass. Now, at closer range, she could see that the man on the porch with her grandmother was not her Uncle Joe at all. It was the man she had only ever seen in a photograph. It was Buddy Delacorte.

CHAPTER 16

★ ★ ★

IT HAD BEEN NEARLY TWO and a half years since she had last seen Father Joe, when he had first brought her to live with her Grandmother Abigail right after Katie's seventh birthday. There had been word soon after that he would be leaving the US to travel abroad to a missionary assignment in Africa, way across the ocean. Faithfully, he had kept his promise to stay in touch, and monthly letters were a much-awaited gift from her beloved uncle, explaining his priestly travels, and even forwarding to her on occasion, the most exquisite little gifts and trinkets from the faraway places where he brought Christianity to the heathen people. It was important work, God's work. And God needed Father Joe's help, so Katie understood why he had to go, and that was why she could not stay at Saint Martin's where he would be able to look after her.

"Meemaw is well enough to watch over you now," he had told her, explaining the reason why it had taken seven years for her to meet her beloved grandmother, and yet another bent truth that was so craftily woven to protect his family. "You'll love New Orleans, Katie, I promise. You'll begin a whole new life, and so will I, but we'll always be connected to one another. You know why, don't you?" he would ask, holding her azure gaze. "Because we're *family*."

She was told that her mother had died soon after she was born, and that Buddy could not raise her all on his own and needed some help. Since her grandmother was ill at the time, Buddy asked Father Joe to let her live with the other children and sisters and priests at Saint Martin's, where she would be surrounded with lots of people to love and care for her when she was very young, until the day that he would return.

"My daddy will be coming back someday to get me, won't he?" Katie asked only once.

Father Joe held her squarely by her little shoulders and spoke plainly. "I honestly don't know when. I wish I could tell you that. All I know for certain is that God knows every answer and no matter what, he'll never leave or abandon you—ever. Remember what I taught you about that?"

The little girl nodded, although she understood less about a God who would allow a father to drop his only child off at an orphanage when she was not really even an orphan at all.

His eyes filled with tears. Katie wondered why Father Joe seemed so sad.

"I love you, sweetheart," he whispered. "You know that, right?"

It frightened her to see him this way. His weakness confused her. But she did not let on and reached to receive his embrace. He drew her close and squeezed her tight.

"I love you too, Uncle Joe," she had said, squeezing back. Little did she know how she could heal a man's soul with just such words.

She didn't ask about her father again until right when she turned nine. It was the photograph of a tall, slender boy with dark brown hair and piercing blue eyes looking contemptuously from a photo frame on her grandmother's credenza that started the conversation.

"That's your great-grandfather, Waltman Champard," Abigail explained. "He was a brilliant man. The woman beside him is your great-grandmother, Rose. This was their house many years ago."

Before Katie could ask, Abigail had produced a second framed photograph and placed it next to the other. "This is my husband, Kenswick Franklin Delacorte III—your granddaddy."

Katie examined the aged photograph, studying the faces of the people whose genes comprised half of her known heritage at best. She noted Kenswick's striking eyes, recognizing them to be similar to Father Joe's and somewhat like her own. Still, there was something very different about her that she did not find in any of the faces of the Delacortes or the Champards. Something that troubled her about the mysterious color of her skin and the feel of her hair that was unlike anyone else's. At times, she felt more akin to Ms. Gretta, their beloved black housemaid and cook, than to her own family.

Finally, Abigail retrieved a dusty portrait from the highest shelf and motioned for Katie to join her on the couch. "This here, baby, are my boys. Warren, Franklin, Joseph, and Buddy—your daddy. There he is on the end."

She scanned the faces of her uncles, locating Father Joe right away. The gangly young boy with disheveled hair and a contemptuous smirk that her grandmother had identified as her father had a calling card that could not be mistaken—those eyes.

CHAPTER 17

★ ★ ★

AT FIRST GLANCE, HE MIGHT have looked like Father Joe's twin, except he had a younger, more angular face. He had an abundance of dark chestnut hair that betrayed convention and parted and fell quite haphazardly above distinctively stunning blue eyes, revealing what might be taken by some as movie star looks. The stranger in his Sunday suit was none other than Buddy Delacorte. There was no denying it.

They had been standing there for quite some time, Katie guessed, drinking peach tea and discussing things; about changing things, no doubt. She could see that a few pieces of her luggage had been moved out onto the porch, and she knew that could only mean one thing. A gray Chevy Impala was parked in the gravel driveway beside the house. A woman wearing sunglasses and a chiffon red scarf waited behind the wheel, filing her nails in concert to a George Jones tune on the radio. A second suitcase had been placed near the trunk of the car.

It had been weeks since she announced that under no circumstances did she care to be reunited with her father and, least of all, go to live with him.

One other time, about two years prior, Buddy had shown

up with the red scarf lady at Katie's school and tried to coax her into their car, calling her by name from the fence on the play lot. The incident had frightened Katie, and she ran inside the school to tell Miss Bradly who called her grandmother promptly. There was a meeting with Abigail, the schoolmaster, as well as a social worker from family services.

Father Joe was notified by wire, but could not return from his missionary assignment in Kenya until the following winter. He wired her back with large block letters that simply read: YOU DON'T HAVE TO GO. STAY WITH MEEMAW. SEE YOU IN TWO CHRISTMASES. LOVE YOU, PUMPKIN! FR. JOE.

"I want to stay with Grandmother. I don't want to be sent away! This is my home!" Katie pleaded. "This is my place. Rose Gate Manor is my home forever. I won't go with them!"

Katie had been fully aware that the man who fathered her and left her at the mercy of a relative and the orphan's door, had never intended on returning to claim possession of a "deeply regrettable mistake of the past." She had heard the adults talking in quiet, hushed tones. Whispers of *changed man*, *reasonable means*, and *settling down* rumbled throughout their secret and incessant conversations.

But Katie Delacorte would have none of it. Buddy was a virtual stranger to her. Just because she resembled him and came from him, partly, did not mean that she had to automatically love him. In fact, she did not even really hate him. What she had felt was indifference, and Buddy knew it. It was too late for promises. When Buddy had sat her down and tried to put his arms around her to tell her how sorry he was for all the past mistakes and how determined he was to make it all up to her in every way, she stiffened, recoiling at his touch.

The worse thing that Buddy Delacorte could have ever done to her was to give her up, and that was unforgivable.

No matter what Father Joe had said about it. It was evident right then and there that the best thing in the world Buddy Delacorte could ever hope to do for her then would be to stay away for good.

And so he did. For two years more—until today. Now, he was back to finally take her away.

"NO!" she screamed, dropping the other shoe and running as fast and far as she could away from the house, until she could no longer hear her grandmother's voice calling to her, her name reverberating on the wind.

CHAPTER 18

★ ★ ★

WEEKS AFTER THE INCIDENT, NEW things started to happen. A social worker and a lawyer each were assigned to Katie's case at the school's request. It would be in the "best interest of the child" to enforce regular visitation with the natural father, they said.

Buddy got his wish and relished in the cherished visits, while Katie endured them, taking the long, tedious drive every second weekend of the month to where Buddy and his new wife, Reeba, lived just outside of New Orleans. They had a low-rent apartment with threadbare carpeting, mismatched furnishings, and a shaggy mutt named Trubeudoux.

Reeba called herself a flower child and liked to run around the house half-dressed, but only when Buddy was not around. He did not approve of "communing with nature" as Reeba liked to call it. So, she would wait for him to leave for work before she would get "comfortable." She would strip down to just her panties and brassiere and carry on just as normal as could be, playing gin rummy with Katie or fixing up a pot of popcorn on the stove. Reeba was amazing that way. No inhibitions at all.

Buddy had a job at a bindery, where he supervised a

crew of nine on sorting machines. On weekends, he would sometimes have to substitute as a lift-driver whenever they were short of help, or when orders were particularly high. This happened a lot. Katie didn't mind. She liked it best when he was away and she and Reeba were left to play cards, or to talk, or to paint their toenails in front of the television.

Reeba became like a big sister to Katie who, at age eleven, was getting the education of a lifetime. Reeba explained all about kissing and petting, makeup, monthly periods, and best of all, dating boys.

"It's never too soon to practice good skin maintenance," Reeba would explain as the two would recline on a stack of lumpy sofa cushions, covered in gooey homemade facial masks comprised of oatmeal and egg whites with cucumber slices covering their eyes.

"Oh, I know what you mean, *dar-ling!*" Katie would quip in her best grownup voice with exaggerated bravado, legs crossed, wearing fuzzy slippers and her stepmother's slip as a dress. The two would giggle until they nearly peed in their pants. Well, when Reeba was ever wearing pants.

The two were becoming the best of friends, and it made Buddy feel left out in the cold. He felt shut out of his daughter's life in every way. A weekend trip to Baton Rouge was, for Katie and Reeba, one big slumber party.

In the fall of Katie's thirteenth year, Buddy announced that he and Reeba would be moving to New Mexico, where they could get great jobs working on the reservations. If things did not pan out, he reasoned, they could always keep moving, proving once again, that Buddy just could never stay in one place for very long. Once again, he was leaving Katie behind.

She had to adjust to the concept all over again of her father and Reeba not being around. It mostly made her sad to know that Buddy was taking her best friend with him. Reeba had been Katie's only real role model, and she had grown to love her like an aunt. Katie was a teenager now, and needed things only a mother or aunt could offer.

"Your Daddy says that he'll be comin' back for you, darlin' . . . onc't we get settled in our new place."

Katie's face saddened, and she nodded. She knew better than to hold her breath. "Sure. I got my friends here at school and all," Katie said, her voice trailing. "Maybe I'll come and visit."

"Sure. Sure, you can come and visit. Anytime at all, sugar. And once the baby comes, we'll be needing all the help we can get."

Katie's heart sank even further. "Baby?"

"Yep. You're going to have a little brother or sister!" Reeba rubbed her slightly swollen stomach. "You write us now . . . on that special daisy writing paper I gave you, okay? An' be good for your meemaw."

One week later, Katie watched as the wobbly Buick eased out of the carport. Reeba and Buddy had packed everything they owned into the car. Reeba put her feet up on the dashboard, rolled down the window, and called Katie over. Buddy stopped the car. Reeba reached up to unloosen the red scarf she had tied in a knot behind her neck and gave it to Katie. "You take care now. Wear this all them ways I showed you, and always be someone people will remember, okay? Pretty is smart!" She blew Katie a kiss and waved at Abigail, who was standing on the curb, dabbing her eyes.

"I will, Reeba," Katie said, pulling her insides in tight, trying not to burst into a million pieces.

"Be good, girl!" Buddy said as he slid the car into drive. "We'll keep in touch."

Katie twisted the scarf around her hand and gave a little wave. The sheer chiffon flapped in the warm wind as she watched the Buick sputter out of sight.

The terrible news that Father Joe had been one of several American casualties killed in a car bomb attack near the South African Capital in Pretoria reached New Orleans on the television well before the certified letter. It was hand-delivered to Abigail, addressed to Mrs. Kenswick Franklin Delacorte III, by a diocesan bishop, Father O'Shaughnessy. It sat unopened on the hall credenza for days before she could bring herself to open it. Instead, she sat in paralyzed grief, praying feverishly and lighting candles, keeping vigil for her brave son's sacred soul.

She would not take food or drink, refusing sixteen-year-old Katie's comfort as she knelt at her grandmother's side, pouring her despondent tears into Abigail's lap. Since he had brought Katie home to Rose Gate Manor, they had only seen each other a handful more times, the last being the previous Christmas. The two were utterly inconsolable. Their beloved Joseph would not be coming back. Never would they see his sweet smile again, or his kind, knowing eyes. The shock and pain was unbearable. Joseph had been the only real father Katie had ever known. Selfishly and secretly, she cursed God. *How could you do this to us? How?*

She knew not the answers to life's cruelest injustices. Being left behind to face the emptiness alone seemed to be Katie's unshakable destiny.

The memorial was a quiet, dignified ceremony, held on the chapel grounds of Saint Louis Cathedral near the seminary where Father Joseph had once prepared for his vocation. Warren, Franklin, and their wives had gathered to grieve for the brave, dedicated fallen priest. Buddy, Reeba, and the baby, a fidgety boy toddler, arrived late and snuck into one of the back pews noisily.

Archbishop Canton presided, calling Father Joe a

"devoted soldier of peace who never lost sight of the true Christian mission of helping mankind to know Christ." The Bishop said that Father Joseph was an extraordinary man who loved the Lord with all his heart, but Katie knew better. She knew just how much of his extraordinary heart belonged to her as well.

She laid a single rose atop the draped metal coffin that was said to contain the remains of the body of the greatest man Katie had ever known. In it, she had asked to place a copy of her favorite book, the one that he had often read to her at the orphanage, night after night, *A Home for Sara.* How she loved hearing it read in his soft, melodic voice.

His personal Bible was retrieved from his belongings, along with a rosary and a small platinum holy medal of Saint Jude, whom Father Joe had said was the patron saint of lost causes. The items had been shipped to Abigail from overseas. She gave them all to Katie and said that they were hers to keep. She would treasure them for the rest of her life.

Katie leaned down close to the casket, and whispered so softly that only an angel could hear her words, "Goodbye, Father."

CHAPTER 19
★ ★ ★

KATIE'S HIGH SCHOOL WAS BUILT on sixty-two years of tradition. Founded by the Missionary Sisters of the Sacred Heart of Jesus, the private all-girls school was named for their foundress, Mother Cabrini. The original building was on Esplanade Street, and it was there that renowned Mother Cabrini lived and worked, serving the needs of the city's orphaned and abandoned in the mission until it was converted into a high school in 1905.

Several years prior, the new location opened its doors on Moss Street, and Katie was one of the privileged first to attend. Tradition was what Katie liked most about her school. Right away, she felt a connection with its rich and revered history. She loved what it stood for, and she loved the stunning ornate architecture and stately dark wood-laden halls of the original building that smelled old and rich with knowledge and holy reverence.

It was Abigail's idea to send Katie to Saint Cabrini's in the Garden District for a "proper education." It was her grandmother's belief that one could not receive as genuine an academic experience in the presence of pubescent young men as such were the designs of the lesser public schools. The Delacortes were well-to-do, and it was no secret that Abigail was one of the wealthiest women in the parish, though regarded by some as being a bit reclusive and eccentric in her ways, much to Katie's embarrassment. Abigail chose her charities selectively, opting to allocate more funds to the preservation of gardens and parish parks rather than to the needy and homeless. It was her money, she would argue stubbornly. And it was indeed hers to do with as she pleased.

Abigail encouraged Katie's desire to study English and the liberal arts, as she, too, had once enjoyed. Katie had a lovely speaking voice, compelling and engaging, which won her instant recruitment on the sophomore debate team.

"Education is everything," Abigail would say, echoing the words of her dear dead father, Professor Champard. Abigail had nothing but high hopes for Katie, who, in spite of her rough beginning in life, would, she was certain, amount to more than all of the Delacortes put together.

She just had to. Katie was the future.

The young women of Saint Cabrini were extraordinary students, each having been hand-selected for enrollment in the highly exclusive institution. Katie was a shoo-in with her brilliant test scores and highly regarded family name. Abigail saw to that. It was her sincerest desire to see Katie graduate from the prestigious school that would guarantee her transfer and acceptance to any of the finest universities.

It was easy to see that Katie had come from fine stock, although she did not flaunt her good fortunes like some of the other girls did. Katie had grown into a fine young woman, with regal good looks. She was tall, nearly five foot eight, with slim, delicate features, high cheekbones, and sharply intelligent blue eyes that had the power to mesmerize. Her unruly dark mane was kept taunt off her face with hair clips and headbands, or left naturally to fall about her smooth and tawny shoulders that warmed to a rich tan hue in the summer months easily giving an exotic edge to her already striking appearance. Katie made friends quickly. She was outgoing and approachable. She didn't choose her friends solely by status, or reputation, rather she trusted her instincts and let her heart lead the way.

"Wait up!" a classmate called from across the schoolyard. Father Michael had just finished morning Mass, and the junior class was filing out of church onto the massive lawn, where the bell would soon sound, signaling first period. The girl, a tiny waif in a glen plaid skirt and iron-pressed button-down blouse, bounded toward Katie excitedly. The two were friends and had been since freshman year when they first met in geometry class. Lorelai Wagner was a *real* orphan. Both of her parents had been murdered in a freak burglary in their home in Birmingham, where three-month-old Lorelai lay safely in her crib, along with two older siblings nearby, who also slept through the ordeal and were miraculously left unharmed. The children were later split and sent to three separate foster homes. Lorelai's first new family was a fate worse than death.

She was abused brutally by a woman who called herself Miss Mother, in her third foster placement at age seven. The woman suffered from delusional psychotic episodes during which time of total irrationality she would subject Lorelai to unspeakable tortures of neglect and abuse; locking her away in a closet for days on end, feeding her rotten food, and doling frequent beatings for crying or showing any form of fear or weakness.

Lorelai's days were terror-filled minefields of at which at any turn, her foster mother would one minute appear perfectly sane and loving, and then the next, mysteriously transform into a horrifying monster, tying young Lorelai to her bed and whipping her brutally with any object she had on hand—electric cords were her weapon of choice.

Mr. Father was a cold, disengaged ogre who ate his supper in front of the television set, night after night, ignoring them both. He occasionally would make casual mention of the cuts and bruises on Lorelai's body.

"Shouldn't you take the girl to a doctor for that arm, Mother? It don't look right," he would ask, over his chicken-fried steak and peas, only to receive her sharp retort.

"Aw, shut up! The little bitch gets no doctoring til she learns to mind. She threw up her goddamn breakfast again!"

The vomit had been scooped from the floor and served back to her in a bowl for her dinner. Mrs. Mother would scream and shout orders during her ranting tirades, wrenching Lorelai like a rag doll by the arms, causing her little bones to break and heal on their own.

Finally, after six torturous months, a teacher at Lorelai's school intervened when the little girl nearly collapsed from hunger while standing in line at recess. The teacher, Ms. Nolan, had noticed that Lorelai had curiously been wearing the same soiled clothes to school for five straight days. She explained that she had been told by her foster mother not to come home, and to "fend for herself" because she had ruined Ms. Mother's picture puzzle by bumping the coffee table when she got too close, causing the pieces to shift out of place. Lorelai then was forced to sleep in the family's garage behind the house, where she ate scraps from the garbage cans, miraculously making it to school each day, filthy and frightened.

She was promptly taken out of foster care and placed in a juvenile home in Alabama, where later she was later adopted at age nine by Mark and Julia Wagner.

Katie cried when she heard Lorelai's tragic life story, imagining all the cruelties her friend had to endure as a helpless child. She detested people who had no business raising children. "I'm so sorry that those horrible things happened to you, Lorelai. You were just a defenseless kid. You deserved better. They were sick—your foster parents."

"Yeah. I know," the sullen girl with willowy limbs and dish-blonde hair twisted into two neat braids behind her ears, said. "The angels, though. They were always watching over me. You know, Katie?"

Katie believed that she did. *Some people should just never have children*, she thought.

Lorelai appreciated Katie letting her talk about all that had happened to her back then, or not talk about it, whenever she didn't feel like talking. Either way, Katie was always there for her.

"What are friends for?" Katie would say, vowing secretly never to lose sight of how lucky she was to be so loved and to be living in the comfort and security of her home at Rose Gate with a grandmother who was all the family Katie really had—or needed.

"I'm not planning on ever having children," Katie said one day as she studied her blossoming form in the full-length mirror, admiring her budding breasts and covetous hips at varying angles. "I don't want to ever get fat or have my breasts all filled with milk—yuck!"

Lorelai nodded from the sidelines, reclining lazily on Katie's bed. She reached for the small teddy bear resting against the headboard and quickly stuffed it beneath her shirt. "There!"

The two adolescent girls burst into laughter at the lumpy, furry bulge beneath Lorelai s blouse that plopped to the floor when she stood up.

"Hey!" Katie rallied. "Do you want me to show you how to fix up an oatmeal facial? My stepmom, Reeba, taught me."

"Sure," said Lorelai.

Katie had never had a best friend like Lorelai, and it felt really good. The two shared nearly all the same classes, clothes, and crushes. They had a secret language in which they talked in code, had a key to each other's diary, and pledged a sisterhood locked in blood, achieved by pricking their pinkies and pressing them together, mingling their blood to seal the deal. Katie and Lorelai were inseparable.

The best of friends two girls could ever be, calling them-selves the Two Musketeers, challenging anyone to come between them.

On weekends, Katie took sewing classes from Miss Ramona, a local seamstress who owned a small dress shop in the Quarter. The cheerful old woman taught the local girls out of a converted back room of her shot gun-style cottage on Saint Ann Street that only had four rooms to it in total. Katie loved Miss Ramona's stories almost as much as she loved to watch her sew, especially the ones about Marie Laveau, the Voodoo witch-lady who cut hair as well as fleeced her victims.

Katie had hoped to be as skilled as Miss Ramona some-day in the fine art of dressmaking. She had first fallen in love with the art of piecing together patterns and prints in home economic class back in freshmen year at school. That was when Sister Claire had first suggested that Katie pursue the skill further, whereby giving her Miss Ramo-na's address.

Katie worked closely with her mentor and eventually learned the fine art of constructing gowns for debutantes and blushing brides, even designing and constructing some of the most prized parade costumes for Mardi Gras patrons that she had ever seen. And remarkably, to Katie's surprise, they were not all for women only.

Miss Ramona saw in Katie a talent far beyond the usual. She had a way with fabrics and ideas of her own—good ones for enhancing a garment's classic look as well as creat-ing unique twists on some old designs. She had talent and a flair for style. "That ain't something can be taught, girl," Ms. Ramona would say. "You got the gift. *Losh pa la pa tot!*" Katie knew from that point forward that she wanted to pursue fashion design more than anything.

It delighted Abigail that Katie had a calling and excelled

in it masterfully. She regarded the gift of having such skills as cooking and sewing as fine and necessary credentials for a young lady to possess, especially when one was as beautiful and talented as her Katie, whom, Abigail was hopeful, would soon be ready for marriage and a family of her own. While Katie did not share in her dear grandmother's vision for her future, she had grown into quite a stunning beauty. And it was all Abigail could do to keep the wolves at bay. At age eighteen, in her final years of high school, young Katie had no lack of wanting suitors.

Well before graduation, Katie had already created her very own dress for the senior dance. A stunning body-skimming sheath gown with yards of cream satin fabric with stunning sequins accenting the bodice and train. She had just the figure to pour into it, too. The look would be in the accessories—a double strand of pearls encircling her neck a la Jacqueline Kennedy, and tiny vintage drop earrings borrowed from her grandmother that had once belonged to *her* mother. The clincher was to be a matching shawl that Katie would drape alluringly across her smooth-toned shoulders in the event that the chaperoning sisters would object and find her indecently underdressed. It was going to be pure perfection. She modeled the prototype for Lorelai, complete with sections of the sequins glued into place for the test fitting.

"You definitely should consider going to design school, Katie. You're a genius with a needle and thread," Lorelai said. "I've never seen anything so beautiful."

"It's not even finished yet. Just wait!" Katie winked.

Lorelai was already slated for Louisiana University in the fall. The Wagner's insisted that she attend a local school with good programs and friendly campuses. "My grades aren't so good, but my father says that I should just muddle through as best I can, at least until I land a potential husband."

Lorelai would be entering into pre-law the following

fall.

God help the criminals, Katie thought to herself in amusement. Even though there was much truth to Lorelai's plan, most of Cabrini's graduating class of 1985 sought college campuses for one of three reasons: innovation, recreation, or escapism. Then there were those like Lorelai, who just hoped like hell to get through it with a bona fide pre-med or law-bound suitor. Everyone had his or her priorities.

Katie knew what hers were—a four-year program at New York's acclaimed private fashion design institute, Couture. Sure, there would still be term papers and tests to plow through, but the real fun would be in learning the ins and outs of the garment industry. Katie's ultimate goal was to someday have her name be synonymous with beautiful fashions for women in a way that had not been seen before.

CHAPTER 20

★ ★ ★

THE SUMMER BEFORE GRADUATION, KATIE was spending more time out of the house. She took a job as a counter girl after school at Biltmore's department store scooping ice cream and making sundaes for power shoppers and tourists.

Work at the food counter was easy and she preferred to earn her own money, which made her grandmother bust with pride. Most shifts Katie kept occupied cleaning off the equipment and dining area, rearranging chairs, and waiting on customers. One such favorite was a brooding artsy-type drifter named Jason Royal, who showed up each and every day around five. He ordered coffee, black, and a slice of pie. He fit in with the Punk Rock set and wore a cluster of keys that jingled on his hip when he walked.

The regulars at the counter had said that he played acoustic guitar at Rent's Kitchen, an upscale restaurant in the Quarter. Katie wondered why on earth, if he already worked in a restaurant, would he come to Biltmore's for chocolate pie day after day? The place was a dump compared to the finer restaurants in the area.

One day, she simply asked him. "What is it about our pie that you like so much that you keep comin' back, Jason?"

He just grinned and shrugged.

"Especially," Katie added, "seeing as how these here pies are fresh-baked and shipped in daily to your restaurant as well."

He actually blushed. "Well, we do carry these pies, I reckon', but they ain't as sweet and delicious as the ones served up by you, Miss Katie."

Katie and Jason did not need fate to convince them that stranger things than love have developed over a good dish of ice cream or a perfect slice of pie. It was the corniest and sweetest line she had ever heard, but it worked. She was hooked on the boy with his avant-garde looks and bad-boy smile.

By mid summer, they were a full-fledged couple, going out on Saturday night dates, to football games, and concerts out on the square near Saint Louis' Cathedral. Jason was older than Katie by several years. He worked as a custodian of an elementary school five nights a week, starting after his restaurant shift promptly at six p.m. Right after he finished his dishwashing job, he would stop off at Biltmore's to see her. There, he would fill his thermos with hot coffee and order a slice of pie, before going to his second job. Every night, Katie awaited his arrival with butterflies in her stomach.

Jason was the most intriguing person Katie had ever known. Sure, there were other boys, but none like Jason Royal. He was different. Besides being dark and mysterious-looking, he possessed a sweetness about him that melted Katie's heart every time they were together. He did not even have to tell her that she was beautiful; she could simply feel his captivating and carefree spirit pulling at her soul from across the room.

Jason was, among other things, a street artist and musician. He had a regular spot on the sidewalk just outside the

Cathedral, where he sketched charcoal portraits of pass-ersby for ten dollars each. He also played guitar, original songs that he had written himself. He shared a flat above a souvenir shop in the Quarter with his friend Chucky.

Love was a slow bloom, starting from the first time she saw him take a seat at the corner table some few months ago, wearing a POW T-shirt, over which he wore a cam-ouflage shirt with the sleeves cut off. He carried a tattered portfolio and wore a thin red bandana on his head. A leather and macramé choker traced his tan neck and he smelled like the sweetest musk—like wet soil and citrus. Katie especially loved his wavy hair. It was a dusky sandy brown that parted and fell in all directions past his ears and neck and swept up off his forehead—a throwback to every sexy screen hunk and leading man on the Holly-wood A-List. All she could remember thinking was how much she wanted to run her fingers through his hair from the first moment she saw him. Somewhere, deep within his soulful and contemplative brown eyes, she saw some-thing beckoning her to obey the feelings that his presence stirred. He was magnetic, mesmerizing, unimaginably irre-sistible. Katie would not have been able to taste life and all its magnificent promises if she could not, for any reason, love this boy. And so she did, with all the passion and inno-cence of a young girl's heart.

Katie had hoped to wait until they were married to sleep with him, but several weeks passed and Jason's persistence and promises had begun to finally wear her down. "Sis-ter Constance says that if a man truly loves you, he will respect a woman's honor and God's command for celibacy up until the marriage night," she said as Jason fumbled for her bra hooks beneath her gauzy sweater. "Maybe we should wait?"

Jason was not a Catholic and was appearing to grow

impatient with Katie's inclination to remain so, and a devout one at that. Her indecision seemed to be driving him even crazier.

One such occasion, when they had been necking for nearly an hour and she had permitted him to feel her breasts beneath her blouse, things changed decidedly. This was further evidenced by the moisture that had soaked clear through her blue jeans, indicating that she was convincible.

So came the words that she longed to hear. "I love you, Katie. I love you, baby, like I never felt for no one else. Not ever. Let me show you. Please, baby. *Please* let me show you how good I can make you feel. God! You're so beautiful . . ." It was nearly eleven and his roommate, Chucky, would be bounding in within the hour, ready to hit the bars that he and Jason frequented regularly, after Jason escorted Katie home in time to make curfew.

Pressing his throbbing groin into hers, he roughly guided her hand. She could feel his erection swell at her touch through his jeans. She stroked him gingerly, fighting with a fleeting pang of conscience, hearing only Jason's sweet words, "I love you, baby. C'mon . . ."

He moaned like a man possessed—possessed with desire, for *her*. The feeling swept deep throughout her body. Jason seized her face, kissing her hard and deep. Darting his tongue in and out of her mouth, skillfully grinding into the inevitable pleasure between her legs, causing an insatiable ache mixed with dizzy urgency to which she would finally surrender.

He yanked off her sweater, expertly unfastened her bra, and gazed at her bare breasts in the flickering candlelight. Her nipples were like crimson rose petals against mounds of lighter flesh. He unfastened her jeans, and she wriggled free, tossing them onto the floor somewhere in a heap.

Her breath quivered, "Jason, I— "

"Shhh . . ." He kissed her doubt away.

A Fleetwood Mac song streamed from the stereo speakers atop orange crates stacked near the windowsill. Katie could feel the vibrations from the bass surging through the floor, coursing through her body. Closing her eyes, she let the feeling of Jason's touch take her to places unknown.

He caressed her breasts, kissing and sucking a trail down along her stomach. Then, all at once his tongue was inside her, probing, licking, and stroking. It was a remarkable feeling that filled Katie up in all the empty places inside. She did not ever want the sensation to end.

She gasped, gripping tightly around Jason back. Just as she feared that the sensation would cause her to transcend the universe, Jason stopped. He fumbled with his belt and unzipped his jeans quickly, exposing his ready cock with a proud pause, allowing her to be notably impressed. Then, he poked and prodded roughly with the tip until he forced his way inside her, causing yet another sensation altogether—*pain!* The sudden sharp tearing seared through her, releasing a warm rush of blood between her legs. She winced and bit her bottom lip as he vigorously began to pump wildly, faster and faster, oblivious to the increasing pain that burned deep within her as he forced her tender flesh. She feared that she would split in two, but rather than stop him, she counted silently the brutal seconds until it was over. *Fifteen . . . sixteen . . . seventeen . . .*

Jason shifted his weight and thrust harder, pounding away at her with what felt like a hot steel rod. Faster and faster . . . grunting now like some sort of animal.

Finally, his face froze in a contorted grimace. He fitfully writhed fitfully, drawing in air in quick, sharp gasps, finally collapsing back down upon her, sweating and spent. His limp cock slid out of her, soft and puffy, covered with her blood.

Jason rolled over and examined himself.

"Shit, baby. Guess you weren't lying about that cherry! Don't move."

He stood up and stepped into his briefs and his Levis all in one motion and fished a Marlboro from his shirt, which was hanging on a nearby chair. He lit the cigarette and disappeared, returning a moment later with a dirty dishtowel.

"It's all I could find . . . just keep it."

Katie refused the greasy rag. "No, thanks, I'll just get cleaned up in the bathroom."

She was stunned at his matter-of-fact attitude. *What just happened here?* she had wondered to herself as she closed the bathroom door. Her vagina was burning sorely, and there was blood on her thighs. She heard him call through the door before turning up the stereo.

"Hurry up, Katie . . . put a fire under it! I've got to get you home. Chucky's picking me up at midnight."

She turned on the faucet and started to cry.

CHAPTER 21

★ ★ ★

ABIGAIL'S HEALTH WAS CONTINUING TO fail, having been diagnosed with a chronic heart condition caused most likely from childhood that had often left her progressively short of breath, swollen in her limbs, and with a persistent cough that plagued most of her waking hours. She had grown progressively weaker with the passing months and often spent her days confined to her bed or in the parlor. She had little hope for much else in life. All that was left for her now were her dreams for her granddaughter; for Katie to have a family of her own someday, and to hopefully carry on the many Delacorte traditions, or what was left of them.

It was no secret that Katie had been pawned off eleven years earlier on her grandmother by the youngest Delacorte son, who was too irresponsible to take care of himself, let alone to raise a child. This true version of events, however, was a direct contrast to Abigail's account of how it was that her dear little granddaughter first came to live with her from the early age of seven.

Katie, it was explained, resided with her in New Orleans in order to receive better care after taking ill with a diabetic state, and thus would receive better medical attention in the clinics and hospitals of Louisiana, while her father, a despondent widower, traveled extensively for his important work. Abigail had painted Katie's dear deceased mother as having been the daughter of a wealthy Kentucky land developer.

Society politely accepted Abigail's fabrication as the truth, and no one ever questioned the peculiar circumstance of a devoted grandmother raising one of her grandchildren as her own. Regardless of the fallacies of rumor, no one could deny the facts of Katie's undeniable mulatto features and coarse dark hair, which blended in concert with the traditional Delacorte characteristics, giving Katie a unique and extraordinary beauty unlike anyone else in her family.

By the time that Katie had come of age, Abigail could barely keep the questions at bay.

"What *am* I, Meemaw?" thirteen-year-old Katie had asked one night at dinner, putting the question to Abigail for nearly the hundredth time. She had always known that she looked different from everyone else in the family. Different from the other girls at school, even.

"Is it true what everyone is always saying about me? I have a right to know," she had demanded. She had both surprised Abigail and angered her as well.

"Katie! Abigail exploded, "What on earth has gotten a hold of you? You're too emotional sometimes, child, for your own good. That's what you are." She then stopped herself short. She collected herself and looked intently at her granddaughter for a long measure, and then decided to say what she deserved to know; to let her hear it from her instead of from the whispers of strangers. It was the moment Abigail had dreaded for years. It was the impossible moment that Buddy had left for her to bear. She could hear Joseph's words: *"It's always the strong ones who are left to bear the load . . ."*

"The truth is, Katie, your mother was . . ."

"*Negro.* Isn't that right, Meemaw?"

"Well, yes, that's right, dear. She was. The birth, it was . . . apparently, there were complications, and she—died. It just happened. Your father was heartbroken. He loved your mother very much," she added. "And he loved you. He took you to the orphanage to be with your uncle because he realized that he could not raise you alone. Now that's on him, not on you. He was too ashamed to ask me for help, I suppose. He had intended to come back for you, he had said, but for whatever reason . . . things worked out this way and here you are, with me."

Katie nodded. She had, it seemed, always known on some level. It was good to have the truth finally spoken. She was well familiar with the rest of the story.

"That makes you—"

"Mulatto." Katie concluded, as Abigail could not bring herself to utter the word.

Abigail nodded.

"May I be excused then?" Katie asked as she rose from the table.

"Yes, dear. Of course you may."

Time would heal Katie's shock, Abigail was certain. She was a strong girl and knew how very special and loved she was. But the one aspect that was far too insurmountable for Abigail to bear from that day forward would be the shame in everyone else knowing it. What if the truth of her half-breed grandchild got out, for everyone to know and to judge her? Surely Katie would know to keep such information discreet as she herself had managed to do for so many years. Abigail could only hope.

Lorelai was Katie's sole consolation, a friend who understood more sorrows than any being should be allowed. They changed classrooms at the eleven-thirty bell and met up in the corridor outside of the cafeteria for lunch just two weeks into the semester. Katie was despondent and barely touched her food. She picked at the bread crust of a chicken salad sandwich, while Lorelai feasted on corn chips and cold chocolate milk, as was her practice each and every day, claiming that cafeteria food was too wretched to eat.

Lorelai's hair, now bleached baby-doll white from sunshine and chlorine, after just four weeks on the swim team, made her look like a stunning California model. She had since grown and matured since the summer, with ultra-modern looks and a tall willowy frame. Katherine had thought that Lorelai should consider modeling. She was skinny as a twig in spite of her voracious appetite. If her nose weren't so crooked, Katie often thought, a problem that could easily be remedied with the right powders and concealers, she just might be able to pull it off. Katie was a whiz with such things and knew a winning face when she saw one. She loved to experiment with shadows and eyeliner. It came easy to her. Katie had an eye for fashion and beauty and, apparently, a quick-developing head for business in knowing that Lorelai had the type of look that could sell things.

"What's the big deal?" Lorelai said, when Katie brought up the subject about her heritage just at the start of lunch period. Lorelai was tearing at the cellophane of a Twinkie. "So you're bi-racial. So what? Actually, I think it's kind of cool. Hey, you said that you've known who you are since you were thirteen and where you came from. That's what matters."

"But what about Jason? Do you think I should tell him?" Katie asked.

"Oh, Jason doesn't mind, I'm sure."

"I guess you're—what? Jason knows?"

Lorelai tried to skillfully change the subject. "Yeah, I guess so. How did it go with you and lover-boy last night, anyway?"

"Wait a minute. *How* does Jason Royal know that about me?"

Lorelai's face softened. She looked so innocent at times it was impossible to be angry with her. "Everyone knows it, Katie. People talk, that's all."

"And what are 'people' saying?"

Lorelai sighed. "The story goes that your mom was black, yes—but she wasn't from Kentucky at all. She was from here."

Katie puzzled.

"The family's name is Del Ray. They're river people. They placed you in a linen basket days after you were born and delivered you to your father. Some friends who know him confirmed this. That's what folks say. The young black girl who died giving birth to you never was married to your dad. I'm sorry, Katie. It's just a story. I'm really sorry." She reached to touch her hand.

"And everyone believes this disgusting lie?" Katie spat, clearly in shock. The story did not match the version she had heard told from her grandmother. Her voice carried loudly over to where a table of other seniors were gathered, who were amusedly observing. The snickers infuriated her even further. "Well, I certainly don't believe it," she said, growing angrier by the moment. She had not eaten since dinner the evening before, and her blood sugar levels had dipped dangerously low.

"Forget it, Katie. It's probably bullshit, okay? People can be cruel. What do they know, anyway?"

Katie felt sick. She didn't care what other people thought, just what Jason *really* thought of her, that was all that mattered. He had been so rough and matter-of-fact with her the night before when she gave herself to him. He said that he loved her, but why did she feel so empty inside?

She needed to see him. She needed his comfort. He would understand how lost she was feeling right now. He was the one person in the entire world only who could make everything seem right again.

She went to the nurse's station for a shot of insulin and began feeling like herself by the end of her sixth period World History class.

After school, Katie ran to Rents Kitchen to see Jason. It was her night off at the department store, and she thought she would surprise him right when he got off. Maybe they would go down to the Brentwood and see a movie or something. *The Breakfast Club* was playing, and she was dying to see it.

She entered through the employee entrance and looked all around, but there was no sign of Jason. She bumped into a harried short-order cook in a greasy apron.

"Sorry, Miss, comin' through—behind you!"

She spun around right into a waiter.

"Hey, girly. Watch it!"

"Oh—I'm so sorry. I'm looking for Jason Royal."

The Latino waiter was stacking his tray with steamy plates of crawfish and motioned to a man near the salads, who was picking over a bowl of bib lettuce.

"See him."

The waiter skillfully perched the massive tray onto his shoulder, and headed out through the perpetually swinging door leading to the main dining area.

"Mr. G, somebody want to talk with you here!"

"Excuse me, sir." Katie approached man called "Mr. G."

The manager did not lift his eyes from the task of studying the expensive lettuce.

"Excuse me, please," she pressed. "Could you tell me where to find Jason Royal? He works here."

"Gone!" the manager barked.

"Gone? Gone where?" she asked, frantically.

The manager didn't look up. "I don't know, and I don't

give a fuck. But his ass is fired if he ever shows up here again. He left about an hour ago. Who's askin'?" He paused from his salads to study her.

"I'm . . . Katie Delacorte."

He gave her the five-second once-over, eyeing her credentials from front to back.

"Are you lookin' for work, Katie Delacorte? Can you serve *cock*-tails?"

He was the smarmiest-looking creature Katie had ever seen. *Not on your life would I ever work for a termite like you!*

"No, sir. I'm not looking for—I'm only seventeen."

"Could have fooled me, hot-stuff!" He cracked his Juicy Fruit and smirked. "I don't know where the hell the kid is. He took his pay and left. Musicians!"

Katie bolted out of the restaurant and down the alley, hurrying the four blocks over to Jason's flat above the Dirty Dog Tavern. When she arrived at his door, she was sweating and panting. *A jump in his shower would feel heavenly,* she thought. She just wanted to feel his body against hers. She would be better this time with the sex. She knew she could do better, and then he wouldn't leave her so quickly, but stay with her instead, cuddling under the sheets. Isn't that what people do? She would have to ask him why he quit the restaurant. They had talked about him joining her after graduation the following year, when the two of them would head off to New York—she, for her dreams and he, for his music. Maybe he was ready to break away. They had only discussed it briefly; about whether or not they would stay until she finished school there in Louisiana, or if she should transfer to a school in New York City next fall. They were going to find a place in Manhattan, where he would work as a short-order cook by day and play his music in the clubs at night. Maybe even get some of his wonderful songs published. She loved to imagine the dream. She replayed it all the time, over and over in her mind.

Climbing the flight of stairs to his apartment, she began to feel a little better. Soon, she would be lying there in his strong arms, and they would talk it all out. He would be all the healing she would need.

She knocked on the weathered door marked 2-D. She could hear Fleetwood Mac blaring on the stereo, so she had to knock harder. The door latch finally clicked from the inside, and a woman wearing Jason's flannel shirt, and nothing else, peered over the door chain.

Katie gasped. "Lorelai!"

CHAPTER 22

★ ★ ★

IT WAS NOT WITHOUT THE price of great self-sacrifice that Abigail paid for her children's passage into life at the ultimate and irreclaimable cost of, perhaps, her own happiness. A happiness, she reasoned, that had died many years ago with first, her dear twin sister, and then her precious angel infant daughter; followed by Kenswick—the only one true light in her life, and then finally, Joseph. What would be left to lose? Abigail's life was at best, a tragic litany of angst and battle for no apparent reason known to man, other than to say that it was her private and puzzling destiny.

Now that Katie had been told the whole truth about her birth from her back-stabbing classmate, she was free to tell the world the shameful secret that Abigail worked so very hard to conceal. That is why she had to do it. To consult with her dear dead sister Genevieve from the grave and through the gifted spirit reader—she had to find out what she should do next.

Sister Santiana, a gypsy medium, read Abigail's fortune in the tea leaves not seven nights prior, warning Abigail of a deep, dark secret about to be unleashed onto the world that had brought sadness and heartbreak to the women who lived at Rose Gate Manor. She was a Negress with opaque skin that glistened in the firelight. Her silk-spun turban covered her hair, except for the gray ones that sprouted from her brows and a few strays above her upper lip. She had a small tattoo on her right wrist that appeared to be a flaming cross. Sister Santiana was in the business of making people feel uneasy, but still, they came to her again and again.

"It lives within the walls of your house," she said with gravity.

She went on to explain that the command was from Genevieve's tormented soul, who begged for prayers to be released from the place where she was held bound, after all these years, along with all of the departed souls of the Delacorte family. Sister Santiana chanted Genevieve's pleas to cleanse Rose Gate Manor of the darkened curse, by the dripping of hot wax from seven holy candles. As she did so, Sister Santiana named each tortured soul one by one: *Genevieve . . . Rose . . .Waltman . . . Marietta . . . Kenswick . . .Joseph.*

"Stop! Please stop!" Abigail cried out. "I can hear this no more. What am I to do?"

"Destroy the curse by fire's flame on All Souls Day, and they will be released."

The medium went on. "The curse moves throughout every room of your house, Ms. Abigail. It is trapping your beloved in its prison walls." Sister Santiana then opened one beady eye. "The light has gone out. That is all, I'm afraid."

Sister Santiana was successfully terrifying Abigail into hysteria. The old woman took every word to heart, believing that the shadowy figure of light that danced on the wall behind her moments earlier was that of Genevieve, pleading for the release of her ancestors' tortured souls.

Petrified and confused, Abigail stood to leave. There was so little time left, she feared. She paid the woman the usual fee.

"Go take care of matters as you have been advised, Ms. Abigail. God's peace is with you."

The taxi had waited the forty minutes it took for the session. Sister Santiana had to assist Abigail, who was too frail to manage herself into the car. The driver recognized Charleen Del Ray and shook his head knowingly. She was the slickest con in the town, making her way by preying on the fears of unsuspecting pawns such as the old Delacorte woman. But he did make a handsome dollar for bringing the patrons there to her gypsy lean-to tent of fortune.

Only, tonight was different. Charleen had waited many years for this special customer. They all came to her tent eventually, desperate and broken, in search of spiritual guidance. And Ms. Abigail was no different. She had been ready for her.

The cab slowly headed westward from the river shanty, back toward town.

The next several weeks were a blur. Katie went on a rampage, destroying every card, letter, and trinket that they had given her—both of them. Lorelai, her dear, poor misunderstood double-crossing best friend, and Jason, the deceitful, lying snake to whom she foolishly and regretfully gave her heart and virginity. She hated them both and chastised herself severely for ever trusting anyone. The feelings of betrayal only fueled her desire to leave town. And the sooner, the better.

Graduation was still many months away, but she decided to research and apply to as many design schools throughout the country that she could.

She had high hopes of being accepted at New York's renowned Couture, where she figured that she could go if she could earn a scholarship, coupled with the college fund that Abigail had set aside for Tulane or Princeton. She would rent a small studio apartment; maybe get a couple of cats, and a part-time job in a clothing boutique—to learn the business. It was important that she would be as self-sufficient as possible and not to expect anyone—even her family—to carry her. She would attend classes full-time, while pursuing her design major. As long as it was a million miles from Louisiana, boarding schools, and mausoleum mansions where people like her grandmother remained locked in imagined and distant pasts, where women threw socials, drank tea, and knitted tiny doilies, waiting for their men to come rescue them from their enchanted prisons.

There were only a handful of such design schools in the States as backups. With her grades and talent, Katie was certain that she could attend any one of them, while hoping for the one of her choice. Nothing sounded as wonderful to Katie as the big city with all its chaos and commotion, theaters, restaurants, dress shops—real dress shops. Boutiques on Fifth Avenue, where big name designers displayed their clothing lines.

This was the dream that fired Katie's imagination. She burned the midnight oil designing sketches for her portfolio and typed entrance exam essays, set up recruitment interviews, and made preparations to leave New Orleans and her life, with all its heartbreaks and disappointments, behind.

When homecoming approached, Katie did her best to get into the spirit of things. She had not spoken to Lorelai since the night she had found her at Jason's apartment, and word through the grapevine was that the two were very much an item and that they were planning on heading for Nashville right after Lorelai finished at Cabrini, where Jason hoped to launch a recording career.

Katie was particularly shocked to learn that Lorelai had made plans to have Jason escort her to the senior dance. *How could she even think of it?* Katie wondered. *The little tramp!*

She was more than welcome to him and his pathetic aspiring "music career," Katie huffed. Boys like Jason Royal were a dime a dozen on music row, and they would soon find that out.

Katie vowed that no matter what happened, she would not let them, or anything else, spoil her own happiness. *Let them flaunt their relationship if they want.* She did not care. She was already counting down the months until graduation and, in her mind, was already on her way to her dreams.

Instead of sulking, Katie got to work finishing her gown for the dance and asked the most popular guy on the varsity team, Scott Schrader, if he would like to accompany her. She had asked him exactly two days prior to the dance. It was on a tip-off from Miss Ramona, who knew about such things. Apparently, Scott had just broken off with Linda "Pom-Pom" Potter earlier that day and was suddenly available. Katie was able to snatch him up before he even had time to return the rented tux!

Katie wore Linda's intended corsage, and Scott sulked most of the night, missing his pom-pom girl, for certain. It was a fine arrangement, and it suited Katie perfectly. Regardless, she managed to hold her head high, even when she passed Jason and Lorelai's table, wearing the remarkable cream satin gown that was the talk of the party, along with her impressive beef-cake escort, making all the girls so envious of Katie that they spent most of the evening despising her duly. Katie could not have been more pleased.

Early the next morning, she awoke to the sounds of a red cardinal in the magnolias outside her window. The warmer winds had retreated, and a serene, easy breeze was stirring up the gardens, sending fragrant wafts from the fruiting trees into the air. Ms. Gretta was frying bacon in the kitchen downstairs. Katie caught the scent immediately when she awoke, as almost instantly, it hit her stomach with a churning jolt.

She raced to the bathroom just in time and vomited.

"Should I tell your grandmother, or will you?" Dr. Gartou handed Katie another tissue, along with the shocking confirmation of the news she had suspected, but had been praying was wrong.

"Are you certain? I mean, really, it was only the one time, I swear." She broke down again, sobbing into her hands, although she did not need a blood test to confirm that she was pregnant.

"I'm going to college," Katie pronounced defiantly. With each wave of nausea, the missed periods, the fatigue, she actively denied what she feared to be true, reiterating to herself, *I'm going to be a designer . . . starting classes at Couture next fall . . . this is not happening to me . . . this is not happening.*

"Katie?"

The doctor was finishing making some notes in her file. "I could tell her with you, if you prefer. Of course, you've already contacted the boy, I presume?"

Katie hesitated. It was starting to sink in all too fast. *Was the room actually spinning?*

"We'll have to monitor the pregnancy very closely due to your diabetes, and given your age, well, there are risks to consider, so I'll be needing your full cooperation. Do you understand?"

"Yes, sir."

Katie was numb. *Oh God, what have I done?*

"It's going to be a tough road, I'm afraid. You'll be showing soon. Your grandmother will have to make arrangements with your school. I warn you, they won't keep you on once they find out. These matters are far too indecent for the Catholics."

He called the nurse, and the two talked in whispers. Something about a place in Minnesota that he knew might "take" her.

"We're getting you the number."

"Doctor Gartou . . .?" Katie said, feeling as if her voice was outside of her body.

"Yes, Katie?"

"Can I get dressed now? I want to go home."

He nodded, patting her knee. "We're finished here. I'd like to see you again in four weeks, then. Good luck, young lady. You're certainly going to need it."

CHAPTER 23

★ ★ ★

ABIGAIL HAD ALWAYS BEEN SUPERSTITIOUS and religiously skeptical, but a growing anxiety and knowing dread compelled her to search deeper for answers as she grew older. She was convinced that time and again, her dear departed sister and husband were calling her from the grave, trying to communicate with her.

Memories of conversations with Genevieve, in the garden, so many years ago, and unexplained provocations, which Abigail was convinced occurred at the hand of her dear deceased infant daughter, Marietta, taunted Abigail incessantly and tested her sanity. The lullabies never went out from her head. She needed to know. *Am I going crazy?* Abigail wondered when she heard voices and a baby's cry around the turn of a hall corner, or bellowing up from the cellar. Even the eaves about the exterior of the house chatted noisily like so many voices all at once, beckoning to her.

Abigail lit candles and burned incense. She pored over books that she had found in the metaphysical religions section of the library. She had to use a large magnifying glass as her vision had become as fuzzy as her brain. She acquiesced to the teachings of voodoo practice with compelling curiosity. It was when she could not see well any longer to read, and her mind was not as quick as before, that she turned to Sister Santiana.

One day, not three months prior, she received a flyer on her door announcing the psychic services of one, Sister Santiana, who had a small pop-up tent shop near the bayou, where she performed mystic readings and voodoo incantations, touting herself to the tourists as a spiritual clairvoyant counselor.

Three separate times Abigail picked up the flyer from in front of her porch door, and tossed it away. Each time, one would reappear somewhere unexpected, such as in the flower boxes, on the garden shed, or in the parcels from the grocery. Abigail was dumbfounded. When the fourth flyer mysteriously appeared wedged beneath her Bible on the mantle, Abigail relented and went to pay a visit to Sister Santiana, citing her sister's otherworldly intervention as the cause. *Okay, Genevieve, dear. You win.*

Sister Santiana had special powder dust and a smooth, polished "healing" stone that she would rub into Abigail's palms to soothe her rheumatism and to calm her nerves. Abigail complained that she often felt anxious during the night.

"Those voices, you know . . . sometimes I hear them. When everything is still in the house. I can hear them calling out at night."

The woman nodded. "Yes'm. Indeed they do."

Sister Santiana would chant peculiarly, evoking the spirits to rise and present themselves. And so Abigail believed that the shadowy figures and flickering light show that played out in her magic tent was all the proof she needed of the old woman's powers.

Once, Sister Santiana even slipped into a deep trance and evoked the deceased Delacorte spirits to move objects and even to ring a tiny bell to prove their presence during an elaborate séance that lasted for up to fifteen minutes. It was nothing short of remarkable.

Sister Santiana held onto Abigail's hands, one in each of hers, and invited her to rest her feet atop her shoes beneath the tiny card table. Abigail and other equally duped unsuspecting patrons never caught on when Charleen Del Ray, posing as Sister Santiana coyly sneaked her bare foot from out of the dummy cast to manipulate the strings of fishing wire and rods that activated the said objects, making them move and levitate on cue.

The night that Abigail returned home from her visit with Sister Santiana, she began to grow faint and dizzy. She struggled to calm herself. She crept gingerly to the cupboard in the kitchen hall and poured herself a stiff brandy. Sister Santiana's stern command still lingered in her mind, *"Destroy the curse by fire's flame on All Souls Day and they will be released."*

The fire-liquid went down like kerosene, which gave her a chilling idea.

She prepared the brew with calm, controlled valor the way that ladies did back when the men were dying and the children were crying, hungry for milk. She could remember her grandmother's stories about the old times. It had been so hard back then. Never was there a prouder family name than that of the Delacortes, or the Champards, who survived every imaginable distress and tragedy that life could serve up. Her pappy's daddy had a hundred slaves and saw them freed on emancipation day. Thirty-three stayed on in Mr. Champard's employ, though, to clean their stables, cook their meals, and to nurse their babies, but never was it permissible for the Negroes to mix with the white folk in blood. *Never!* It would corrupt the race, casting shame and defilement on the family . . . on the sacred family name.

CHAPTER 24

★ ★ ★

ALL SOULS DAY
1985

KATIE'S NOVA SPUTTERED IN THE dark twilight up Rampart and west on Canal. She wanted to avoid the Quarter, where a host of ghouls and goblins were most likely taking to the bars and restaurants after their trick or treating, now filling the streets. Most of the frolickers traipsing up and down the hedge-lined walkways of the Garden District were the last of the lot. It was getting late. The large, lighted mansions glowed invitingly with eerie jack-o-lanterns grinning on the ornate antebellum porches of the stately plantation homes.

She turned the corner onto Saint Charles Road, thinking all the while about the words she was about to say. Telling her grandmother that she was pregnant would not be the hardest part. It would be facing the disappointment in her eyes.

Abigail had such high hopes for Katie, as did she, for herself. Now what would she do? Whatever the case, she was convinced that her grandmother would know. She would take Katie into her arms and say that everything was going to be all right. Meemaw would fix it— she hoped.

The fair-haired elderly woman with the bright, shinning eyes once had nerves of steel, but lately it seemed, she had become distant and fretful. Often she would just drift off to some distant faraway place, with a glassy-eyed stare that concerned Katie deeply. To where was her dear grandmother retreating? Why had she become so paranoid and moody as of late? Katie wondered. It was apparent that Abigail's inner light and vibrancy was starting to fade. She was edgy and paranoid, suspicious even. She was, Katie feared, starting to grow regrettably delusional.

Katie would talk herself out of such thoughts, not wanting to believe them. She would soothe her grandmother's worries with a nice cup of chamomile tea, or by a reading from her favorite book. Still, deep down inside, Katie knew that something mysterious was slowly robbing her grandmother of herself. Bit by bit . . . piece by piece, erasing parts of Abigail with each passing month . . . week . . . day.

Katie was not a half block from the house when she heard the sirens. She had turned onto the street right into the center of a tumultuous scene. Police cars and emergency vehicles were everywhere. A uniformed officer was directing disorientated traffic in alternate directions. In the distance, the night sky was alight with a tremendous glow and a waft of thick, black smoke permeated the humid night air.

Then she saw it. A house halfway down the block—it was *her* house. Rose Gate Manor was ablaze.

Fiery orange flames shot into the sky, and a sickening disengaging of its structure collapsed into charred heaps onto the street and the scalded lawn below. Windows popped like pop-tops, and fiery projectiles made arching trails in the night sky.

Katie could not believe her eyes. Rose Gate Manor was burning, slipping from her sight as awestruck onlookers gawked, straining to view the spectacle. A glimmering passing of New Orleans' history succumbing to the perils of the mighty flames.

Katie could not move. It was all she could do to look on in utter disbelief and horror amid the chaos. And then, finding her full voice, a cry sprang up in her throat, jolting her to her full senses, rattling her to the core as she screamed, *"Meemaw!"*

Katie bolted from her car, leaving the motor running, and raced toward the blazing inferno, deaf to the shouts of the fire officials and police calling out for her to stop.

A burly officer covered in soot, all but for his eyes, caught her arm just as she was about to charge the steps of the inflamed portico.

"No! Get back!"

In a flash of a millisecond, it erupted from the weight of the massive roof that slid like a fallen giant down to one side, displacing the stately pillars, which first teetered, then collapsed in a grotesque contortion onto the blackened rubble that was once her home.

Katie was frantic. "My grandmother! She's in there! Please . . . somebody! You have to find her . . . Meemaw! Please, God, help her!"

She watched the old mansion tumble to ruins before her disbelieving eyes.

A second official appeared, and a half a dozen more were turning open water hoses onto the burning house, to no avail.

They led her to the back of an ambulance, where a body lay, covered with a sheet atop a gurney. No one made a move to resuscitate the victim. A paramedic was re-packing some tubing and supplies. His partner spoke in low tones, motioning toward the corpse.

"Miss, we believe that we have retrieved Mrs. Delacorte. Pulled her from the bedroom not ten minutes ago. The body, it's indistinguishable."

Katie regarded what appeared to be part of a leg protruding from the soiled sheet. Barely attached to the charred, mangled limb was a partial foot with a floral embroidered house slipper fused to the skin. It was the only recognizable thing that Katie could identify, or needed to, in order to confirm the unspeakable.

Somewhere in the distance, she heard someone call her name.

"Miss Delacorte . . . ? Can you hear me?" Someone's hands bore down about her shoulders. Voices and images blurred, and a distant incessant humming rose up in her ears. Then, everything around her started swirling and slipping farther and farther away, until, all at once, everything went black.

CHAPTER 25

★ ★ ★

1986

THE AIRPLANE CONNECTED WITH THE asphalt with a jolt, and the flight attendant's voice came on over the speaker. "*Welcome to Houston Intercontinental Airport, where the temperature is currently seventy-five degrees Fahrenheit, and the local time is nine thirty-five a.m. Please keep your seatbelts fastened until the aircraft has completely pulled into the gate.*"

Kathryn pressed her nose against the plastic window. Everything looked green the way she had remembered. Even in the heart of winter, it was always green south of the Mason-Dixon Line. She would not need a sweater or coat anymore. After a year and a half in the cool and often frigid temperatures of Winona, Minnesota, she vowed never to leave her beloved South ever again.

The chimes toned, and the passengers quickly disengaged their seat belts in rapid succession. She was alone—completely and finally alone—once again. And she was more than ready to begin a new life.

The first thing she did was to check in at an economy hotel near the airport with dismal walls and a poor excuse for air-conditioning. It was a quick cab ride from the terminal. She had saved a small cash reserve that would have to do for the time being, as her share of the inheritance money would not be given to her directly until she would turn twenty-one. Living with any of her known relatives in the interim, was not an option. The situation, she had decided, called for a clean slate.

Next, she would be in need of a good used vehicle. She walked several miles to the nearest town of Humble, pronounced by the locals as *Um-bul*. There, she plunked down nearly eight hundred fifty dollars on a 1978 Sherwood Green, Pontiac LeMans right off the lot. She talked the salesman down, considering herself quite a shrewd negotiator, scoring new floor mats and a road atlas in the deal.

She had lunch at the Humble Diner. A real honest-to-goodness Southern feast of beef barbecue, mashed potatoes, gravy, turnip greens, and slaw. She washed it down with several glasses of iced tea. How she'd missed the pleasure of sweet tea! She felt strangely conspicuous sitting alone with the noontime regular diners who made notice of the obvious stranger who had settled in the corner booth, poring over the apartment listings and want ads diligently.

"Excuse me ...?" Kathryn asked, as the waitress retrieved a whole rhubarb pie from the dessert carousel. "Could I get fruit salad, please? No whipped cream. Oh—and I'll have another glass of tea with that."

Kathryn had not eaten so well in months. She knew that if she played her cards right, everything was going to work out just fine. She had been planning everything out to the letter when all she had was time and a million hours to dream her next moves. It was a fresh start in a brand-new place where no one knew her name, or her past, or any of the secrets she had left behind. No one ever would. As far as she was concerned, Texas was the place where she could shed her old life and begin all over again. Starting with her name.

Gone was the innocent childhood moniker. From this point forward, she would be known as *Kathryn*, her full name—the only true thing that her birth mother, or her other family, had given her. A truth that was relayed to Father Joseph who had kept the weathered Bible that she had been found with until it was handed down to her after his passing. Now, it was a prized treasure tucked safely in a small brown satchel beside her in the booth. It was a beautiful, strong name that she would live up to, with pride and sophistication, just like her grandmother's name had served her. Kathryn Wanda Delacorte had *arrived*.

She checked on several apartments from a phone booth outside of the Texaco, noting their locations on the back of the road map. There were hundreds of miles of roads and freeways that comprised the city, and by the day's end, she felt as if she had covered each and every one of them. She found a small apartment in West University not far from downtown, close to the college, which was right in the heart and pulse of the city. It was where she wanted to be, in the thick of things; as close as possible to the movers and shakers of Houston's high society. If she was going to make something of her life, it would have to come from the right opportunities. It would be up to her to put herself in the path of potential success at every turn.

The apartment was not far from the city's renowned Galleria district, with its prestigious restaurants and hotels and sprawling shopping mall and the nearby affluent neighborhood of River Oaks, where she hoped to find quick work in one of the exclusive new boutiques. These served the wealthy and fashion-savvy residents who could be, for her, potential customers.

The city was bustling with the hum of fortune-seekers and oil company tycoons who had once fled south to partake in Houston's boomtown promise of petroleum rivers and liquid gold mines. The city was friendly, and Kathryn felt instantly certain that she was going to enjoy her new home.

She unloaded the car and was able to carry all of her worldly belongings into the split-level flat in just five trips. She had the first-floor unit with a single bedroom and open kitchen and living room combination that made the apartment feel like a large studio. The bathroom was so small that it only offered a commode and standing shower.

The walls were stucco and painted a pale cream, and the burnt-orange carpet felt like it had seen better days. The kitchen was walnut and olive green with amber fixtures over light bulbs in every room. It was not much, but it would do. Kathryn did not own a stick of furniture, but to her, it was a palace. It was her brand-new start.

Within a week, she had a phone, a flea-market sofa, and one end table. She bought some groceries and a small houseplant. The place was starting to slowly take shape. For her first official dinner in her new place, Kathryn prepared a grilled cheese sandwich with tomato soup, just like Ms. Gretta used to make for her when she would get home from school. The meal tasted good, but made her sad thinking about Rose Gate, her grandmother, and her life back in New Orleans.

Kathryn felt nostalgic after the solitary dinner and decided to rummage through some packing cartons that she had shipped from Louisiana to the main post office downtown. She retrieved a small metal strongbox and from the satchel in which she kept all her worldly treasures, she unpacked: Father Joe's Bible, Saint Jude medal, and his onyx rosary, along with a jade brooch, miraculously unharmed from the fire. It had belonged to Abigail, and it was the only thing on earth that was left of her grandmother from the char and ashes that took everything they owned. She touched it gingerly and placed it along with the other items into the strongbox as if it were a thing of gold. A few color snapshots were wedged beneath the Bible, but Kathryn could not bring herself to look at them. Not yet anyway, she decided, and closed the lid.

Matthew and Ryan Masters waited on the front steps in quiet, controlled anticipation. They lurched at the ready at the sound of each approaching car in hopes that it would be them. Their grandmother tinkered in the kitchen with Aunt Lorraine and Uncle Mack. It was the warmest day so far since Easter, and the grass was starting to come in nice and green. Soon they would be able to ride their bikes to school. But that was not at all what five-year-old Ryan was thinking as he fidgeted with the clip-on tie and itchy trousers he was forced to wear—under great protest—and on a Saturday afternoon no less! He was wondering what she would be like. He wondered about babies; how his important status in the household was about to change. From that point, it had been *him* who had gotten all the attention and fuss. Now, everything was going to be different. Sure, he told Mom and Dad that it was okay with him that they turn the playroom into a nursery so that he would not have to share a room with Matt. So what was the big deal? Babies didn't take much space. They were little. And it would be years before she would want his toys anyway. Right?

Somebody shouted from the porch, and everyone scrambled onto the lawn. Grandma, Grandfather, Aunt Lorraine, Uncle Mack, Cousin Viv, and some neighbors too.

"The car is here!" someone called.

Ryan was the first to spring from the porch onto the

sidewalk to meet them. The station wagon pulled gingerly up to the curb, and everyone crowded around.

'C'mon, Matt!" Ryan called. "Our new baby sister! She's here!"

CHAPTER 26

★ ★ ★

THE FIRST FEW WEEKS WERE tough. No one was hiring at the local retail stores. Kathryn had gone on countless interviews and had spent entire days at placement agencies talking with recruiters and taking typing drills, which made her palms sweat. She never was good with a keyboard, but give her a sewing machine and she could really shine. There were plenty of entry-level receptionist positions available, but Kathryn was not interested in working for oil companies or banks, stuck behind a desk. She did not want to answer phones, take messages, or juggle anyone's appointment book. She had a certificate of completion for passing the GED exam with certification from the night school she had attended in Minnesota while living at McKenna House. All the girls there were required to finish their high school education as part of the house rules, and to work part-time in one of the nearby towns. Kathryn had been placed in quality control at a canning factory in Fountain City just one week after she had arrived in Winona. She inspected and packed lids for pickle jars and ketchup bottles, four hours a day. It was tedious and grueling work. She then worked in the back office near the end of her pregnancy at the women's home, stuffing envelopes and filing paperwork with three other girls from the house, who were also awaiting the birth and impending adoptions for their babies.

Kathryn had little hope for a real future in Houston if she did not further her education, but at the same time, she needed to work. No one seemed to need a seamstress's services within a forty-mile radius of her apartment. She posted flyers everywhere: the North and East Loop areas, near the Medical Center, the downtown district, in the affluent suburban burrows, and even near the NASA Space Center. She even tried an upscale chain of department stores, looking for work in alterations, but was only offered a cashier post on weekends in women's better dresses. She took the position, along with a full-time receptionist temp job at an offshore drilling corporation on the west end of town, much to her displeasure. She knew that the schedule would be brutal and the work dull, but it was necessary in order to stay afloat and to save enough money to attend business courses at the University to complete the next phase of her plan, which was to ultimately create and market her own custom line of fashions and accessories to the private sector. It beat counting pickle jars. She was on her way.

CHAPTER 27
★ ★ ★

IN TWO YEARS' TIME, KATHRYN had successfully acquired an Associate's Degree in business management and had squirreled away enough savings to quit the department store and get started on her business venture. She would keep working as a temp to pay the rent. Her first task was to produce a line of distinctive fashion prototypes that would identify her brand as being fresh, unique, and new to the scene. She settled on creating some fun, bold pieces that would be distinctive and eye-catching, and that most women could incorporate into their existing wardrobes.

Kathryn worked her magic with liquid craft paints, glue, rhinestones, studs, and appliqués to adorn everything from jean jackets to baseball caps to knee socks with glitzy bursts of color and artful abstract designs creating novelty casual wear and accessories, which all bore her cursive signature in silver thread on stunning silk labels, aptly deemed, *Katie D. Designs.*

One day, when she brought some of the samples to her current temp office job to show them off, Babette Stockton, her boss's wife, who was visiting for the afternoon, fell instantly in love with the designs, buying up every item

Kathryn had. When she inquired about how she could see additional items, Kathryn had to confess to Babette that she had just cleaned her out of her entire inventory.

"My word!" Babette gushed. "If I took these samples along to my Thursday night wine club, I can guarantee that you would get at least a dozen or more orders. They're simply fabulous."

Kathryn felt a thrill of excitement.

"You really think so, Mrs. Stockton? I have a million ideas for this line, and some others for—you don't think it's too flashy, do you?"

"Flashy? Oh, dear," Babette quipped, tossing back a mane of three-tone bleached blonde tresses and fanning out five hot-pink dagger-pointed fingernails like a peacock. "This is Texas, honey—there ain't no such thing as being too 'anything!'"

The consequence of Mrs. Stockton's love affair with Kathryn's rhinestone-studded and beaded shirts, hats, boots, and handbags resulted in an order for twenty more items, which Kathryn would have to custom-make for her and her equally enamored society friends.

With the money she made from the sales, Kathryn produced additional inventory with the intention of presenting the samples to the local merchants around town. She knew that the large chains would not even consider doing business with an independent, so she focused on the smaller boutiques located just outside of the city.

The shops of the little town of Spring featured folk art and handmade crafts where visitors and locals could stroll through the historic streets of yesteryear, or old-time Texas, as it was affectionately known, where original cottages and farm homes had been converted into charming country stores and boutiques.

Kathryn had some crude business cards printed up on

lavender card stock with matching letterhead and labels and opened a company business account at the local bank near the Pick 'N Save. Happily, she was officially in business.

She solicited fifty stores in all, including the confectionary and ice cream parlor for good measure. Kathryn visited each one in person, presenting her line to the proprietors of the women's apparel shops. Five out of twenty-five boutiques agreed to display her merchandise on a consignment basis, and one bought a dozen Madonna-style ankle socks and lace headbands outright. She received one hundred forty-five dollars written out as a check to Katie D. Designs, which she did not even cash right away. Finally, before she had to cash it for more seed money, she made a photocopy of it and placed it in a frame above her headboard, keeping it as a trophy and sign of things to come.

Babette Stockton kept Kathryn hopping with orders for months. Between her steady stream of requests and replenishing the Spring Towne boutiques, which really started to take off, and with the pending holiday season quickly approaching, it was all Kathryn could do just to keep up. It was clear that she was going to need help.

She promptly hired a seamstress named, Nina, a Hispanic woman who answered her ad in the *Chronicle* to do part-time work out of her home. She was a shut-in with a flair for sewing, and she was very fast. Kathryn trained her quickly on how to apply the sequins, appliqués, and studs that adorned her signature garments. Together, they filled the orders for hats, belts, T-shirts, and vests for vendors throughout the area.

Kathryn began designing and trying out some new patterns that she tested in the local country boutiques, and soon her fledgling company was producing and selling custom- made garments that bore the Katie D. Designs label uptown as well in the high-priced storefronts. Her little company was growing at such a rapid rate that she and Nina could scarcely keep up with the demand.

Within two months, Kathryn found it necessary to rent a small twelve-hundred-square-foot office in a warehouse just off of the Beltway, where she officially set up shop, bringing on two additional seamstresses and a part-time shipping and receiving clerk. She also contracted a twenty-four-hour answering service to handle the overflow of incoming calls.

Kathryn's duties of serving as designer, customer service, operations, sales clerk, and general manager, put her officially at the helm of her own ship. The feeling was both thrilling and terrifying at the same time. Needless to say, she loved every minute of it and was right on track with her dreams.

CHAPTER 28

★ ★ ★

1989

KATHRYN WORKED DAY AND NIGHT, long, tedious hours, sometimes spending twelve to eighteen hours at a time at the warehouse. There was always something keeping her busy. It was all she could do just to keep up, managing the staff, filling orders, maintaining the production lines, and in her spare time, designing new merchandise to offer her vendors. It was no small task, and the work kept Kathryn pretty much exhausted.

She was voracious in her quest for success, constantly shopping the high-end chain stores and catalogs for trends; taking frequent buying trips to Dallas and Atlanta for new merchandise, and when time and funds would allow, she would head to New York City, filling her sketch pads and notebooks with pages of color notes and designs. She would then bring home new concepts and cutting-edge garments, acquired from sample racks and trunk sales, influenced from the real world, gleaned right off the city streets and runways; inspired from the back alleys and urban schoolyards of the city. The posh glut and panache of Broadway and Fifth Avenue, she knew, would also play well in the South.

Kathryn used it all, applying her extraordinary talents to finding just the right blend of style and substance, altitude and attitude, to suit the esteemed women of Houston's couture set, who were her main customers. And that she did with enough grace, style, and success to eventually earn one of the community's most prestigious awards.

That next year, Kathryn received the Chamber of Commerce's highly exalted "Women of Achievement" award for business excellence and entrepreneurship, which was, in her recollection, the first award she had ever received. The honor was to be presented to her at the annual Fall Fashion Gala, with the entire fashion industry—and all of Texas—watching.

The grand lobby of the famed Houstonian was themed "Lost in a Masquerade" and featured a cotillion of Texas's finest festooned in black-and-white regalia cleverly disguised in elaborate sequenced and feathered papier-mâché masks and feathered fans. Some of the guests were in sixteenth-century full face and costume, resembling period barons, baronesses, and jesters. It was a Mardi Gras parade of sorts for the elite high-society set, and it was a spectacle to behold.

Kathryn received her award shortly after a splendorous dinner culminating with flaming Baked Alaska paraded around the room to the orchestra's lively rendition of "When the Saints Go Marching In." It was a moment that instantly produced a tug upon her heart, reminding her keenly of her bayou home back in New Orleans. A place she often thought of, but that seemed so far away. She had to quickly steer her thoughts from her reverie, lest she lose her cool composure that had become her defense against an uncertain world.

Kathryn was no longer a little girl, or a young adolescent

forced to grow up sooner than she should have. She was an accomplished businesswoman now at only twenty-three years old. She would have fooled anyone with her poise, grace, and effortless natural beauty. Her raven hair had since been made smooth with relaxers and was spun in a fashionable up-do off her angular face revealing a flawless caramel complexion, the only real indicator of her mixed heritage. She had a genuine smile and pageant queen looks with translucent azure eyes that turned heads everywhere. She looked stunning and sufficiently understated in a sleeveless Christian Dior black gown with an incredible flowing chiffon scarf—her signature statement—cascading over her bronze, toned shoulders. She gave the appearance of being much older than her years standing at the podium accepting the prestigious achievement award. Success indeed agreed with her. Cool and stoic, she embraced the moment, knowing it to be merely the beginning of her dreams. There would be so much more to come.

Kathryn sipped a delightful chardonnay in a quiet corner of the room, thinking ardently about her escape once the orchestra finally began and the dancers took the floor. This night, in the enchanted walls of extravagance and masked fantasy, no other world existed. Kathryn's business was remarkably running a forty-percent profit margin; the Women of Achievement award that had been snagged for her mantle was well-deserved, and she could not have been happier, or felt more empowered. She was an accomplished woman who was writing her own destiny by shattering the past with a vow to never look back. Never again would she let herself be fooled by feelings of desire or attraction. Never would she love and lose so prodigiously. She simply would never let it happen.

So when a masked stranger who had been staring at her all night slipped her a note scrawled on the back of his business card in Monteblanc ink, requesting to meet with her, she was quick to disregard it, tossing it onto a nearby bus tray like trash, making full certain that her mysterious admirer saw her do it.

Denver Ralston had been studying Kathryn intently all evening from across the room. Never before had he seen such a stunning woman as she. He was mesmerized by her acceptance speech hours earlier and had noted, much to his surprise, that she was at the Gala unescorted.

He decided that he would drop off his flavor-of-the-month companion early that evening. Natasha had seen him eyeing Kathryn unabashedly all night long and was dully perturbed.

What was it about some women that simply drew him in like a fly into a widow's web? Was it her smile? Her eyes? The way she carried herself? Yes to all of those, he decided—and a dynamite figure to boot. Kathryn was perfection, Denver thought. And he knew perfect when he saw it.

He would have her. Of this, he was certain. Her disregard for his little message did not discourage him in the least. In fact, it amused him. Of course, Ms. Delacorte had no use for cheap schoolboy tactics. He would wait until the time was right to make his move. It only made him want her more.

CHAPTER 29

★ ★ ★

A NON-STOP STREAM OF ROSES KEPT coming, one by one at first, and then in great bunches. Day and night, they arrived. Long-stem red roses—everywhere—at her office, by the front door to her new apartment in Memorial Village, on her car. There were floral deliveries at all times of the day and night. It was a curious occurrence. No notes. No messages, just gorgeous roses appearing, singularly and in bunches around the clock.

Someone was playing the most curious game, Kathryn thought. And to be honest, the secrecy and intrigue excited her. Who was this mystery admirer? she wondered. She didn't have a single inkling whom it could be—at first.

At least not until one week later, when Kathryn received a box of cocktail napkins bearing the Houstonian logo, each one printed with the same message in Monteblanc ink: *Dinner at eight? Say yes!* And in parenthesis below: *(Please don't throw this chance away . . . if you do, here's ninety-nine more . . . and ninety-eight . . . and ninety-seven . . .* Kathryn smiled. It was the masked admirer from the award banquet. Each napkin was individually numbered in descending order. She had to admit, her mystery suitor certainly had style, and was most persistent.

No name or number appeared on the napkins or box, so Kathryn waited aptly, and sure enough, in three days' time, the unnamed stranger surfaced once again, sending a delivery to her door. It was a case of vintage Chardonnay, the very wine she had been enjoying the evening of the Gala when he saw her for the first time. A note was attached to the crate on a large, colorful tag: *Beautiful Lady, call me. I await your answer. Denver H. Ralston.*

Kathryn paused. She recognized the name right away. He was a business tycoon right out of the pages of Sandra Scope's Society feature in the *Chronicle*—a wealthy bachelor with enough clout and assets to be deemed one of the top eligible catches in all of Texas, a state that considered itself to be a nation unto itself, so he was a bit of a big deal.

She couldn't believe it. What on earth did Denver Ralston want with her? She figured it must be some sort of joke, or publicity stunt. *What could it hurt? I'm in control of things.* She had mustered the nerve to call the number provided, and Denver himself answered on his private line.

"Hello? Is this Mr. Ralston, please?"

Her voice was timid and soft, not at all how she wanted to come across—hardly the self-assured, ball-busting businesswoman who won achievement awards. She felt her face redden and her palms grow moist. She had chickened out three times prior, and this time was pay dirt. *Who was she fooling?* The moment was unnerving her.

Denver sounded like he could not have possibly been more thrilled.

"Miss Delacorte?"

"Yes."

"Finally, she speaks! I am Denver Ralston. I'm so glad that you called. Tell me, are you enjoying the wine I sent you?"

Ten minutes more and they had agreed to meet for dinner and cocktails at The Brownstone. By the time Kathryn had hung up the receiver, her heart was pounding. Little

Katie Delacorte had bagged a date with a bona fide billionaire. *God bless Texas!*

She cranked the stereo and ran through her apartment to her bedroom and jumped up and down the on the giant mattress. She felt giddy and silly, which was a feeling she had not experienced—ever. For an instant, she thought about Reeba, and wondered what she would do. Then, in a Southern second, it was clear as crystal—an oatmeal facial was in order.

Denver was amazing. Kathryn had never met anyone quite like him before. She had fully expected him to be stodgy and arrogant—ruthless in business, a common misconception taken of self-made moguls, he explained. But it was the opposite with him. Kathryn found her date to be attentive and genteel. He had old Southern charm that Kathryn took to immediately and found addictively endearing. He had a strong, athletic physique that Kathryn later learned was earned from four years playing football for Georgia State. Twenty years older than she, Denver had a rugged, handsome face, a strong chin, and inquisitive steel-gray eyes. His once-dark hair now gleamed silver and was brushed back, short around the ears, neat as a pin. His smile was slow in coming, but it shone ninety watts in all its glory. He smelled like leather, and scotch and Cartier. He was Irish and Greek on his father's side, and his mother was one quarter Cherokee. He was the most beautiful man she had ever seen.

He was the perfect gentleman and remained so for the full four months that they dated. He never once made a harsh or crude remark, or even tried to so much as kiss her except for an innocent brush on the cheek or pat on the hand at the end of a particularly wonderful night of dining, theater, or occasionally, two-stepping at The Post Oak Ranch.

Denver waited. Never pushing himself on her, he wined and dined Kathryn until she was dizzy from his charms and truly mad with longing for the object of her desire—*him*.

Suave, cool, and controlled, Denver commanded her attentions and every emotion simply by building a sexual tension and suspense that Kathryn thought would cause her to burst. And when first and finally they touched and kissed, Kathryn did just that.

She positively exploded with passion, allowing Denver to stroke and caress her everywhere, offering him her breasts and buttocks, pressing her hips hard against his leg as she took his eager tongue into her mouth. Right there in the hall at her apartment, what at first was an ordinary goodnight kiss, sent them both into oblivion, locking them in a lustful embrace that resulted in several hours of the most glorious lovemaking Kathryn had ever experienced, or knew that she could. There had been no one since her adolescent crush that cost her so dearly—until tonight. The reality of it all thoroughly convinced her that she and Denver were destined for more and fated to be one.

The two were married one week later in an Episcopal chapel in Galveston, followed by a champagne brunch with just a few choice family and friends, including, Denver's adult son, David, and his elderly mother, Hortence. Following the ceremony and reception they headed for the airport, where Denver's private plane awaited to shuttle them first to Corpus Christi for the night, and then on to Madrid for a three-week honeymoon at the Ritz, exploring the vibrant city and its many treasures.

"She's such a little angel, isn't she?"

The happy five-year old in pink tights and tutu padded across the stage at Miss Pearson's direction at the Silly

Goose preschool parents' night pageant.

The Masters sat forward, teetering on the edges of their seats to get a better view. Dr. Masters fumbled with the lens of his new Nikon. Even from twelve rows back, he could clearly frame up her cherubic face perfectly with the telephoto lens. She grinned impishly, playing the crowd like a fiddle.

"That's it, Ellie . . . great job! Hey, sweetheart, give us a smile!" Dr. Masters beamed, clicking away.

The crowd gave a rousing round of applause to a chorus of "Awwws" as the little girl with the big blue eyes spontaneously threw her father a kiss, stealing the show and not least of all, the hearts of everyone present.

CHAPTER 30

★ ★ ★

1995

THE RYDER TRUCK PULLED UP to the weathered two story Georgian house with the rusted- out swing set in the backyard. The perfectly pruned azalea bushes tucked neatly beneath the large picture window overlooked the cobblestone street on the corner of the block where the Masters children grew up and ran and played. It was where they rode their bicycles up and down the neighborhood streets, never too far out of earshot from their mother's dinner call.

Ellie was ten, sitting between her brothers in the back seat of a very-packed family van. The awkward teen boys were jabbing elbows and kicking up trouble astride her, when they suddenly paused momentarily from their Gameboys to watch it all fade behind them in the rearview mirror. It was moving day.

What would Texas be like? Ellie wondered. All she could imagine were tumbleweeds and prickly cactus plants and ranch-hand cowboys running around. Her father had said that Houston would be nothing like that. Her imagined scenario of life in Texas filled her with dread. "What if I don't make any new friends?" Ellie had asked, fearing that her distinctive East Coast accent would set her apart from her classmates right from the start. Why did her father have to take another job so many miles from everything they knew? He was a surgeon, probably the best in the world, her brother Matt had said. People needed him there to help them get better. Ellie could not argue with that. Luckily for the Masters children and others like them, many of the area schools were filled with transplants from northern and eastern cities whose families had similarly been relocated to Houston due to their fathers' jobs with the hospitals and large oil corporations.

Happily, it was not as difficult to get acclimated, as Ellie had feared. Seventeen out of thirty-one of her classmates were also transplants. Ellie's new friend, McKenzie was from Queens, making her mild East Coast accent seem nonexistent by comparison.

The Masters moved into a large lavish home located in an affluent suburban region called the Woodlands, just on the outskirts of downtown Houston. The sprawling corporate and residential mini-mecca featured newly con-structed luxury homes and businesses dotting the fairways of competition-worthy championship golf courses and glistening man-made lakes.

It was a lush and luxurious setting, with the constant waft of sweet cedar and pine baking in the heat and humidity held prevalent in the thick, stifling air drifting in from the Gulf. In a word, it was H-O-T. The Masters felt more like they had moved to Honduras than Houston. It was defi-nitely going to take some getting used to.

Kathryn loved her new husband Denver, with all her heart. She was thrilled to be Mrs. Denver Ralston III, and played the role to the hilt. Denver's fortune was mainly in a string of construction companies, a few hardware chains, and new emerging big-box stores, where people could buy everything from tank tops to tires. Next to pleasing her virile and dashingly handsome husband, Kathryn pleasured in spending his money, decorating their new forty-room estate in Houston's Bellaire, the beach house in Corpus Christi, and the ranch in Austin. Denver traveled extensively, leaving Kathryn to oversee matters of running the households. She sold off her business immediately in order to free up her time for him exclusively, but, unfortunately, spent most of her spare time waiting for Denver to return from international business trips, late-night meetings, or weekend golf outings. While Kathryn was generally happy with her marriage, she realized that the price she paid for the fairy tale was great.

"I'm lonely." There. She said it. She had confessed her woes to a two-hundred-fifty dollar-an-hour shrink wearing designer clothes far better reserved for the body of runway models and sporting enough expensive artwork on the walls to start her own gallery. Halfway through her litany of childhood angst and abandonment, Kathryn realized that the woman was not really listening. She was just going through the motions.

"What do you think I should do?" Kathryn asked.

"I don't know, Kathryn. The important thing is what do *you* think you should do?"

"What do *I* think? I think that for the small fortune that you're making off of my dysfunctional and unfortunate past and upbringing that you should at least have one fucking constructive piece of advice as to what I should do to make my marriage work. That's what I think!"

Dr. Lesser blinked, showing little reaction to her patient's outburst.

"I see. Anything else, Kathryn?"

Kathryn got up from the couch, scooped up her designer bag, and smugly spat, "Yeah. Your clothes suck. I think that too. How's that for brutal honesty? *Geeze!* I feel better already. You're a goddamn genius, Doc!"

Kathryn stormed out past the receptionist, startling her with a cool breeze as she whizzed on past in her Prada pumps.

The harried girl bounded from her chair. "Mrs. Ralston. Will you be needing another appointment?"

Firing her shrink was just the first step. Second, Kathryn had to find a way to cope with Denver's absences and the growing fear in her gut that said that things had changed. She didn't know how, or when, but they had. The downtime made her incurably restless. She had already learned to play the part of a "perfect" society wife, complete with tennis lessons, lunch at the club, socialite friends, and a *Town & Country* picture-perfect home with maid servants, gardeners, and cooks.

She attended so many lunches and socials that she could barely look at another plate of seared salmon. It was a byproduct of chairing on simultaneous humanitarian counsels and committees. She had a private workout trainer, a chef and chauffeur at her disposal, along with a closet full of designer clothes, one hundred twenty pairs of Italian shoes, a white Mercedes, and a stable full of thoroughbred horses on the ranch in Austin.

It had always been one of her life's goals to learn to ride horses. It was a skill that, proudly, she had grown impressively proficient at. Kathryn had a favorite, a mare, which she tended to with particular attention, often driving over to Austin two to three times per week to train her. Alex, the Syrian stablehand was the only other person, besides Kathryn, whom the mare trusted. All other staff members were off-limits to the magnificent honey-brown mare that Kathryn simply called Baby.

Something about the gentle yet powerful horse soothed Kathryn's spirit like nothing else. When she and Baby would ride, they became one with the wind, the sky, the sun, and the dew-kissed rolling grassland. It was a feeling of complete and utter connection that could not be explained. It freed Kathryn of the shackles of her too often-tormented thoughts, carrying her farther and farther away from the places she left behind and the newer fear that was now threatening her perfect world.

"What's the matter, dear?" Denver asked from behind his *Wall Street Journal*. It was the end of the year, and once again, he would be taking a trip to Hong Kong before the holidays. They were planning a week in the Caymans to spend a very unorthodox Christmas up to their ankles in white sand and seashells. It was his decision that they would enjoy a much-needed respite from the erratic and demanding schedule that kept them from actually enjoying their now fifth year of wedded bliss.

"To hell with all the holiday fuss and hoopla," Denver had said. His family and associates would just have to celebrate without them. Kathryn seemed glad that he was carving out some time for just the two of them. She had no connection to her family on Buddy's side to speak of, as they lived their separate lives and communicated rarely, if at all, so the opportunity to spend the holidays, just the two of them alone, was what she and Denver needed. It was sure to make her happy. In just three short weeks, they would be on their way to a tropical paradise. But first—he had to take this business trip to Hong Kong. What could he do?

"I miss you, Denver . . . I miss us. That's all." She purred, smoothing his hair over his brow.

Too much time on a beautiful woman's hands was not a good thing. The last thing in the world that he needed was a discontented bride.

"Hey, I have a great idea," he proposed, lowering the newspaper as Sue Lee, the kitchen maid, promptly refilled his coffee cup. "Why don't we move the trip up a few days? You go on ahead of me and I'll fly down and join you at the end of the week right when I get back from Hong Kong."

Kathryn sighed. "It's just that—"

He frowned. How could she find fault in his offer? He was making an effort to spend quality time with her soon, wasn't he? "It's just *what*, dear?"

She seemed to catch herself once again being selfish and childlike. Didn't she see that he was doing his best to make time for them?

"Oh, it's nothing, really," Kathryn said. "That sounds absolutely perfect. I'll go on ahead."

She bent over the buttered toast and kissed him gently on the cheek. "But you'd better hurry back, old man, or I'm going to run off with one of those hot little cabana boys if you're not careful!"

His mobile phone rang, and he got up to retrieve it from his briefcase. Sue Lee hurried off to summon the car.

"Ralston here," he said, giving her a smile.

He covered the mouthpiece of the huge contraption with its long, rubbery antenna. "It's Mr. Yakioshi, sweet-heart . . . can we discuss this later?" He grabbed his suit coat and patted her affectionately on the behind. He spoke loudly across the ocean into the large plastic phone—a technological wonder. "Someday they will make a portable phone no bigger than a compact," he would tell Kathryn, amused. He liked being in the know of things, and he felt that in many ways, he was an innovator. He only wished more people saw things his way. Starting with his beautiful wife.

A horn sounded from outside. It was his driver.

He blew Kathryn a kiss and, backing out the door, once again covered the receiver discreetly.

"I'll have Triston book us a table tonight at Lagniappe, okay?"

Kathryn nodded and blew him a kiss.

Safely inside the limo, Denver slid the privacy window closed and signaled on the intercom for the driver to take him to the Galleria office. He was still on the clunky portable phone, and did not miss a beat.

"So we're all set, then . . . I've booked the flight. Next time we see each other, we'll be in Hong Kong, *Mister Yakioshi!*"

A sultry female voice on the other end of the line cooed the ready reply, "I can hardly wait, my darling . . . *Sayonara!*"

CHAPTER 31
★ ★ ★

1995

KATHRYN GOT BUSY. AS USUAL, once she decided on something, she had no choice but to follow through. Her days of padding around in house slippers ordering roomfuls of furniture and "doing lunch" with dinosaur society matrons were over. She did not need a two-hundred-fifty-dollar an-hour therapist to tell her what she needed. It was obvious. Kathryn was stifled. She was sweetly and slowly beginning to wither on the vine from lack of nourishment. She needed more. She needed a *purpose*.

The idea hit her while she stood beneath the glistening shower jets, letting the soothing steam filter through her pores, stirring her senses. *What if Denver let me run one of his smaller offshoot businesses?* There had been so many in the last acquisition, surely there would be something she could manage with her talents.

Of particular interest to her was a fledgling cosmetic company called Beauty Essence. It was a line of inexpensive simple ingredient cleansers and lotions, as well as a small collection of blush and eye shadow palettes, eye pencil, and lip-gloss products. Kathryn was not entirely sure exactly what the concept was all about, but she was determined to find out. The product intrigued her, and the potential for mass marketing such a beauty line positively excited her entrepreneur instincts even more.

She skipped her morning jazzercise class, driving right on past the fitness complex and on to the local library. Strolling purposefully toward the reference desk, she gleaned some curious stares from the other library patrons, med students and legal types in business suits and dress shirts, as she plopped down at a large table in her Lycra leotard and bright pink leg warmers.

For hours she pored over the financial listings and marketing data for skin care and cosmetic companies in varying demographics for several competing industries. What she found when she was finished, was what appeared to be a viable opportunity.

She jumped on the personal computer screen with the help of the librarian to dial up and read countless reports on the Internet line that pulled information from data banks on the World Wide Web. She researched tediously for comparison data on the ingredients of currently marketed products manufactured in the United States and abroad. She rifled through page after page filled with new and innovative ideas about the changing direction of beauty. And changing it was. According to Kathryn's armchair analysis, everything pointed in one inevitable direction—back to basics.

The way of the future would be a step back to simpler, more natural methods. Like any entrepreneur worth her salt, she decided that she would test her theory. Kathryn consulted with dermatologists, scientists, botanists, and countless beauty experts over the next two weeks, each providing mountains of useful data and research to support her vision. The business plan would practically write itself.

She completed the financial prospectus just minutes before the car arrived to take her to the airport. She would carry it with her to the Caymans and present it to Denver once they were alone and he was relaxed, giving her his full attention. She basked in the possibilities for her idea. It had been too long since Kathryn had thrilled at the prospect of having a good idea. Actually, she had plenty of them—big ideas that she was dying to share with Denver—but it never seemed like the right time. Perhaps it would be better once they were in the islands away from it all, when she would have her handsome and brilliant husband all to herself for seven entire days. She had helped him pack prior to his trip to Hong Kong the night before he left, slipping various trinkets into his luggage in anticipation of the following week, when he would join her on the island. She pictured his delight when he would find them, one by one.

There was a post card with a powder-white beach and a huge, bright blue ocean that made the palm trees depicted look small; a bottle of suntan oil, and a smooth pink sea-shell. She hoped that he would find the treasures as he unpacked and think of her with wild anticipation.

She would be ready too. In just seven glorious days she would have her beloved husband all to herself. Kathryn felt like a queen. Never, in all of her life, could she remember feeling so full of utter joy and contentment. This was it, she decided. The thing that people search all their lives for. And it was her turn at last, to revel in it. How far she had come, indeed. What a price she'd paid to get here. *Not bad for a little mulatto girl from Louisiana!* she told herself.

The taxi's horn sounded. She gave a quick wave from the window, signaling that she would be right down. Gathering her bags, she hurried for the stairs, nearly forgetting the business plan she had placed on Denver's desk. She went back and snatched it hurriedly; inadvertently dislodging a stack of papers left unbound that fell to the floor. She quickly picked them up and rearranged the papers on his desk. She noticed a receipt from Tiffany's on top of the stack for a very large sum.

"What do we have here?" Kathryn said aloud. She smiled coyly as chuckled at the irony. She had caught her husband's loose attempt at hiding the evidence for an extravagant purchase for his endearing wife. She could hardly contain her excitement. Denver had hoped to surprise *her* with a gift of his own. They were simply made for one another. No one had ever been so good to her in all her life. She wondered what she had done to deserve him.

Burying the receipt carefully back in the stack of papers, she promised herself that she would act surprised when he presented the gift to her. "I do love you, sweetheart," she whispered. "Thank you so much for finding me."

CHAPTER 32

★ ★ ★

KATHRYN LOVED SUNRISES. SINCE SHE was usually up with the chickens, she rarely missed the tireless spectacle of watching the dawn creep across the expansive blue sky, little by little, slowly bringing the day to full light. Next to a cup of her favorite dark-roasted coffee, it was the most glorious wake-up call around. She could hardly wait for the dull and distant light far off on the horizon to break through, and to behold the sensational unfurling of a different, exotic sky. It was an exquisite pleasure to be sipping this morning's coffee on a veranda overlooking Seven Mile Beach on the brink of a glorious Caribbean sunrise. The sea air and the waves were absolutely breathtaking. She slipped on her designer sunglasses and tilted her exquisite face to the sun.

If only Denver were here with me, she thought wistfully. *I can't wait to tell him about my business plan.* She decided that she would take a dip in the hotel pool after breakfast and then do some shopping on the island to help make the time pass. He would soon be there with her.

Life was full of so much uncertainty and strife. She felt so lucky to be Mrs. Denver Ralston, and to have found her place in the world. Theirs was a love that was here to stay.

Still, she did feel that there was so much more she could be doing, and she could not wait to share her ideas about that with Denver too. With the man she loved and trusted more than any living soul. While she didn't need his approval, she did want him take notice of her capabilities. She would show him that there was more to his beautiful wife than makeup and manicures—plenty more. And she fully intended to turn those assets into gold.

Kathryn sat in the lobby of the hotel. The open-air bar was aptly filled with tourists and retired snowbirds who had permanently fled the chilly winters of the north for sandy beaches and perpetual summer winds. A few locals in suits and ties were conducting business at a small table in the corner over cold Coronas. It was after six p.m., and happy hour was well underway. A Calypso band was playing on the pavilion stage overlooking the beach, and people were beginning to gather on the crude wooden plank dance floor, in cut-offs and flip-flops, some bare-footed, gyrating to the drone of the steele drums creating melodic pulses that carried the spirit and made one's troubles seem as tiny as a grain of sand.

Kathryn was stunning. Tan and lean in a Halston halter dress, she perched regally atop a bamboo barstool, holding the attention of every man in the room, as was her prac-tice. She would let them look, but nothing more. She was a one-man woman, and Denver was all the man she would ever need. In just three short days, he would be there. She truly believed that she could do anything. He made her feel that way.

Her heart leapt when he appeared in the foyer. They exchanged smiles, and then, in a swift moment, were locked in each other's arms as if they had never been apart.

"I've missed you, my darling. Have you kept yourself entertained?"

"I've managed," She smiled, smoothing his silver hair and tracing a line behind his ear. "Although I thought I would die waiting! Are you hungry?"

Denver grabbed her waist and loosened his tie. He growled playfully, quite out of character for himself as of late, but refreshingly delightful nonetheless. "Just hungry for you, baby!"

She grabbed the room key, scooping up her purse as she slid from the barstool, certain to flash him just long enough to show him what she was wearing beneath the flimsy sundress, playfully daring him to notice.

Denver squinted and then smiled. "Are you *wearing—?*"

She smiled coyly and nodded, jingling the key. "Room five twenty-two . . . in *five minutes.*"

She was waiting for him. When he knocked eagerly on the hotel room door, a sex goddess greeted him therein, wearing nothing but a garter belt, bra, and heels. A thin film of black chiffon was all that stood between him and pure ecstasy. He worked his way up her astonishingly firm thighs, scarcely able to keep his eyes off of her garter belt and lace push-up bra. It was every man's choicest stripper fantasy. This, she knew.

She drew him into the dimly lit room and began to undress him slowly.

The sensations were thrilling. She worked like a pro, further unfastening his tie, unbuttoning his shirt, teasing his ears with hot flicks of her probing tongue, giving him shock waves from head to toe.

When she bent down to address the massive bulge in his pants, he truly thought he had died and gone to heaven. What a rare treat this was! He strained to imagine the last time he could remember Kathryn ever pleasuring his cock this way and came up blank. He just couldn't recall, and frankly, at the moment, it did not matter a whole hell of a lot. He was being gratified in the most delightful way, and that was all that mattered.

"Whowwee! Crystal—you are fucking *amazing!*" he said as he fell backward onto the bed. She mounted him and began rocking slowly back and forth. His body shook as he clutched her ass and pumped away, taking in quick, sharp breaths, feeling her silky Asian hair fall across his face, which excited him all the more.

He moaned in rising crescendo, and then he stiffened and fell limp beneath her.

Distressed, she could immediately see that he had stopped breathing altogether. "Denver!"

Shaking him violently, she pressed down on his bare chest with both hands, delivering frantic thrusts with all her strength above his heart, cracking two ribs in the process. She lunged for the phone, knocking the lamp to the floor. "Help! Please!" she begged the foreign voice at the front desk. "My God! He's having a heart attack! Call someone—hurry, please!"

Denver Ralston was pronounced dead upon arrival at Queen Elizabeth Hospital in Kowloon, Hong Kong, at seven thirty-five p.m.

CHAPTER 33

★ ★ ★

THE PHONE RANG ON DEAF ears. Kathryn was not talking to anyone. She had not eaten or slept in five days. The flight back to the States had been a blur. She did not remember much. Denver's chief advisor, Rand Biderman, flew down immediately to bring her home. The body would remain in Hong Kong until details could be cleared with the authorities. Discretion was of utmost importance.

The woman was being held for questioning. Everyone, with the exception of Kathryn, seemed to know things. Secret things. Rand blubbered in the limo on the ride back to Houston, but she was too drugged-up to join him. The doctors had given Kathryn sedatives to help her through the shock. Rand had been a friend and confidant of Denver's for thirty-five years. There would be a mountain of details to drudge through.

"Don't worry, Kathryn. I'll take care of everything," he told her, patting her listless hand.

Rand Biderman's physician saw to it that frequent Valium cocktails were administered on a regular basis, keeping reality as far away from Kathryn's jumbled consciousness as possible. They were fearful of her slipping into a diabetic coma and had to watch her constantly. Arrangements still needed to be made for the body, which remained on ice nearly seventeen hours across the ocean.

Mostly, Kathryn slept from exhaustion and grief. Occasionally, when she would come to, she would shriek loudly, thrashing about the bed like a wild animal. Two nurses were assigned to her bedside at Biderman's request, force-feeding her intravenously, seeing to her insulin treatments, and keeping her comfortably sedated.

It was two weeks before Denver's corpse finally arrived back in the States where he was buried in an undisclosed location.

An astonishing crowd of mourners gathered at the Ralston estate, and TV reporters incessantly hounded the family and cohorts of the dead billionaire. Denver's son, David, gave a valiant and exemplary eulogy, standing alongside his life partner, Gregory, as the only immediate relatives in company with some seven hundred friends and associates.

Denver was well loved and admired by so many. Kathryn was too ill to attend the service and had the excruciating torment of having to view the highlights of the memorial covered on the local nightly newscast.

Rand visited her frequently, checking up on her and tending to Denver's remaining business affairs. Kathryn rarely emerged from her darkened bedroom, often refusing meals, and not bothering to bathe for days on end.

One Sunday he found her standing at the foot of the bed, staring out into the garden. Her hair was freshly washed and wrapped in a bath towel. He was happy to see her looking alive.

"Good morning, Kathryn!"

She did not answer. She just regarded him with a cool glare. He felt strangely uneasy, but tried to remain light. He had brought her a small velvet satchel that he was certain would cheer her. The item had been found in Denver's suit coat the night of his death. He showed it to her. It contained an exquisite white coral brooch surrounded with Austrian cut diamonds. She took it from his hand. The brooch was valued at fifteen thousand dollars. She knew this from the receipt slip she had discovered just a few weeks ago.

"I thought you might want to keep this . . . he probably had intentions of giving this to you on your trip."

Kathryn's sallow continence remained unchanged, although fury raged inside her, behind the dull, swollen eyes and the thin, pale frown. "For me? Ha! It was intended for his whore!" she spat. *How stupid could this asshole be? How dare he bring this worthless token into my house!*

The agony was maddening. Rand balked as she coolly tossed the bauble over to her housemaid, who was tending to the bedsheets as if it were simply a box of chocolate truffles.

"Sue Lee, you'll enjoy the brooch, won't you?"

The young woman stood, stunned. "No, ma'am. I couldn't. It's much too—"

"Don't be silly, Sue Lee. Take it and wear it in good health. It's yours. Now, if you would, please, quickly pack up my things. I'm going to be taking a little trip."

Rand was incredulous. "Trip? What trip? Where?" he bumbled, reeling from the scene with the brooch. "I must insist you tell me, Kathryn. Where are you going?" He squeezed her arm.

Bad move.

She exploded. "DON'T TOUCH ME! Don't you ever touch me again! Got that?"

At one time, she had high regard for Rand Biderman, but now, she simply hated the sight of him, as everything about him reminded her of Denver. Surely he had known about her husband's indiscretions, *surely*. In her eyes, he was equally as guilty as her lecherous departed spouse, whose soul she was most hopeful was charring black at that very moment in a fiery burning inferno in hell.

"I'll have my lawyer contact you, Rand. Just be ready. I intend to take everything that is coming to me, and I mean *everything*. That bastard is going to pay from his grave!"

She pounded across the floor to show him the door. "That's right, the free ride is over, I'm afraid. Do not hesitate to spread the word to your cohorts. I am back, and I will fight for what's mine."

Biderman's voice tightened. "Oh, really, you will? Well, there's the matter of legalities, my dear, and from the looks of things as they are, it does seem that there is one rather large glitch. That woman in Hong Kong found alongside Denver, well, she too just also happened to be legally married to him. They wed not three months ago in the British Isles."

CHAPTER 34
★ ★ ★

CLEARING UP DENVER'S BUSINESS AND financial affairs was swift and easy, seeing as how the billionaire magnate managed to have willed almost everything to humanitarian foundations, namely in the areas of cancer and AIDS research, of which three research centers, a hospital library wing, and a street outside of the medical university was named after him. The remaining spoils, the largest portion being the construction and hardware companies, were bequeathed astonishingly to neither of his wives, nor his son. Instead, the baffling billionaire had intentionally left the greater bulk of his fortune to his originally intended beneficiaries, as was his wish all along. The fabulous Ralston fortune primarily went to Denver's prize-winning Shih Tzu show dogs: Tossie, Tina, Tiny, and Dane—a move that would keep his lawyers busy for eternity to sort out.

It was a shock to everyone, not least of all, the shareholders in the chain of some twenty-odd Building Barns across the South.

The remaining holdings, a handful of small corporations, stock portfolios, real estate, cars, and other liquid assets were divided among his two wives and his son, David, although it was Denver's willful intent to deny his gay son any due inheritance of the Ralston fortune, which really did not come as a shock to David.

But so it came to pass that David was counted in, thanks to the work of savvy family attorney Karl Christensen, whose ethics nobody thought to question. He alone also held the manifesto for the Shih Tzus' named ownership of the chain of home-building stores, until something could be decided as to what to do. He was also working on annulling the second marriage to Crystal Chung.

When all was said and done, Kathryn would walk away virtually debt-free, and the CEO of Ralston Enterprises, which, in turn, owned twelve unrelated companies ranging from a chemical fertilizer plant to a small radio station in Oklahoma. She quickly sold the house in Houston, and took possession of the ranch and stables in Austin. It was quite an impressive haul for a widowed bride of just five years, but she would need to hire a crew to manage the assets she did retain.

Biderman's lawyers made her sign an affidavit forbidding her to share her story with the media. Rand managed to keep the press from exploding with the juicy story of the billionaire bigamist and his bizarre exploits. In fact, Denver Ralston was instead revered for his generous support in the field of medicine and the fine arts, heralded as a hero to humanity, snuffed out all too soon in his prime.

Word of the Building Barn's "change in ownership" caused an instant panic in the market, inspiring the company's investors to sell, as buyers from several international conglomerate chains chomped at the bit to snatch up the plummeting precious shares.

Kathryn had to get away, as far away from the madness as she could run. She retreated to the only place in the world she could ever remember having known true solace.

She headed back to San Antonio and to the gates of Saint Martin's Mission.

On a swing set in the play lot, she remembered it all. The children on the ward, the sisters with their kerchiefs tucked into their sleeves . . . their round, kind faces. Tempera paints and Elmer's Glue . . . scratchy red mittens and Father Joe, with his soothing voice and gentle smile; the musky smell of his neck and vespers . . . the scrape of his beard. She closed her eyes and imagined being five again and enveloped in her uncle's arms. She had not a single recollection of Buddy prior to being nine years old, except for what she saw in photographs. It was Father Joe who had held her heart.

A school bell rang, and a cluster of young elementary age children burst from the gymnasium on their way back into the brown brick building. A Franciscan priest gathered them in at the door. He smiled when he saw Kathryn staring.

In a way, she regarded all of them as kindred spirits, waiting to be found. She suddenly wondered if *her* little girl ever felt that way, angry with her like she was with Buddy for abandoning her.

Kathryn wondered about the child she had secretly named, Brittany, who would now be ten and surely wondering about her past by now; trying to imagine her mother's face, perhaps. It was too painful a thought to consider. Kathryn had done such a good job of shutting the thoughts out. Not giving in to the imaginings, the *what-ifs*. It was simply too painful. She had convinced herself that she had done the right thing—the only thing she could have done under the circumstances. She never even told Denver about her daughter. She was ashamed and never wanted to open the door to the past. She had a new life. Now, it was all shown to be a lie. In a way, perhaps she deserved it. She fought the tears. No. She had done the right thing by her daughter, and that was all there was to it. Thanks to her, her daughter never had to spend a single day of her life in the walls of an institution or had to wait for someone to rescue her, as she had been able to place her into the arms of her new parents, the blissful couple with the soothing voices.

Kathryn walked from the deserted play lot and made a vow at last and for good never to look back. She would now have to find a way to save herself. Again.

CHAPTER 35

★ ★ ★

KATHRYN BURST INTO RAND BIDERMAN'S office, catching him mid-bite into a mountain of roast beef on rye.

"That'll kill you, son. Hasn't anyone ever warned you about heart disease?"

Rand wiped the traces of Dijon from his chin, stood, and fumbled for words. "Hello, Kathryn. Come right in, won't you?" The nerve! She grated on him like a bad itch. If only she weren't so damned beautiful . . . it made it so much tougher to hate her.

She plopped her perfect ass squarely in the chair across from his desk and balanced a slim briefcase on her lap.

What the hell is this? He braced himself for what would come next.

"Two words," Kathryn pitched. "Ecco Labs."

Rand's furled brows indicated exactly what she expected. He drew a decisive blank.

Kathryn threw him an inner tube. "The chemical plant, Rand. It's one of David's holdings. I want to trade one of my companies for it."

David Ralston had retained Rand Biderman, appointing him as chief executive officer of the remaining businesses of the Ralston Empire—excluding, of course, the Shih Tzus' construction and hardware store chains. David was loath to profit one cent from his estranged father's dynasty and chose to carve his own fortune on the fruits of his own labor and talents. He ran a respectable and reasonably successful art gallery in Houston's River Oaks, where he and Gregory, his life-partner of seven years, resided.

Rand was aware that Kathryn's holdings could be worth far more split into separate companies if they were managed properly. The possibilities intrigued him.

"What have you got to trade?" he asked, knowing full well that she had no idea of the true potential and value of her portfolio.

"Some real estate . . . industrial tenant units along the Beltway . . . a dairy farm in Porter . . . several old warehouses in Liberty, and a Quick Mart in East Texas—I think that's everything—oh, and the Austin ranch, *minus* the stallions and my mare."

Rand paused. He felt a twinge of elation. *The Austin ranch? Was she kidding?* He did a quick assessment—the warehouses in Liberty were nothing more than useless storage housing some outdated farming equipment from an estate buy-out. The land it sat on, however, was gold for sure, and would be prime for future expansion. *All of this for Ecco Labs?* The tiny chemical plant in Sulphur, might have once held potential. It manufactured, among other things, industrial and household cleaners, and pesticides, along with a small cosmetics division. In comparison, though, to the current real estate value of the other holdings, it was worthless.

Stupid woman! Rand suppressed a smile, and a bit of an erection, causing his jaw to twitch. "Okay," I'll speak with David. You're *entire* portfolio for Ecco Labs, correct?"

Kathryn nodded and stood to leave. "Make the deal, Rand."

Who did this broad think she was? He started to stand, but then thought better of it. Instead, he stayed seated, careful to stifle the stiffy that was growing in his trousers. "I'll be in touch as soon as I hear back from David."

"You do that," Kathryn said coolly. Then she turned and slammed the door in her wake.

Once outside, and safely in the Mercedes, she slumped forward and let out a relieved sigh. Kathryn despised the fact that Rand held most of the cards when it came to Denver's misplaced fortune. She had needed to bait him just enough to get him to give her the one thing she really wanted in the deal—a shot at developing and growing Beauty Essence into the new cosmetic line she had conceptualized prior to Denver's death. She had already transported all of her horses safely to an undisclosed stable in Dallas, prepared to abandon residence of the Austin ranch house immediately if need be, and *if* the bargaining got ugly. She knew how very fond Rand was of the Austin ranch. It was her ace in the hole.

Five days later, Rand phoned with the news. "David will deal. I'll have the paperwork drawn up."

"Terrific," Kathryn breathed into the phone. "I'll be there in an hour."

Kathryn showed up at Biderman's office, sans her own lawyer, with briefcase in hand. It amused Rand to watch her in action, thinking herself so savvy and ball-busting. It was his pleasure to relieve her of prime retail real estate in exchange for a dilapidated fertilizer factory that specialized in hennas and hand lotion. One hundred forty acres of prime Texas dirt would soon be his to turn into a small fortune. David knew nothing of the value, or ever would if he could help it. *Why bother him with details he cared little about?* David Ralston was Denver's son, but did not have a business savvy bone in his body. He was not even present for the transaction. The kid trusted him, as well he should. David was set for life—in spite of his father's wishes. Rand was about to make David an even richer son-of-a-bitch, and himself so too, in the process. He had plans to develop and manage the prime real estate that would have the big-name merchants clamoring for positioning. If he played his cards right, maybe he could even talk David into letting him eventually purchase the Austin ranch down the line for a quarter of what it was worth.

The exchange was swift. There were several documents to sign, with only a notary present.

"Drink?" Rand offered, ever the gentleman, motioning to his fine scotch decanter glistening atop a mahogany credenza.

"No, thank you," Kathryn said, glacial and focused. She wore her poker face even then. But all he could see was a looker in a killer designer suit with three-and-a-half-inch power pumps, looking quite the executive vixen; alluring and tantalizing in the provocative slit skirt that defied the conventional code of conservativeness. She had great legs. He hated to admit it. Kathryn was a damn hot woman. *If only things were different*, he thought.

Kathryn scanned the contracts, narrowing her sharp blue eyes, poising the pen tip above the dotted line. Then, suddenly, she quipped, "Oh, just one more little thing before I sign this, Rand . . ."

He stiffened. "What's that?"

"The radio station in Albuquerque. Is that negotiable too?"

Rand snorted. *What was this all about? Now she was interested in a single-channel AM carrier?*

Rand recalled the holding—part of a broadcast company with a two-bit radio station that featured a deejay named, Captain Wayne Scanner, who reported on paranormal ghost stories that ran syndicated on a handful of radio stations throughout the country. Word was, though, that he actually broadcast from a mobile trailer somewhere in the middle of New Mexico. His listening population numbered less than a small church choir.

He wondered why she would be the least bit interested in a freak like Scanner and his nightly spook-show anyway.

He pushed back. "The broadcast company is not a part of the deal." *What did she know that he didn't?* he began to wonder. A cool sweat broke out beneath his hair weave. "I'm really sorry, Kathryn. I'm afraid I can only offer Ecco Labs, like we discussed, or no deal."

Kathryn nodded pensively. She closed the pen matter-of-factly with a decisive click, and frowned. "I see. Well, I guess we have no deal, then."

She left without a further word, letting her spiked heels rake the carpet as she strutted out the door.

In less than forty-eight hours, Biderman had rescinded, sending Kathryn a bouquet of pricey exotic flowers and a fresh stack of contracts to sign. She had called his bluff and won.

The very next morning, she was on a flight heading to Albuquerque.

CHAPTER 36

★ ★ ★

THE ONLY WAY TO REACH Laguna, New Mexico, from the airport in Albuquerque was by jeep. It was a fifty-two-mile drive to the ancient Indian reservation. Kathryn could have hired a driver, but opted to be adventurous and make the drive herself. The rental outlet had given her directions on a crude map.

"No one's real sure exactly where his setup is," the befuddled station manager of WKOL explained when Kathryn appeared, unannounced, in the middle of his lunch break. He was just about to tear into his fry bread and hominy stew take-out seeping from a paper sack. "We tell our listeners that it's smack dab in the middle of nowhere—they eat it up. Our affiliates say that it enhances the mystique."

Kathryn had requested statistics on the radio station's listenership and sponsors. The figures were anemic, at best. The station offered little more than hourly weather and farm reports, local ads, and occasional world news; mostly town square chatter hosted by a former clergyman turned disc jockey. There was no music programming to speak of, with the exception of an occasional commercial jingle.

The highlight feature was Wayne Scanner's eerie four-hour show, which delved nightly into the world of the paranormal and extraterrestrial. It was pointedly a favorite of the locals, and surprisingly a veritable "hit" with the syndicates, whose paltry fees for licensing rights, according to WKOL's Dick Natallie, was what kept the station running.

"They purchase carts of Wayne's show, edit them for time, and air it as part of their evening line up. It's recorded at two p.m., but most stations play him at midnight to four a.m. It has really developed a rather remarkable 'cult' following in the northern states and Canada."

"I see," Kathryn had said, taking it all in.

"Without the syndicates," Natallie had elaborated, "we'd all be screwed!"

Kathryn stayed on at a local B&B that night after having Natalie walk her through the books and numbers. She further learned that local advertisers paid little for air time during Scanner's show, while Arbitron reports indicated that national stations were getting top billing for ads running during recordings of the very same broadcasts.

It was evident that if managed properly, WKOL's desert deejay could make Kathryn a veritable fortune, at least enough to fund her business plan for the advent of an innovative and revolutionary new beauty line that would take the cosmetic industry by storm, as was her newest passion and goal.

First and foremost, she would need capital, and Wacky Wayne Scanner and WKOL would be just the ticket to bankroll her new venture.

"I'm going out to see Wayne Scanner myself," she had announced. "I'll be sending my controller down just as soon as possible. He'll need an office and a list of each and every national syndicate we sell to. We'll put a freeze on any contractual deals we cannot renegotiate for twice the going rate for stations to sign on for two-to four-year deals. Otherwise, the cost of carrying Desert Hauntings has just risen to *quadruple* the going rate!"

The next morning Kathryn was off. She started on I-40 in a rented four-by-four, finding the drive to be enjoyable, although the wide-open terrain and expansive skies made her miss her horses back in Austin. She called her stable-hand Alex, from her new cell phone. The Nokia had a new modified design with a shorter antenna, which made it just about fit all the way in her purse. She wanted to check up on her precious stallions and her beloved mare, Baby. Kathryn hated the thought of keeping them in a rented stable.

She would be back in a day and a half before heading for Sulphur to meet with her staff at Ecco Labs. *Her* staff. She relished the sound of it. There was so much to be done in the business of getting on with one's life, she thought.

The desert air was incredible. In spite of the blasted heat, she opted to turn off the air- conditioning and roll down every window, letting the arid winds stir her senses. She drove, reveling in her thoughts. She was, indeed, a survivor. Telling herself over and over—*Don't forget about your dreams, girl. Delacortes never give up!*

The dilapidated camper looked worse than she had imagined. It was set up on cinder blocks, had three-tone aluminum siding and rusted out handrails leading to a screen door that hung permanently crooked on its hinges. A few plastic flamingos and a decapitated acrylic Santa Claus served as yard art on the patch of brown grass that defined the front lawn.

A collection of antennae and electronic equipment and cables jutted out from the roof of the trailer, and a mammoth-size satellite dish pointed due south into the sky not fifty yards way. It was a desolate location, all right, taking two road maps, four filling station attendants, and a call back to the radio station on her newfangled cellular phone to finally locate it.

Kathryn pulled the jeep up to the monstrosity, kicking up red dust and gravel; a commotion that sent a scraggly tan and orange mutt into a barking frenzy, announcing the intruder's arrival.

Wayne Scanner looked every bit the "mountain man" and eccentric recluse with full grizzly beard, bare feet, and native beads strung in his long gray hair. His skin was the color of a paper bag. Kathryn could not say that she was the least bit surprised by his appearance. She would not have expected anything less.

The man was a desert legend, an insomniac's friend, and a trucker's companion on those long, endless stretches of blacktop. Scanner's four-hour show broadcast from his remote makeshift studio running on just enough wattage to reach back to the station's antenna, located at about seventy feet high on a gas company-owned tower back in town. There, the main station, or "Translator" rebroadcast the show by relaying the signal to nearly two dozen syndicates nationwide, including Houston, Oklahoma, Arkansas, Mississippi, Tennessee, Louisiana, and even as far north as Wisconsin. Locally, though, with the hilly terrain, he was lucky enough to reach a twelve-to fifteen-mile radius to factory-installed car radios and the occasional portable receiver in the area just on his own juice.

Scanner appeared surprised that Kathryn was not escorted by an entourage of corporate-types and was outwardly taken by her seemingly young age. "So you're the new boss lady, eh?"

"Yes, sir, Mr. Scanner. I came all this way to introduce myself to you and to have ourselves a talk. I wanted to see your setup for myself." She indicated, looking all around. "Just wanted to see how it is that you do what you do."

"No one ever comes out here, Ms. Ralston. Forgive my manners. Let's go inside. You'll fry your fanny in this heat!"

He led her to the trailer, which was meat-locker cold inside, for the sake of the technical gadgets, she'd guessed.

"Are you hungry any?"

"A bit," she said. Truth being, she was famished from the drive.

They settled down at a wobbly card table. He filled two paper cups with lemonade from a glass thermos and then promptly produced a tray of square sandwiches, which he explained he had made earlier that morning in anticipation of her visit.

"They're not fancy, now. I didn't know what you might like, so I mixed them up. There's a little of everything: peanut butter with sweet jelly, chicken salad, bologna and cheese . . ."

She reached for one of the small wedges. "Thank you. You didn't have to fuss. Really."

"No trouble. Believe me, ole Duke and I don't get too many visitors out here, especially ones like you. Now then, tell me, Ms. Ralston, you really came all the way out here to unplug me, right?"

His gaze was unchanged.

"What? No. Of course not," Kathryn gushed. "On the contrary, Mr. Scanner, I think your show is great. I've never heard of anything like it. The numbers don't lie. Did you know that over half of the stations that carry Desert Hauntings have been receiving weekly increases in their listenership and ad sales at every syndication across the board?"

Scanner scratched his head. "No, I don't believe that I did."

"That's right," Kathryn continued. "Our findings indicate that your little show is going gangbusters out there, and I'm here to discuss signing you on exclusively for several more years. Of course, that is only if you want to, Mr. Scanner. I have some fabulous marketing ideas on how we can pitch your show to the East Coast and have you interact more with the callers, and such."

"Excuse me for saying, ma'am, but your husband never did have me sign a single paper to tell my stories to people on the air. He just gave me the means to do what I love to do, and that's talkin' to the world into this here little microphone 'bout what I know."

"I'm not here to change that, Mr. Scanner. I want you to continue to do what you're doing the way you like doing it. Okay? That's what I'm asking."

Kathryn patted him assuredly on the hand and looked kindly into his gray eyes. He smiled, looking a bit relieved.

"Oh," Kathryn added, "there is one last matter, of course, regarding the renegotiation of your salary. We are, of course, committed to retaining your services for a long time to come."

The old man looked puzzled and then chuckled heartily as if it were the very first belly laugh he had had in a very long time.

"Salary? You mean, you're actually going to start *paying* me to do this?"

Denver Ralston never actually employed Wayne Scanner, a former military buddy who served with him in Saigon 1972, when they were both just twenty-five years old. Scanner had worked overnights on programs produced by the Armed Forces Radio Service. Denver liked Wayne's style and often listened to his broadcasts. The two had become fast friends and kept in touch throughout the years. Not less than seven years ago, Scanner and Ralston had reconnected, and that's when Ralston agreed to lease Scanner the use of an old makeshift remote studio, strictly as a favor, that was once said to be the dressing trailer of Marlon Brando in *On the Waterfront*. It had always been Wayne Scanner's dream to have his own radio show since his first crack at the microphone working part-time in the day working civilian duty.

Upon returning from an eighteen year stint as a private cargo pilot for the government, Scanner had retired from the military and settled on a small Indian Reservation deep in the New Mexico desert and began studying ancient folklore, astronomy, and matters of the occult. He had become fascinated with mysteries of science and the supernatural; a hobby that prompted him to share his findings and fascinations with anyone who cared to listen. Wayne Scanner was often credited as being a master story teller. Wise and well-versed, and uniquely engaging, he spun enthralling tales that mesmerized and amazed audiences of all ages and persuasions. He was thrilled to take his friend up on the offer.

Denver generously funded the fully equipped mobile studio for Scanner, which ran feed from his radio station there in Albuquerque, charging Scanner twenty-five dollars a week "rent" to play the prophet on the airwaves, right there from the parking lot of WKOL.

One year later, Scanner moved the radio wagon, as he liked to refer to it, deep into the Nevada desert, and had basically been living out of it ever since; still broadcasting from WKOL's signal for twenty-five dollars a week, paid directly to the station under a corporate pseudonym, Coyote Mountain Enterprises.

Dick Natalie had never put two and two together. "*He's* Coyote Mountain? We never really knew. Figured those payments to be an anonymous benefactor of the station. He never missed a week. The understanding was, that Ralston had compensated Scanner directly, I mean, we just assumed. He never officially appeared on the payroll, but that wouldn't have been unusual for your late husband to have intentionally arranged. He bank-rolled a lot of people discretely."

"I see," Kathryn said, figuring that there was much about the way that Denver did things that could be classified as unusual. She was most likely the least among many who never really truly knew him at all.

\# \# \#

Kathryn's lawyers were commissioned to smooth out the legal agreement between WKOL and Coyote Mountain Enterprises to terms that were amicable to both parties. Scanner's radio trailer got upgraded to state-of-the-art status, and he was officially signed to a five-year contract and game plan that would bring Desert Hauntings from the distant New Mexico valley to over thirty-five high-paying syndicated radio stations nationwide in less than twelve months.

For the first time in his professional radio career, Scanner was placed on the payroll.

CHAPTER 37

★ ★ ★

FOUR WEEKS LATER
SULPHUR, LOUISIANA

KATHRYN ARRIVED UNANNOUNCED, LOOKING MORE like a receptionist or secretary in her Calvin Klein jeans and trendy silk blouse than an executive heavy. She carried a platter of chocolate chip cookies right into the lunchroom, depositing them on the large round laminate table, startling the afternoon crew who had gathered, as they did every day at noon, for ham sandwiches and hot gossip.

"Hello, everyone! I would like to introduce myself. My name is Kathryn Ralst—" she stopped herself short, deciding from that point forward, she would denounce anything in her life that reminded her of Denver, especially his name. "Kathryn Delacorte, formerly Ralston, and now president and CEO of our little company. Let me start by thanking you for your service and dedication to Ecco Labs, especially during the transition."

A mix of blank and seething stares bore holes right through her. Her voice rang empty in the silence her sudden appearance evoked. Still, she remained cool and unflinching. Fifty some-odd staff in all had been mysteriously cut just three days prior to her little cookie visit, preceded by a tag team of corporate types, stiff-lipped business consultants who spent days infiltrating the offices, hallways, and research labs of Ecco. Only five out of ten senior Ecco executives remained, retained for their expertise at questionably exorbitant salaries that no doubt, they would now be required to actually earn.

This left a total of just two hundred sixty-five full-and part-time employees in all, from a population of over five hundred associates. The new boss had come in with a vengeance *and cookies*? In their eyes, Kathryn Delacorte was the enemy, all right.

Kathryn's advisors had worked up a long-term prospectus that would take her original business plan well into the next decade. Soon, Ecco Laboratory's largest offering would be the production of a first-rate line of new earth-friendly personal hygiene, beauty, and household products of revolutionary proportions. Kathryn appointed herself head of the specialty cosmetics division, hiring a brilliant team of researchers and aestheticians to assist with the conception and design of what would be called, Earth's Essence Beauty Line, which was slated to be introduced to the private sector later that spring.

Eventually, the industrial chemical and agricultural divisions would be phased out as the Beauty Care Products line grew. Kathryn's two-, five-, and seven-year plans said so.

"We're going to be a cosmetic giant in less than five years, gentlemen . . . mark my words," Kathryn announced to the entire executive committee, punctuating the prediction with a Raven Red lipstick imprint on a napkin, held up for the entire board to see. They applauded approvingly. Only one officer walked out during her speech, doubting the capability of having a twenty-eight-year-old woman at the helm. Duncan Pearce's resignation was no great loss to Kathryn. She was secretly relieved that the Doubting Thomas dropped off from the start. She would require total dedication—one hundred percent commitment from her managers and directors. Everyone would have to be a team player, or they were simply out. Without this, Kathryn and Ecco would not stand a chance, and as chances went, this was what she deemed to be the biggest undertaking of her life.

Kathryn worked seventy-hour weeks, overseeing all aspects of Ecco's operations, learning as she went, to fend off the fear of failure, dispel naysayers, and to rise to the challenges of running a company she knew very little about. It was frustrating at best, but Kathryn was determined to persevere and dedicate her energy to learning and developing every way she could to make her mark once again in the business world. This time, though, the stakes were much higher, and the lessons learned were more often than not hard-earned.

It cost Kathryn the loss of three more senior officers in all, the retention of two additional consultant firms, a new advertising agency, and four different business managers over sixteen months' time, before things finally began to click.

The trend suggested "back to basics" and Earth's Essence Beauty Line was at the ready to answer the call, delivering high-quality cosmetics and personal body products created completely from all-natural components; derived directly from Mother Earth and enhanced and processed in the specialty laboratories of Ecco Corporation. The exclusive products not only carried an eco-friendly message, but an impressive money-back guarantee—all at a price point that set Kathryn far apart from her competitors. *Beauty*, as was her winning slogan, *doesn't have to break the bank.* Earth's Essence would be an affordable alternative to pricey, department store chemical-laden jars of empty promises. Women would receive the benefits of quality, youth-enhancing products that were as affordable as they were pure. Earth's Essence not only promised, but delivered, honest beauty.

The radio station was doing splendid. Kathryn poured profits from Scanner's show into the corporation, growing Earth's Essence at impressive strides. The concept was catching on, and the demand for products nationwide enabled the division to hire on new employees until the need for additional space was imminent.

In just three years time and ahead of plan, the new beauty line officially branched off from its parent company to new headquarters in Dallas. Kathryn, as the sole shareholder, then began to offer hefty stock options to her dedicated team in lieu of bonuses, giving them co-ownership of the wealth. It was an unprecedented move, winning her accolades in the business community, and no less, the attention of Wall Street.

Kathryn moved herself into a sixty-six-hundred-square foot two-story penthouse that had four bedrooms, six bathrooms, walnut floors, a twenty-two-hundred-bottle wine room, and a full chef's kitchen. The luxury condo had city views that went on for miles. On weekends, she would make the drive to San Antonio to tend to her horses at a newly purchased ranch not far from the Franciscan mission where her life began.

The Earth's Essence beauty line put natural beauty first and foremost in women's minds. The attractive and effective ad campaigns cable TV spots, and in-store point of purchase displays, and chain store counter promotions drove sales to epic heights.

In the summer of 1999, Earth's Essence went public, trading for nearly sixty-seven dollars a share, and growing.

Once again, Kathryn had proven that she had the stuff to rise above adversity, and the feeling of victory was beautifully sweet!

CHAPTER 38

★ ★ ★

HOUSTON. TEXAS 2003

A SEA OF BLACK CAPS AND gowns assembled onto the grounds in front of Saint Basilica's chapel. Classmates clung to one another, arm in arm, in a chain of gleeful embraces. Joyful cheers, bright, gladdened smiles, and tears ensued; many dreams were made ready for the promise of bright futures ahead. Libby directed her husband, who was single-handedly recording the entire day's event on a camcorder as Matt and Ryan closed in on their teenage sister with bear hugs and brotherly shoves. Grabbing her commencement cap, they tossed it about like a Frisbee.

"Hey, you turds. Cut it out! I'm warning you—*really?*" she pleaded.

Her brothers were grown men, but they still loved to torment her. Dr. Masters paused and zoomed the camera in for a better angle of the action, laughing, quite amused with the impromptu drama unfolding. It was real slice-of-life stuff.

Ellie shrieked. "C'mon, you guys . . . you're *embarrassing* me. Give it back!"

She snatched wildly at the air for her prized cap, but her towering tormentors would not relent. Eighteen years of beating up on their baby sister only made them pros at the sport of sibling superiority. With Ellie moving away into a dorm on the college campus in August, and both boys away at their respective colleges in Austin and Louisiana, there would be no more kids left at the Masters's household. The reality was not lost on their mother, who was trying to hold back the tears as it was.

"Matt! Ryan! *Stop it*, won't you?" Give your sister her cap for goodness sake," Libby said. It was always she who had kept the peace in the family, managing to raise three beautiful children while maintaining an accounting practice and tending to the needs of her husband, the esteemed surgeon.

Garrett Masters had only recently turned in his scalpel at the hospital for a research desk at the University, a promotion that couldn't have come at a better time. It would mean that he would now have even more time to spend with Libby—and Ellie, who would be attending the very same school, the University of Houston where he worked.

Dr. and Mrs. Masters were extremely supportive of their daughter, encouraging her creative aspirations right from the start, as they did for each of their children, cheering them on to pursue their life careers with vigor. It was no surprise when Ellie received a four-year scholarship, earned for her academic excellence in liberal arts and the sciences.

Ellie intended to minor in English while studying chemistry and biology, toward her major. Her hope would be to apply for a pre-vet program in the fall of her senior year at Texas A & M University. It was clearly evident that whatever career path their Ellie decided to take, she would succeed. She had what it took to make great things happen for herself. The Masters couldn't have been prouder, and they couldn't have loved her more.

From the day that Garrett and Libby Masters first saw Ellie, they knew that the decision to adopt her was certain. Of all the available infants, she was simply the most special. Little did they know just how significantly their choice would change the dynamic of their family in a way that would bring joy and light into all their already bountiful lives.

Libby had been devastated two years earlier to learn that, at thirty-five, she needed a preventative hysterectomy due to the probable threat of her developing the ovarian cancer that had claimed the lives of her mother and her sister in a span of only fifteen years. The risk was too great not to go through with the procedure. The promise from Libby's loving husband, in return, for undergoing the procedure, would be the selection and adoption of a baby girl.

Libby and Garrett Masters agreed that somewhere, somehow, there was a little angel meant just for them. Besides, they had read so much about the rising teen pregnancy rate and knew that they could more than do their share to be part of the solution.

And so it was that through the advice of helpful friends, who had also adopted recently, the Masters were referred to Jim and Mary Lou McKenna. The two were the proprietors of Hester's House, named for literature's fated heroine and unwed mother, Hester Prynne of Hawthorne's famed classic, *The Scarlet Letter*. Hester's House was located in Winona, about one hundred twenty miles from Minneapolis. It was a home for unwed and teenage mothers seeking couples just like the Masters to privately adopt their infants into loving and caring homes.

Libby would never forget the day that Mary Lou McKenna finally called to say that the arrangements were in place. They would follow and finance an unnamed teen's pregnancy throughout the duration and for the final weeks of her recovery once the baby arrived.

Katie was that teen and was not informed who the

new parents would be, only that a viable couple had been located.

On the day that Katie gave birth, the couple was there. Waiting for their brand new daughter to arrive. They loved her even then—and Katie too—mystified at her resolve and yet indebted to her at the same time, for having the strength to do it. To give her baby up.

Katie saw the child only briefly when she first emerged, all wet and shiny. She refused to hold her, though, and simply turned her head. She could surely hear the staccato, tiny cries, but only shut her eyes to the pain.

The nurse cleaned and dressed the baby beneath a warm lamp, then placed a pink stocking cap on her perfectly round head. She presented the swaddled infant to the woman who was standing just inside the door of the birthing room.

"I cannot take her. Not yet, anyway," the woman had said. "Not until her mother holds her first. I can take this child as God would have it, from her mother's arms, but not from her womb."

Libby pleaded with the nurse to encourage Katie to hold the baby. Please do this. For *her* sake."

Tears streamed down Katie's face as she conceded, taking her newborn daughter to her heart and glancing only with a moment's pass over its form to confirm the count of fingers and toes. She was perfect.

She gazed at the infant and communicated silent words that could only have been known by mother and child. Five eternal moments passed. With the magic of a mother's kiss, and a whisper, she gave her daughter a secret name— *Brittany.*

Libby heard this and vowed right then and there to give her "Brittany" as her middle name. Ellen Brittany Masters.

Katie motioned for the nurse, indicating that it was

time. She lifted the child upward and watched as the nurse placed her in the woman's arms.

And without a further word, she gave her away.

CHAPTER 39

★ ★ ★

THREE YEARS LATER

A CLAN OF NOISY PAJAMA-CLAD CO-EDS filled the dorm halls with chatter and laughter, making it difficult for Ellie to hear herself think. Quarterly final exams were just three days away, and she had to ace biochemistry if she had any prayer of making it through the semester. Biochemistry was brutal. Truly, the faint of heart and sub-genius minded were clearly eliminated well before the second term, *if* they survived that long.

Ellie was an exemplary student, pretty and smart in a no-frills, wholesome kind of way. She was tall and lean with a thin, angular face and an honest smile. She was more than bright, still, she struggled through a tundra of classes and course work that earned her nothing more than a solid "C" grade point average, a fact that often brought her to tears of frustration. Surrendering to understandable limitations, Ellie reluctantly decided to change her major mid-point and entered her junior year with a new declared area of study. A field, which not only interested her, but one she was quite proficient at, combining both her love of art with a knack for the written word. Ellie was a keen communicator, and decided to put away the laboratory test tubes in exchange for a camera as she prepared for a career as a photojournalist.

Ellie aspired to report news and evoke inspiration through photographs, to capture time and truth with her ever-changing lens. By the following semester, Ellie's grade point average had returned to a respectable "A" status, and with the onslaught of aced project assignments and midterm exams, Ellie knew that she had found her niche and was back on track.

Upon graduating from the university the following year, Ellie's professor had given her a lead on a staff assistant position at the *Houston Chronicle*, where she had worked for sixteen months at the assignment desk before landing a job as the assistant editor of *Habitat*, the official newsletter of the Houston City Zoo Organization. There, Ellie found her toughest clients to be the incorrigible and unpredictable furry-haired and sometimes scaly subjects she often got to photograph.

Loving animals was easy—photographing them, was another thing altogether. Ellie was good, one of the best. She worked tirelessly just to get the timing right—the critical four-hour window when a sleepy sloth would awake in his treetop home just long enough for her to line up a shot with all the lights and filters needed to catch him, lumbering and yawning, just getting up from his twenty-hour nap. Or, just in time to catch a full-length shot of him scratching his belly in contentment after a tasty meal.

She had patience and a keen eye for knowing when an animal was ready to be admired and for when it would be best to leave it alone. Climbing fifty feet above a rocky ravine to get a perfect angle of a harbor seal emerging from a cold-water swim and sunning himself on a make-shift sand bar, his short, thick coat glistening in the warm

Texas sun, won for Ellie a prized shot that was ultimately featured on the cover of *American Zoo's* magazine.

Ellie worked odd hours, to say the least, and reveled in her newfound freedom as a full-fledged adult with a one-bedroom apartment, utility bills, and a sporty red pickup truck that was a gift from the Masters for her graduation. She was happy and hopeful for a future with limitless possibilities. After all, she knew that in so many ways, she had been born under the luckiest of stars.

CHAPTER 40

★ ★ ★

2008

ROSS LOGAN WAS THE PRIDE of Abilene, a small town in West Texas about one hundred fifty miles west of Fort Worth, where he brought accolades to Abilene High School his junior and senior year as the school's all-star triathlon state champion three years running. He later returned after college to coach the boys' varsity basketball team to victory: three all-star state championships in a row.

A divorcé with two bright, athletic sons in middle school, he actively participated in their lives early on, and later, after the divorce, traveling back to Texas in spite of a busy schedule, to honor his visitation agreement as often as he could. He had recently taken a position as zoo director at the Houston City Zoo after several management stints heading wildlife conservation facilities in some of the most prestigious and largest zoos in the country, namely in New York, Ohio, and California, which was, for him, a huge win as his ex-wife had recently relocated herself and the two boys to San Antonio. Now, Tucker and Cameron would be just a four-hour drive away. Dr. Ross Logan was a highly accredited and respected veterinarian with multiple degrees in medicine, zoological studies, and microbiology. His area of specialty was aquatics, and that is where Ellie first met him—at the fish tank.

The "tank" as it was called, was a chlorinated one-hundred-forty-eight thousand- gallon aquarium, eight feet deep, filtered at four hundred gallons per minute. It was where Dr. Logan was supervising the transfer of a very sick sea lion that would be flown to Florida for treatment in their specialized marine facility.

It took Ellie nearly one hour to track him down, and when she finally did, she could certainly see why. Ross Logan was moving at warp speed, giving directives and deploying crews in all directions. He was laden with several two-way radios, a mobile phone, and a series of clipboards and a computer device on a portable cart looking more like a techno-robot or creature from *Star Wars* than like a man. *But he is a man . . . and a fine specimen at that*, Ellie thought as she approached the wildly gesticulating maestro as he choreographed the dance of some sixteen staff technicians and zookeeps, who assisted in the tranquilizing and netting of the frightened creature, readying her for transport in a specially designed crate that had to be air lifted by chopper.

Time was a determining factor in the race to get the sea lion, affectionately called Lola, to the medical facility in Orlando.

"Dr. Logan? How do you do? I'm Ellie Masters, from the *Habitat*," Ellie said, walking alongside his double-time gait. "I'm here to conduct an interview and to get some shots of the new primate wing."

He continued working as she talked to him, slowing down only briefly to extend his hand to shake hers, giving a moment's heed, it seemed, to her snug tank top and bare, toned shoulders. She was sporting two cameras around her neck and a water canteen on her hip.

He then stopped short, looking upward at the horizon.

"Right. I'm sorry, we are having a bit of an emergency here."

Was he talking to her? She wasn't sure.

Four men were carrying the creature, which had been successfully sedated, in a large wooden container. A chopper was just landing some fifty yards off in the field on a patch of wild grass as a harried crew attended to their tasks. Dr. Ross Logan paused, wiping beads of sweat from his forehead with a red bandana. He had the looks of a Hollywood leading man and about all the charm of Indiana Jones, himself. His striking green eyes suggested that he was an old soul, for sure, but his buff physique suggested otherwise. He looked like he could run an iron-man triathlon in record time.

Ellie's heart fluttered a bit when he grinned apologetically her way. His smile was kryptonite.

"Sorry about all this. Duty calls, you know."

He was begging off—no! Now what was she going to do? Go back and tell her boss Dale Hunter, that she didn't get the story? That the sea lion had the flu?

Ross Logan was, if not many things, *resourceful*. Grabbing his gear and leatherbound briefcase, he dismissed one of the technicians from the job and then motioned to Ellie.

"Hey, you're a reporter—have you ever flown in a helicopter with a sea lion before?"

Ellie gasped. Instantly, she had forgotten her fear of such things as heights and prop planes. "Well, no, but—"

"Good! Let's go, then!" Logan called, motioning for her to get into the chopper. He quickly belted her in, brushing his massive forearm across her chest, leaving her little chance of backing out—or wanting to. "You can get the interview on the way," he said, directly into her ear, then jumping into the seat next to her. "We'll be back by dusk," he said over the whirring blades.

Oh my God! Ellie's mind whirred as well, as her heart did a full leap.

"All right, then," she said as the chopper lifted skyward. "Let's do this!"

Ellie got her interview, some remarkable shots for the magazine, *and* landed a date with the reticent Dr. Ross Logan after co-assisting with the safe patient transfer. That led to several more dates, and eventually, an exclusive arrangement that offered a never-look-back storybook-worthy romance that quickly catapulted her soon-to-be nonexistent single life into the star-kissed stratosphere of true love.

Later that spring, Ross proposed to Ellie, and the two were married at a sunrise civil ceremony held, of all places, on the zoo grounds, on the twentieth of May, just one year to the day after they had met. Lola and her new pups were present, along with a cadre of every beast, fowl, and fish known to mankind, as well as friends and family. As far as Ellie was concerned, there could not have been a more perfect place or way to marry her life's true soul mate.

In spite of it all, though, as the bright Texas sun rose over the northeast gates of the magnificent historical landmark zoo that day, Ellie could not help but wonder, as brides often do, about her birth mother. It was yet another milestone in her life that brought to mind the burning question that she had carried somewhat familiarly in her heart since childhood. *Where?* she wondered. *Where did destiny place my birth mother?* She was, to Ellie, a nameless woman who did not know the intricate details of her daughter's life, or would ever be able to know the thousand ways that Ellie felt lost and found among the many valleys and peaks of being just who she was—a part of someone else; someone with a whole past with bloodlines and family she would never know. That, and a biological father with no claim to her birth. In spite of the incredible and blessed life that her adoptive parents had given her, still . . . on some level, Ellie longed for answers that just were not possible.

Today, she would have liked her real mother to somehow know, along with her adoptive parents, the gladness she had found in loving Ross . . . a love that she was certain would last forever and never leave her wanting.

The following year, when Earth's Essence hit six million dollars in sales, Kathryn threw the party of the century in New Orleans. Erased would be the memories of loss, rejection, and betrayal that caused her to once to flee, only to return triumphant. The *Queen of the Mississippi* was a magnificent jeweled Southern vessel, glistening elegant and proud on the mystical waters of the mightiest of magical rivers. A Dixieland band played jovially on deck, welcoming the honored guests beneath a blanket of Southern stars, who, despite the imposing heat, made merry in their finest gowns and dinner coats on the pier, making their way to the exquisite riverboat, where the most remarkable of nights awaited inside. Chilled champagne, caviar, and a twelve-piece orchestra that played a Dixieland Jazz tune welcomed Kathryn's entire staff as they streamed into the dining room. Two hundred and fifteen of her "closest" friends, brought to New Orleans with spouses and loved ones to celebrate the company's biggest triumph to date—Earth's Essence beauty line had become a household name, thanks to the efforts of all the people in that room. The evening, the trip, and the festivities were all Kathryn's gift to them.

"Look at the magnificent riverboat over there! Isn't it *incredible?*"

Ellie paused, taking in the spectacle, which, in all its glory, looked perfectly aligned with the stars as it drifted proudly on the murky water in the distance.

"Look—they're having some sort of party. It looks formal . . . lot's of black ties and sequins. Oh! And an orchestra too. Don't you just *love* parties, Ross? For some strange reason, I just adore New Orleans."

He drew her closer and kissed her neck. The two gazed from the balcony of their hotel room out at the marina, entwined in a full-body embrace. The quick two-day trip to New Orleans was all the time they could steal away from work for their first anniversary. Ross would have to be back on Monday.

"I love you, Ross Logan. And I love being here with you. This is such a magical place. I don't know . . . it feels strangely soothing to me in a way that no other place on earth does," she said to her husband, while gazing offshore at the glistening riverboat, pulsating with light and sound from its revelries.

"I'm glad you are happy," he whispered, breathing it all in.

She settled further in his embrace, drunk on the moment. She had never felt happier in all her life.

The party-goers cheered and raised their glasses high as their beloved CEO crossed the stage in a stunning beaded gown, waving and blowing kisses to the crowd like a regal queen. They chanted her name in unison: "Kathryn! Kathryn! Kathryn!"

It thrilled her to receive such adulation on the very soil of her formative childhood home, where she later had such fond memories, most of all, of her grandmother, Abigail, and the high school angst that set her off into the world. The memories were bittersweet, causing her to feel strangely empty at the same time. A feeling she quickly checked and then dismissed.

Shouts and cheers erupted from the dance floor.

Heading out onto the deck, she breathed in the fragrant night air. It was, for her, a shining moment. A promise fulfilled. Delacortes don't just win—they *persevere*.

She leaned against the railing and peered far across the water. *Now it was time,* she thought, *time to talk to David.*

CHAPTER 41

★ ★ ★

HOUSTON, TEXAS – 2009

KATHRYN MET DAVID AT A sidewalk café in River Oaks, her favorite one of all with its canopied awnings and exquisite artwork on the stucco walls. The hostess seated them on the patio in a section that had the best vantage point of the historical tree-lined street.

It was hot. Houston hot, but Kathryn never let a thing like humidity cramp her impeccable style. She wore her hair off her face, pulled taut with a sleek black headband. She was tan and lean, back on her daily workout regimen and weekend retreats at the stables in San Antonio.

David was already there, reading *The New Yorker*, looking blissfully content in the shade. He stood, smiling.

"Have I kept you waiting long, love?" Kathryn gushed, all hugs and kisses. *Damn. But did he look like Denver*. She had forgotten how handsome he was.

"Not at all. I love it here. Just catching up on some reading."

He kissed her cheek and they sat.

"So you've eaten here before?" Kathryn asked.

"Oh, quite a lot, in fact. Gregory and I frequent all of

Chef Edmond's restaurants. You might say that we are fans of his. As a matter of fact, I sold him two paintings from the Hale collection not less than six months ago—there they are right over there." He pointed in the direction of the entrance. "That's *Savannah Wheat* and next to it is *Southern Dreams*. Kicker is, Chef hails from Jersey. Go figure!"

Kathryn smiled. She was so pleased for David. He seemed more relaxed than she had ever seen him before. He looked good, happy even. The two waited for the busboy to finish filling their glasses. Mineral waters with miniature round ice cubes bobbing in and out of cucumber rinds. *Tres chic.*

"Ultra success agrees with you, Kathryn" David said with a blinding white grin. "Are you enjoying Dallas over Houston? Not nearly as muggy, eh?"

"That's for sure, but this is not as bad as The Big Easy. Still, nothing *easy* about this heat!" Kathryn said, fanning her pretty face with a menu.

David chortled, flipping his wrist a little too convincingly. "I hear you, honey. You don't have to talk to me about hot. I just don't let it get to me. That, plus I don't wear any underwear. Gregory loves that I run around commando."

Kathryn smiled. David was ever so funny. It did not matter to Kathryn who he was, or whom he loved. She respected and cared about David unconditionally, and he adored her for it.

They feasted on blue corn chips and four-alarm salsa, collecting tiny paper umbrellas in their margaritas until they finally decided to order. Two large sizzling platters of steaming fajitas arrived, and they dug in. Kathryn was famished and preferred to do nothing on an empty stomach. After they finished eating, she whipped out an overpriced compact and a regal tube of lipstick and got right to the point. "I want something from you—*two* somethings, darling," she said while applying the siren-red lacquer.

"The answer is *yes* and *yes,* David said after a sip of espresso. "So why ask?"

She thought for a moment. "Just in case you're curious, I'll fill you in. The first is business. The second, a personal favor."

He took another sip and wiped his goatee mindfully, giving her his full attention.

She continued, "You own Banguard Publishing. It's is a small fifteen-man operation in Lubbock. They produce a bunch of trade magazines and print two local town papers—*The Scribe* and *The Southern Chronicle*—in addition to publishing a handful of independent non-fiction titles, you know, the how-to/self-help psychology sort."

David nodded. "You've done your homework as usual, I see."

"I'm interested in getting to know the business, and I thought a little hands-on would be the best way to learn. You see, I have some ideas, and, well, let's just say I'm ready for a new challenge, and *you* my dear, hold the key."

"And so, you want to borrow this key?" he said cheekily.

"Don't be silly, David. Of course not. I want to *buy* Banguard from you. Will two hundred and twenty thousand be a fair price?"

He gasped and then, giving a little quiver, grinned. "What? Kathryn, are you serious?" He thought a fretful moment more and paused. "I feel as if I'd be taking advantage of you if I said yes. But as you know, I have no interest in any of my father's former holdings. It's all just in name only."

That's what she wanted to hear.

He scribbled something on the back of his business card. "Ben Madison is my personal attorney. He'll work with Biderman and set up the deal. I'll give him the word that you'll be in touch. I'm simply out of the loop on all this, and that's the way I prefer it."

She stared at the splashy business card. "Great. I'll talk to Ben Madison on Monday, then. So we have a deal?" Kathryn leaned forward to shake on it, and instead, he grabbed her hand and pulled her forward, planting a scratchy kiss on her cheek.

"Deal," he said plopping back in his chair. Then, he eyed her fixedly. "Tell me—what possible use to you is a small publishing house like Banguard, anyway, Kathryn? Dare I ask?" David said as an afterthought. "I mean, why in the world would you pay so much to own it? Really, fess up!"

"It's not what it *is,* my dear, it's what it's *going* to be. Those good people there won't know what hit them!"

"I shudder to think," he said, reaching for the check. She could tell that his head was simply reeling. He could certainly buy a lot of art for the haul he was about to make on this sale; it was enough to make him more than grateful. One thing was for certain—she always had a way of getting what she wanted.

"Oh, what was the other thing? The favor you mentioned?" David said as he signed the check.

Kathryn smiled. "I want you to help me find someone."

"Sure," he offered. "Who is it you are trying to find? he asked, nearly dropping his cup when she leaned casually in and delivered the bomb.

"I want you to help me find my daughter."

CHAPTER 42

★ ★ ★

FALL 2010

ELLIE FEARED THAT SHE MIGHT be losing her mind. She noticed him first at the deli counter at the supermarket. Then, again in the cat food aisle. His cart was empty except for two small cantaloupes rolling around in the seat basket. He made a break for it when she circled back and glared at him. Realizing then that she was on to him, he disappeared down the soft drink aisle and out the sliding glass doors.

The next occasion was far more peculiar and unnerving. She could have sworn it was the same stranger, sitting alone just two tables over from her and Ross at Touché. Feeling uneasy, she feigned a headache and convinced Ross to leave before dessert, not wanting to alert him to her paranoid fantasies.

Who was he? Was it the same guy from the deli? She couldn't be sure. The resemblance, from what she could remember, suggested that it was him, wearing the same grimy baseball hat.

The third encounter confirmed her fears. This time, driving home from an off-site shoot, she spotted a black

Ford Ranger tailing her. It followed her never more than two car lengths away all the way from Conroe. She exited onto I-45 heading back toward the city and a high-traffic area to a corporate corridor lined with high-rise hotels, skyscrapers, and retail outlets.

She had two canisters of film that needed to be delivered to a client who was staying at an area hotel. When she slowed down to pull into the sloping driveway of the Westin, it was then that she was certain, as he followed her right into the parking lot, and waited to see her next move.

"That's what you think, *Jerk-o!*" She addressed the huge headlights looming in her rearview mirror and, making a sharp left, she navigated through several rows of parked cars before exiting onto the street and peeling off back in the direction of the freeway. The Ranger followed in pursuit.

She gasped. Then, firmly gripping the wheel for battle, she floored it. "Okay, then, you want to dance? C'mon, *Dickweed*—follow me!"

She took off like a bullet, dodging skillfully in and out of lanes in an effort to lose him on the surface streets and then merged onto the frontage road leading back to the freeway, where she cut him off and left him stalled up against an embankment, waving to his fading reflection in the rearview mirror as a semi screamed past him, laying on the horn. The hulking four-by-four was no match for Ellie's nimble Subaru as she left him fuming in the dust.

CHAPTER 43

★ ★ ★

TWO MONTHS LATER

"WHAT *IS THIS*?" KATHRYN ASKED, shuffling through a stack of grainy photographs strewn on her desk.

"That's her—at least I'm pretty sure it is—speeding off like a bat outta hell jus' after she nearly ran my tank into a guard rail."

Kathryn was clearly annoyed. Even over the phone, Caffey could read that her nose was flaring. Her voice was terse and agitated.

He was no photographer, that was for sure, but she would be hard-pressed to find a better detective. Unfortunately, most of the photos were so badly blurred that they were indistinguishable.

"Look, Mr. Caffey, or Al—*whatever* your name is. I don't know what kind of private investigator you are, but I'm going to need a little more proof than just a few blurry photographs and your gut hunch that you got the right person."

She tossed the envelope into the trash.

"You're just going to have to do better than this if you

want me to continue to retain you."

Caffey argued his case. "Your informant didn't give us much to go on. I mean, we need hard proof, Ms. Delacorte . . . a birth certificate, school records, and such. We got nothin' solid to go on. If you don't mind me sayin' so, I could get farther if I could jes' approach the supposed adoptive parents directly and ask a few questions." They had narrowed his search down to a middle-aged couple in Houston, who fit the bill as potentially being the adoptive parents, but at this point, it was still a guess. "Plus," Caffey hedged, "we don't know for sure if the girl I'm tailing is even your daughter. Why are you goin' about this the hard way?"

Kathryn's secretary walked in, grimacing apologetically. "Ms. Delacorte, your two o'clock is here."

Kathryn motioned for her to wait, clutching the receiver firmly.

"Never mind about that. I'm not paying you to think. I have my reasons. Let's just leave it at that." She squeezed her forehead, indicating that her temples were pounding. The seventy-hour workweeks were definitely starting to take their toll. She had a boardroom filled with corporate suits who were waiting for her. "You're just going to have to try harder then, Mr. Caffey. I'll be in touch."

Click. The line went dead.

"Shit!" Al slammed the receiver down, jamming his thumb in the process. "Son-of-a-bitch!" *Why was it he always got the nutcases? He needed a new profession, all right. Should have studied engineering or forestry instead of dicking around in criminal law.* All it got him was twelve years on the force and an honorable demotion to a desk job for having a little thing like prostate cancer. They had cut the bad stuff out, and he felt better than ever—like a new man, actually—but they weren't going to let him go back. *Jesus-H-Christ! A guy gets one bad break and he's finished. Screw them. And screw Kathryn Delacorte, too!*

CHAPTER 44

★ ★ ★

ONE YEAR EARLIER

KATHRYN'S FIRST INVESTIGATOR, RON BAVARRO was a pricey "people finder" who charged a king's ransom to locate missing persons. He was impersonal, shrewd, and did not return phone calls. Worst of all, he was indiscreet, and that bothered Kathryn. The task of finding her daughter was a private and personal matter, and even though Bavarro came highly recommended by her stepson, David, she decided to wait until Bavarro was able to locate and verify the couple as being the adoptive parents with a possible link to her daughter's identity—before firing him.

The last thing she would need would be bad publicity as a result of a loudmouth spotlight-seeking detective. He was already boasting around town about the "Delacorte case." As it was, it would take another five grand to make him forget that he ever met Kathryn Delacorte, and he was to hand over all contents and notes from her case file.

Bavarro's work, however, turned out to be key. He had managed to deliver the whereabouts of a Houston couple, whose last name was Masters, which alone was no small feat.

Due to the fact that Hester's House was an independently run shelter for unwed mothers and not government funded, adoptions were handled from time to time, under "private contract." This meant that Kathryn's daughter's adoptive parents most likely hired an attorney to "falsify" the adoption proceedings, which amounted to no more than crude "rights of ownership," or contracts similar to ones that would be signed in the transfer of property—leaving no legitimate paper trail. Adoption "fees" were directly paid to Hester's House and no one was the wiser. After all, there were clearly mouths to feed and utilities to be paid; no one ever questioned the integrity of the "backdoor adoptions" that were considerably quicker and cleaner than alternative channels—least of all, the often unsavvy and desperate clients seeking newborns over older children.

The process left little time for the changing of minds, where an unstable and emotional birth mother might choose to keep her newborn instead of putting it up for adoption, as was her original agreement with the safehouse, where for several months prior, she would have received the best of care. The swiftness of the process left little time for filing of forms that would legally link the transfer of guardianship from party to party on public record.

Hester's House closed its doors in 1990, when a former resident indicted the McKennas for infant racketeering when she tried to reclaim her son of fourteen months from a Seattle couple who had paid eleven thousand dollars for "dummy" adoption records and what they thought was legal adoption of the child.

Kathryn Delacorte's baby would have been such an "undisclosed" case. No documentation of any sort existed, or probably ever had.

All Kathryn could recall, she had told Bavarro, was the nurse's faint voice confirming, *"You can tell Dr. and Mrs.*

Masters that they have their little girl."

Later, Kathryn added that at the time, she had been told that the couple had driven up to the house in a car with Minnesota license plates, and that the woman was heard saying that her baby would have siblings—two brothers. There was not much more to go on, but then again, there rarely ever was.

Bavarro had traced fifteen families from public documents and census information with the surname Masters who were living in or around the state of Minnesota in 1985 in which a medical doctor was the head of household and the family had a minimum of two male children. From countless possibilities, he narrowed it down to the four best possible guesses: A Dr. Kenneth and Trudy Masters residing in Saint Paul, Dr. Graham and Cynthia Masters in Pine City, Dr. Thomas and Claudia Masters in Lancaster, and Dr. Garrett and Olivia Masters in Minneapolis.

The process of elimination was swift. The Saint Paul couple checked out with no additional dependents other than one son born in 1987. The Pine City Masters had two sons and two naturally born daughters—all with valid birth records that checked out with the prospective hospitals. Mrs. Thomas Masters had been widowed since 1991 and never remarried, or acquired any children.

This only left Garrett and Olivia Masters, who checked out as eventually having had three dependents in 1985— two boys and one girl of which birth documentation for one Ellen Brittany Masters contained a discrepancy. Her birth certificate, which had been filed with the state of Minnesota, indicated that she was born at Our Lady of Mercy Hospital in Minneapolis on March 15th 1985. Further investigation with the hospital revealed no such birth record to match. Nor was there any record of an Olivia or Libby Masters, as she went by, registered in maternity on or around that day. So, Bavarro deduced from the bogus birth certificate that Garrett and Libby Masters were most likely the adoptive parents. Further investigation confirmed that Dr. and Mrs. Masters were sem-retired and currently residing in The Woodlands in Houston, Texas. Such was the run of Bavarro's usefulness. He was fired.

Al Caffey was hired in the summer of 2010 and read the notes from his predecessor's file with mixed concern. He was charged with the task of finding one Ellen Brittany Masters, and confirming her identity. If he could successfully connect her with the previous Minneapolis couple, now living in Houston, he would have what Kathryn Delacorte had paid dearly for—the discovery of her biological daughter who would have been twenty-five years old by now, the same age as the woman he had been tailing.

"Find her," Kathryn had charged. "But don't reveal a thing to her, or to the adoptive parents. It must be done quietly. I mean it."

Kathryn liked Al Caffey from the moment she met him, and hoped that she could trust him, even though he looked a little shifty and far less polished than Bavarro. He came cheaper too, and seemed hungry for the work. Most appealing, he did not seem to care who she was, or what the rest of the world thought about her or her famed-dead husband. Al Caffey was simple and direct, and Kathryn respected that. They went over Bavarro's information at her ranch home in San Antonio, where they had all the privacy in the world.

"One hundred thousand for her exact whereabouts. Ten now, and the rest later. Deal?" Kathryn said, holding out a freshly signed check in front of his ruddy, eager mug. The guy was nearly salivating for it.

Caffey swallowed hard and smacked his lips. "Yeah, sure. You got a deal, lady."

They shook on it. And within one hour Caffey was on a plane to Houston.

CHAPTER 45

★ ★ ★

HOUSTON, TEXAS

A L CAFFEY HAD STARTED UP his private investigating business in 1989 and ran occasional bodyguard stints when he could to get by, safeguarding rock stars and local athletes from time to time from the wackos. Later, he worked in private service, catering to the endless needs of Hollywood's elite. It kept him in business cards and beer nuts, and that was all that really mattered to him—that and keeping sober, as he had proudly been for six years running. He was back from the chemo now too, and business was beginning to trickle in. Still, every damn day was a challenge all its own.

Here he was, at Christmas, holed up in a Texas studio apartment rented by the week for the duration. It was located in Sharpstown, which he aptly referred to as *Shittown*, located in the southwest section of the city, just a bullet's shot away from the crime-infested mall and freeway. Caffey was originally from Tulsa, but anywhere the work took him, was home. The no-frills studio served as both his home base and his working office.

Once again, Caffey studied the rather pristine file by the

glow of the television screen sputtering a re-run of *Cheers* in the background. Bavarro's notes were mostly typed double spaced with copies and clippings attached neatly in the inside pocket. *Hotshot big city dick . . . anybody could surf the Net for leads and locations. It took more than desktop sleuthing to find a face in a crowd of two million people—to deliver flesh and blood.* Al shoved the file into an empty desk drawer and grabbed a steno pad. He began formulating some notes of his own. Several other leads had loomed flat and vacant of any real potential up until now, such as the ones kept in a stack of tattered files, each leading to dead ends.

Caffey had traced the license plates belonging to one Ellen B. Masters from 2001, to the present day. She would have been residing in Houston then with her adoptive family at which time when she turned sixteen, she would have applied for a state driver's license. Caffey found that Ellen Masters had a valid Texas driver's license only up until August of 2008, after which it was left to expire. No plates were ever reissued with the department of motor records anywhere in the United States under her name after that, which could only mean one of two things— either she no longer owned a vehicle, or had changed her last name.

That's when Caffey scrawled a note to himself in red ink across the margin of his notebook on the probable hunch, *married?*

It would take Al Caffey six and a half months in total to narrow the search down to one from twenty-seven possibilities after researching dozens of current and former Ellen Masters who had resided in the Houston area between 1995 and the present day, with birth records tracing back to the East Coast. There was one former Masters—his original hunch—whose profile checked all the boxes. Ellen B. Masters, who existed up until October of

2008, then became Mrs. Ross Logan.

It was possible that he had finally found his subject. At least he hoped. He had snapped photos of her from a distance and plastered them on the closet door in his studio efficiency. She was tall, slender, and athletic with an almost a tomboy quality. Her auburn hair was parted down the middle and just hit her shoulders. She had a wide smile and a slightly pointed chin. He was certain that she was Kathryn Delacorte's biological daughter. If the information on the marriage records matched the profile linking her to the original East Coast Masters, and the falsified birth records, he would have her. All he needed were nine little digits—her social security number—to match to the documents for Ellen Logan.

CHAPTER 46
★ ★ ★

AL SNAPPED HIS CELLPHONE SHUT and exited the diner, where he had guzzled down three doughnuts and a chocolate milkshake, his idea of a balanced breakfast. He climbed into his truck, or his "mobile office," as he liked to call it, strewn liberally with paper bags and Styrofoam cups, indicating that this was where he spent most of his time. But as far as Al was concerned, the Ranger had better views than his shoebox studio, and besides, he liked to stay at the ready to move on at all times.

He headed downtown to the heart of Houston's central business district and parked in a tow zone just feet from a towering building, where he watched the gleaming revolving door of the mammoth skyscraper and lit a Winston. The entire fifty-second floor belonged to the Allegra Corporation, a billion-dollar ad agency, perched precariously atop a mountain of law firms, investment companies, banks, and retail conglomerates.

Allegra Corp. was king in the ad community. Its talented account executives and ad designers spun magic with catchphrases for everything from cold remedies to talking toys. They produced epic-quality two-minute television commercials that sent viewers scrambling for their credit cards. It was here that Ellen Masters Logan, as her work-issued ID stated, was employed as a staff photographer.

Al reached under the seat and extracted a tan wallet. It was Coach leather. He opened the center pocket and began rifling through the contents once again to assure that it was all there—driver's license, credit cards, checkbook, and even a few stray postage stamps.

Getting it earlier that morning had been easy. He just slipped in unnoticed and lifted it while she was in the shower. He entered and exited through the patio door, which she and her significant other never kept locked. She had left the wallet next to her purse on the counter, along with her work ID badge that was attached to a silver clip. Caffey had waited until the man had left for work. He had to slouch low in the driver's seat to avoid being seen, with the steering wheel pressing uncomfortably against his nuts. Once the man had gone, Caffey made his move.

He had since clipped her ID badge to his visor, which made tracking her down to her workplace a bit of a breeze. Included in the wallet was a photograph of Ellen and the man living with her, who obviously was her husband as evidenced by the shot of their wedding day, which further explained the different last name. There was also a family-type shot with a middle-aged couple and two male siblings that appeared to have been a family portrait taken at NASA at least a decade prior. *It had to be her—Ellen Masters, the daughter of the original Minneapolis couple, Garret and Libby Masters.* He studied the photo on her driver's license. She had a nice smile, for sure. He further noted that there was something peculiarly exotic about the features. He had not gotten close enough to her yet to discern just what. One thing was for certain, Kathryn Delacorte looked far too young to be this girl's mother, but, if the background information checked out . . .

Removing the cash to make it appear that the wallet had been ransacked before a Good Samaritan found it, he placed it into a large manila envelope. He was not a total cad. She would be missing her credit cards and family photos. He had made copies earlier of everything that he needed. He scribbled her name on the front of the envelope with a dying Sharpie and licked the flap. Extricating his bulbous belly from behind the steering wheel, he left the Ranger illegally parked and casually waltzed into the marble lobby and presented the parcel to the security clerk behind the desk.

"Could you see to it that Ms. Ellen Logan with Allegra gets this, please?"

He walked back onto the street in the stifling Houston heat, pondering. He would have a former colleague back home down in records dig up some additional documents with the information he had obtained. The guy owed him the favor and would be obliged to do it. As soon as Big Mike ran the report he would be home free. Or, back to square one with twenty-six more wallets to go . . . it was a crapshoot, all right.

Kathryn got the call from Al one week later, confirming that Ellie had been found. The place of birth indicated on one Ellen Masters Logan's marriage license matched the falsified Minneapolis hospital location on the birth certificate exactly. Kathryn was thrilled. And thanks to her overwhelming gratitude, Al Caffey got to retire three years early.

CHAPTER 47

★ ★ ★

FALL 2011

KATHRYN SPENT ALL HER TIME commuting back and forth from her cosmetic company in Dallas to Banguard, the publishing company in Lubbock. The newspaper company owned and ran a fifty-year-old weekly called *The Scribe*, which was primarily an ad magazine that featured short fiction, general interest stories, advice columns, recipes, and local weather reports. Other publishing interests held by Banguard were a number of niche titles that mostly appealed to a male demographic in boating and outdoor sports-related themes, with the exception of a handful of secondary titles in health and beauty categories—which were of most interest to Kathryn.

But before any restructuring could be done, it would be necessary for Kathryn to learn the business from the ground up as a sort of apprentice.

She worked with a foreman named Carl Lindner, who trained her on the massive printing machines, went on sales calls with the resident account executives, and shadowed editors, copywriters, and reporters. She fielded copy and asked to oversee all advertisement layouts and decisions, so that she could learn the ropes. At first, she was perceived by the staff callously, presumed to be nothing more than the "bored widow" of corporate tycoon Denver Ralston with too much time on her hands and little to offer except for the grief she would most likely impose, demanding change and higher profits at the cost of their professional integrity and talent.

They had seen it before. Banguard Publishing had gone through a dozen buy-outs in the past half-century, and Kathryn Delacorte was lucky number thirteen. And up until now, all had run smoothly. No one was interested in printing their own resumes, so they braced themselves just the same and simply waited. Waited for the bottom to fall out.

It never did.

The announcement had come in mid-June of 2010. For the first time in almost a decade, Banguard Publishing was actually going to turn a profit. From the beginning of her ownership, Kathryn vowed that the company would do what it would take to bring itself up to speed with its competitors. Of primary impact was Kathryn's policy of refusing to negotiate ad rates. Because of this bold move, many of the company's titles were on an upward trend with no end in sight. Consultants were called in, processes restructured, new equipment purchased. For once, downsizing would not be the answer. Instead, money would be spent, and Kathryn had the revenue to play ball.

Kathryn hired a boatload of heavy-hitters from competing companies in the industry to bring in new advertisers and to grow the newspaper's circulation at a rate of double-digit thousands of new subscribers per week, both in print as well as with the new emerging online offering on the Internet. Kathryn rewarded dedicated employees for helping her to build success, stone by stone, just as she had done with Earth's Essence by offering generous bonuses.

Kathryn knew that growth could not be accomplished without a loyal and compensated team. She was quickly becoming known and respected for her unorthodox and unconventional methods as, "The lady with the Midas touch." She was not above shocking her sales team into action. A favorite story was how she challenged her sales staff to sell three hundred additional ad pages for the year by breaking the watch she was wearing right in front of them with a hand weight and then promising the purchase of a new Rolex for each one of them if the goal was met. When the team gladly came through, she made good on her word.

The company continued to take in large printing contracts and maintained a client base of loyal advertisers who quickly doubled and tripled their orders in response to the paper's growing circulation.

In just two short years, *The Scribe* had received the honor as Texas's third largest newspaper in the entire Southern region. In conjunction with Banguard's newly expanded auxiliary book publishing department, and quickly growing online presence, the value of Denver Ralston's original little "pet paper" rose to impressive heights, positioning it nicely, drawing interested investors and hefty dividends on the public market, a feat that Kathryn had predicted would not happen in the first five to seven years.

Business was booming, and in the fall of 2011, Kathryn was able to unload some of the titles ahead of schedule to a UK publisher who had wanted to enter the US market for some time, purchasing the bulk of the titles for a cool forty-five million.

Kathryn strategically kept the health and beauty magazines, and would focus most importantly one fashion title, *The Look*, which was starting to show growth in the women's market. By selling off the specialty interest and smaller titles, and capitalizing on the company's more promising offerings, Kathryn adjusted her portfolio once again, moved the operation to her home base in Dallas, and renamed the company Delacorte Publishing. She recruited and hired on a few choice employees who were willing to relocate, creating a stellar staff who shared her passion and vision for the new and total revamp of *The Look*.

"In spite of poor ad sales, *The Look* consistently posts strong newsstand gains," Kathryn had said as she addressed the core executive team in a closed-door meeting. "American women of a certain age," she'd predicted, "are interested in a magazine that speaks to their issues and concerns about looking and feeling great, not one that bombards them with steamy content and sex quizzes. We're going to change that."

The cohort of hand-picked magazine industry rock stars seated at the table included Canadian-born and former runway model-turned-fashion director, Mingon Perron, a doe-eyed natural beauty who held duo-art degrees from a premiere New York design school, along with credentials assisting for Calvin Klein and Donna Karan in back-to-back internships before being hired on at Christian Dior in Paris. Creative Director and Fashion Guru extraordinaire Kyle Dean, highly credentialed in publishing and design, who had written several books on fashion in the eighties and nineties, and who served as contributing editor for several fashion magazines and blogs. Kyle boasted a Harvard degree, and an eminent family who made their name in textiles, and a former child-star actor turned realtor boyfriend named Tyrique. Kathryn managed to woo Kyle away from a potential job at a men's publication just in the nick of time. Seated next to him, was Senior Fashion Market Editor, Diann Spencer, a smart, hard-working corporate climber who started her career as a fashion assistant in the trenches at the house of Ms. Diane Von Furstenberg.

Later, hired on at *Cosmo*, as assistant to the Fashion Director, eventually working up in the ranks to Fashion Editor, and finally to Senior Fashion Market Editor for a competing woman's magazine, *Beauty Confidential*. Diann's resume was organized, efficient, and unscrupulous, just like her pitch—selling herself and her abilities in an impromptu interview where she and Kathryn had bumped into each other at an industry conference on the East Coast in, of all places, the ladies' room. Diann had whipped out her glossy business card from her Birkin right there at the sink and laid it on thick. She was willing to relocate to Dallas, had an iPhone bursting with industry contacts, and was filled with just enough swagger to convince Kathryn to take a chance on the crass, ball-busting, platinum blonde and former NBA cheerleader who would not take no for an answer.

Further rounding out the core team was Stephanie Anderson, a recruit pick from a pricey headhunting service that sold her as edgy and eager. The Texas-born sorority girl with the shoulder-length wispy auburn bob was a trendy twenty-something with a shameless Twitter feed and aspirations higher than her morals, Kathryn was afraid. But putting her in place as Diann's trusted assistant, she'd figured would do them both some good.

Kathryn chose to bring dark horse Siobhan Cruz on board from accounting obscurity, where she had worked for the past two years for Banguard. Siobhan had impressed Kathryn on more than one occasion in the past. With her heart-shaped face, enormous hazel eyes, and Mexican/Italian features, at just twenty, she was a dead ringer for Mila Kunis. Kathryn had decided that she would mentor and mold Siobhan into a fine executive assistant for herself. She liked the girl's quiet confidence and deft efficiency—qualities often lacking in today's tepid millennial talent pool.

Last but not least, seated at the far end of the conference

table, directly across from Kathryn, was Adam Nichols, Director of Marketing and Strategic Development. Adam had been with Kathryn since the early days of Earth's Essence and had agreed to come on temporarily. He was originally from Baton Rouge, but settled in Dallas when Kathryn moved the cosmetic company's headquarters to Texas. Adam held an MBA, had won numerous industry awards, and had worked for a string of corporations throughout the South before joining on with Earth's Essence. Adam was as trustworthy as the day was long, and there was no way that Kathryn was going to move her business plans forward without his expertise. This was mostly because Kathryn knew that Adam was different. He was not affected by the same ambitions and agendas as of most everyone else in the cutthroat world of corporate greed and gain. At thirty-seven, his neatly cropped salt-and- pepper hair and soulful brown eyes rivaled Clooney. He had a relaxed manner and was, remarkably, in-between jobs at the time Kathryn re-nabbed him. Everything about Adam fostered a trust in Kathryn rarely given to anyone.

The team was in place. Her Dream Team. Their collected efforts, she was certain, could only spell success. She just needed their full buy-in.

"Banguard always suffered from not having a flagship title," Kathryn said boldly. "Now, as Delacorte Publishing, it will have one. Introducing: *High Style*—the magazine that will capture upscale beauty, lifestyle, and fashion advertisers, and turn forty-plus women into a demographic for which advertisers will be willing to pay."

The conference room exploded in approving applause as the image of the new flagship title loomed on the projection screen, featuring a radiant and smiling Julianne Moore gracing the holiday debut cover. It was sealed. Kathryn's choice and auxiliary staff were on board and eager to get to work on the new launch.

Kathryn basked in the moment and all the possibility it held. Finally, she was about to realize her biggest dream yet. The stars were lining up, and she could not have been more excited.

CHAPTER 48

★ ★ ★

JANUARY 2012

THE ROLLOUT OF *HIGH STYLE* was fraught with water cooler chatter.

"Everyone knows that the typical launch fails—"

"Eighty percent of new titles fail over the long term—"

"Half don't live to celebrate their first birthdays—"

Kathryn was well aware that every launch had growing pains. The editorial refocusing, the redesigns, and the turnover were only part of the infancy stage. But she refused to let the naysayers affect her vision. In fact, it spurred her on. When she overheard two junior sales reps who stepped onto her waiting elevator, oblivious to her standing there in the back, pontificating, "Ms. Delacorte is a an excellent ambassador for beauty, but as a strategist, salesperson, and manager, I just don't know if she has what it takes" Kathryn took action. She called an impromptu sales meeting, making sure that the two doubting Thomases were front and center to hear the announcement, and it didn't matter in the least to Kathryn that they were men.

"Currently, our magazine is sorely lacking in ad buys from Regal Color hair coloring products at only six pages.

Our competitors have close to one hundred fifty pages combined. The problem as I see it, is that we simply do not know enough about Regal Color's brand or their products. So, I have taken the liberty of enrolling all of you—including myself—into the Regal Hair Coloring School."

After two weeks of shampooing, cutting, and coloring, the entire sales staff knew the product inside and out. Further, Kathryn made sure to have her assistant chronicle the experience in a series of posts, tweets, and Instagram pictures that hit the target with her millennial-minded client. As a result, Kathryn's brand continued to garner visibility, linking her solidly with the blissful marriage of beauty, fashion, and publishing and creating a new buzz with an ever growing, wider demographic. Sales soared to eighty-six pages within two months, garnering her the loyalty and devotion of everyone on the *High Style* team.

Kathryn knew that finding and retaining loyal and dedicated staff members who matched her level of ambition, intensity, and drive would be the secret to success. Kathryn most enjoyed taking chances on young, driven unknowns to fill out her staff. "I look for people who can become stars," she had said when she first interviewed Siobhan Cruz, a candidate who did not disappoint. Siobhan was a pro, helping Kathryn keep her finger on the pulse of every aspect of the magazine's inner-workings, far beyond simply scheduling her appointments and fostering the team's collective goals. Siobhan kept Kathryn's life on track, and prioritized matters that made Kathryn's day run smoothly; namely, but not limited to, managing the deadlines for creating the editorial boards and final publication approval; working with the business, marketing, and sales departments; finalizing details relating to photo shoots; overseeing Web content; analyzing the business diary, graphics, and new seasonal styles; and engaging in business-related travel, public appearances, and press interviews. Siobhan also choreographed Kathryn's personal life in addition to planning staff meetings, corporate events, and juggling all of Kathryn's work-related social functions. She was valiantly protective of her boss's non-negotiable restorative time, carved out twice weekly with any of her private sessions with either her yogi, spiritual advisor, or tight-lipped plastic surgeon, followed by an aromatic lavender massage by her private masseur, who was on call along with a tribe of health and beauty doyens. Each were at the ready to soothe away the stresses of being a fashion magazine mogul.

"I'm thinking of throwing a company party to celebrate the success of the debut launch," Kathryn said, reading the accolades from a newsfeed on her computer screen to Siobhan, who was standing in the doorway of her office holding a large vase filled with a spray of pink roses out in front of her. "High Style's *debut issue sold out the initial pressrun so quickly that an additional 500,000 copies had to be printed hastily. Ad inventory for the first three issues sold out, and one rival publisher said that at the direction of Ms. Kathryn Delacorte, the maiden magazine set the new 'gold standard' for launches."*

"I know! It's epic—right?" Siobhan said. "I'll just put these down, and then I'll go get my iPad." The bubbly assistant hurried to place the arrangement on a glass credenza near the floor-to-ceiling windows of Kathryn's massive office, which resembled a chic New York-style apartment in upper Manhattan. "They're from a beauty blog that wants an interview. What shall I tell them?"

"Give it to Diann, she loves that sort of thing."

Siobhan returned a moment later with her iPad in one hand and her now-cold morning latte in the other. It was nine thirty a.m. and she was just getting her first sip.

Kathryn reached into the mini fridge behind her desk and retrieved a mineral water. "Okay—ready for this? I'm thinking a Gold Rush-theme party for the gold standard of launches. A full blow-out Western theme night at my ranch home, of course, with the works—full barbecue spread, hayrides, games, huge dance floor, and music. Who is that band I like?" she asked as Siobhan tapped the notes onto her device.

"Lady Antebellum, Siobhan said, not missing a beat. "I will see if we can get them. Won't be cheap. What dates are you thinking?"

"Any time at the end of the month, if possible. Put everyone up at the Marriott on the Riverwalk and we'll need buses to transport everyone to the ranch. What do you think? Line dancing . . . a raffle—oh! And a nice grand prize—like a Silverado."

"Check." Siobhan never paused a moment. This was old hat for them. Already, she and her boss could plan an event on the fly that would take others days or weeks to hash over. Event planning was an area where Siobhan excelled— among other things. She was efficient at multi-tasking. Kathryn's visions were always realized with Siobhan at the helm.

It was not unconventional for Kathryn to throw parties, social outings, and team-building events that rewarded her staff on a regular basis. She knew no better way to say thank you to the people who helped make it all happen.

"The invites must say: 'Western attire required," Kathryn mused, adding further, "But not the dreadful kind with denim and red bandanas. Make it clear that this is Texas high style, ya'll—*tres chic* all the way!"

CHAPTER 49
★ ★ ★

STEPHANIE ANDERSON DESPISED THREE THINGS: cat-haters, whiny, model-types, and people who thought that her job was far more glamorous than it was. Mostly, she hated working for the vile Diann Spencer, Senior Fashion Editor with her tyrannical, prima donna, self-serving agenda. Everything about the woman was fake—from her bottled blonde hair to her silicone boobs. She had everyone, including Kathryn Delacorte, believing that she was the bomb. In reality, she was self-serving, opportunistic, and manipulative. Running personal errands for her majesty made Stephanie feel like a subordinate. Diann had a constant list—cigarettes, dry cleaning, complicated iced lattes—it was never-ending. The implication that she was Diann's personal gopher was degrading. Setting up makeover pictorials, or choosing typesetting for a contest ad would be a far better use of her talents and time than fetching tampons for the dragon lady diva with no soul.

Stephanie stood in front of Diann who was pounding out her final lap on the treadmill near the window in her small corner office, waiting for her to "dismiss" her for the day. The ritual made Stephanie seethe.

The spindly amazon hit the off button and climbed down

from the machine, panting and sweating unattractively. She motioned for Stephanie to sit on the stiff leather couch across from her desk and took a swig from her pricey thermos.

"Close the door," Diann ordered.

Then, she rifled through a stack of chaos on her desk and retrieved a printout of an industry review. Struggling to catch her breath, she began reading, "*Under President-CEO, Kathryn Delacorte,* High Style *has proven to be a strong performer in its early days.*"

Stephanie nodded. This was not news. Everyone knew that the magazine was strong and showed great promise. That was why she would hang on and comply with a smile on her face. It would just be a matter of time until she would impress Ms. Delacorte herself and move out from under she-devil Diann's death grip. She wanted more than anything to be an Art Director, to someday supervise and unify her visions with her own junior assistant to push around.

"There's more," Diann said, holding up an acrylic talon. "*In a recent interview, Delacorte confirmed: 'We have searched for the perfect candidates to spearhead our editorial mission and have found them in Senior Market Fashion Editor, Diann Spencer, and Creative Director . . . blah, blah.'* What do you think of that? It's great, right? Kathryn thinks I'm brilliant."

Stephanie half-smiled and checked her phone. "Really awesome, Diann. Props to you, for sure. You so deserve it, really. Was there anything else you needed, then? It's getting kind of late."

"I'm going to ask for more from you—from both of us. We will need to work harder to help bring this magazine to number one as quickly as possible. I mean it," Diann said, wiping the perspiration from her sun-speckled décolletage. "Brain-storming sessions, late nights, scouring the blogs and feeds for trends coming up on the streets. We'll need to attend all of the designer shows and presentations and plan for non-stop domination that is full-on. It'll be balls to the wall for Fashion Week, of course, coming up next weekend. I'd like for you to get our itineraries in order and post everything noteworthy throughout the events, in real time. Stacey Cummings will be writing a day-by-day recap of our experiences. Oh, and you'll want to get started on booking that humanitarian pictorial in Europe for the holiday issue. I'm going to need your full commitment day and night."

Stephanie bit her lip. She fought to stay cool, peering at her boss from behind the lenses of her chrome-plated designer miniature round frames. She produced a forced a smile.

"Plan on being attached to my goddamn hip—oh, and one more thing," Diann said as she swiped at her iPhone dismissively, "I'll need you to run to the pharmacy before they close and pick up my birth control pills."

One day at a time, Stephanie said to herself, picturing Diann standing in an airport in New York with a double-connecting red-eye on an over-crowed coach flight back to Dallas due to a booking malady. *Hey, it could happen.*

CHAPTER 50
★ ★ ★

"ADAM—" KATHRYN STOPPED SHORT AND waited when she saw that he was on a phone call, stopping just outside of his open office door. Adam Nichols never kept his door closed. The modest, sparsely furnished office was neat and aptly inviting with its array of outdoor-themed framed artwork tacked to the bare walls, small coffee table, and khaki- beige sofa in the far corner with a single thriving potted ficus tree basking in the Texas sunlight. He smiled and motioned for her to come in.

"Okay, John. I'll see you on Sunday, then. Have Stacey pack your tackle box and windbreaker. We'll be going out on the lake and see if they're biting. Okay? Good, then, John . . . see you soon." Adam hung up the phone and stood, slipping his hands into his pockets. He was tall, well over six feet, with kind brown eyes, a serious face that brightened when he smiled, revealing deep laugh lines and a strong chin. He had an athletic build from playing rugby in his early years, but now, at forty-one, he kept his phy-sique in check with morning laps in the pool at the local Y. "My dad," he said. "We have a fishing date out at the lake this weekend."

"In Austin, right? I recall that you have a home there, or

did. Do you still have it?" Kathryn made it her business to know a few personal details about her employees over the years, especially ones as loyal and talented as Adam.

"I do, indeed. I have a small house on Lake Travis. It's perfect for my hound dog, Wrigley, and me. The property juts right up to the dock. My dad really loves it there, and we get to spend time together while he can still enjoy it." His voice trailed a bit into an awkward pause.

Kathryn smiled kindly. She knew that Adam's father was in the onset stages of Alzheimer's disease and that Adam's weekend visits with him were a priority. "Does your father live in Austin?" Kathryn asked, fearing that she might be overstepping by asking.

"No, he lives in an assisted facility in Brookdale Alamo Heights, in San Antonio. He's a real hit over there with all the widows."

"That's really great." Kathryn laughed. "It's wonderful that you two get to use that boat of yours. And speaking of San Antonio, make sure to look for a memo from Siobahn to hold the date for the company event out at Delacorte Ranch. We're going to go ahead with the plans for the party. I'll have Siobahn get on your schedule to run the numbers."

"Will do," Adam said, grinning.

Kathryn checked her watch. "Oh—I've got to get to my ten o'clock. You'll be at the event, right? I mean, you and the corporate credit card."

"I will be there, Kathryn. With spurs on." Adam chuckled. "Wouldn't miss it."

"Wonderful," Kathryn said as she slid out into the hall and headed toward the elevators, calling in her wake, "Save me a line dance!"

CHAPTER 51

★ ★ ★

THE EVENT WENT OFF WITHOUT a hitch. The grounds of Kathryn's ranch estate were luminous. The special event company went all out in creating a truly magical, upscale, Western-inspired gala. Everything was illuminated in clear globe string lights from the majestic entrance gates leading up to the massive house, to the split-rail fencing horse runs, to the state-of-the-art multipurpose barn that served as the dance hall and entertainment pavilion. Capitol Nashville recording artists Lady Antebellum performed on a stage resembling a three-dimensional saloon and Western town complete with livery stable, hitching posts, and a flatbed wagon. Tumbling hay bales and a Texas twister were recreated in concert through the magic of digital technology blasting graphics on a hundred-foot LED wall producing a high-octane show that was nothing short of sensational.

Three hours in, and the party-goers were still going strong. Kathryn couldn't have ordered a more perfect night sky, filled with stars as far as the eye could see. Everyone was enjoying the merriment, letting loose and celebrating what promised to be the beginning of a publishing behemoth for Kathryn Delacorte; a dream she could hardly believe was happening, thanks to the time and talent of so many of her dedicated staff.

She told them so in a speech kept short and sweet. With a glass of Dom Perignon in hand, she addressed her beloved staff into a popping microphone. "I look for three things when hiring smart people: energy, judgment, and creativity—regardless of previous experience or background because I know that if you bring good people to the table, they will do the rest."

A roar of cheers and applause floated to the rafters and shouts of, "We love you, Kathryn!" emanated from the crowd. Kathryn looked like a vision in her couture Western blazer, silk Hermes blouse, and Dior denim. The rhinestones and Swarovski crystals that adorned her mauve and tan Stetson matched her custom-made boots with inlaid color images of her first Katie D. Designs logo from when she was sewing sequins onto sweatshirts in Houston on one boot, and the gold-embossed Delacorte Corporation logo on the other.

"The March issue," she continued, "will carry three hundred twenty pages—one hundred seventy of them will be ads."

The crowd cheered and howled. And then, breaking into a frenzied collective chant, with their fists pumping into the air, they repeated her name, "Kathryn . . .! Kathryn . . .! Kathryn . . .!" The moment caught her off guard and she stood, awestruck at the love and gratitude that poured over her. Cell phones exploded with photos, Intagrams, and tweets. Live video streamed into the stratosphere as the love-fest continued, only to be outdone by the extravagant fireworks display finale that exploded in the sky high above all of them to end the night.

"I'll tell you, that woman sure knows how to throw a fucking party," Diann slurred as she drained her sixth margarita from the glass and consumed the salty residue with her tongue. "Stephanie, can you get me another one of these? No one's driving tonight! Thank God for that, right?" Diann said, pressing her rock-hard silicone into Adam's bicep.

Stephanie turned in the opposite direction from the bar, pretending not to hear her.

That was Adam's cue to leave. He was amused and repulsed at the same time. The two had only been back from the show in New York just over a week—it was a miracle that Stephanie hadn't clocked Diann by now.

"Are you going to catch the bus back to the hotel?" Diann said, trying to steady herself on her teetering leopard-print pumps. "If you want—"

Adam cut her off at the pass. "I think I will go find Kathryn. You enjoy the rest of the night. Be sure to get me those receipts from your trip before Tuesday, right?"

"Yeah, what-*ever!*" Diann pulled a face and swatted him away. A server approached with a tray of freshly poured tequila shots, and she was on him like a rash.

CHAPTER 52

★ ★ ★

FROM THE LARGE BAY WINDOW behind her, Kathryn could see that the party was still going strong. She could even feel the bump of the speakers causing the house to vibrate beneath her feet. Stealing a moment away from the revelry to catch her breath was a different kind of bliss. She rarely spent any time at the ranch since the new acquisition, and now every bit of her time and energy would be needed to keep the momentum with the magazine going. She still had a half glass of champagne from the toast and smiled as she lifted it up toward the framed photograph of her grandmother, Abigail, smiling at her from the corner of her mahogany desk. "I miss you," she whispered, feeling a sense of sadness that she rarely allowed herself to let in. It had been a long day, she told herself.

Her iPhone buzzed on her desk, breaking her from her trance. It was a text from Adam: How about that line dance, Boss?

She tapped the screen with regrets:

Sorry to miss out — already on my way back to Dallas. Going to get an early start on the projections for next month's issue. Enjoy the rest of the evening. -KD

Her smile faded into a yawn. She would call for her

driver and meet him off the kitchen out back, and slip away unnoticed. But for the moment, she just felt like sitting in the dark a little bit longer.

CHAPTER 53

★ ★ ★

FEBRUARY 2013

THE NEXT TWELVE MONTHS SAW further re-organization of Delacorte Publishing's offerings, with an increase in the number of titles to fifteen, with powerhouse *High Style* leading the pack, now reaching 5.5 million readers each month. Other newly acquired categories included: health and fitness, child rearing, travel and leisure, home decorating, gourmet cooking, and entertainment. As a result, Kathryn's empire was growing exponentially. Web-based technology was booming, and many of the titles already addressed a twenty-first-century mindset. The idea for an Internet lifestyle title as well, was already in the works. In spite of all the growth, *High Style* continued to be the jewel in Kathryn Delacorte's crown.

Kathryn's vision was to cross-sell and cross-promote the Kathryn Delacorte name and within two years time, to reach 9.9 million readers a month. It was her ultimate goal to pen her own beauty and fashion books, make special appearances, and offer motivational speeches where her knowledge and story could prove inspiring. She was already in talks with a design house to lend her name and style to a ready-to-wear clothing line to be sold in department stores, in catalogs, and online worldwide.

"Everything should be run out of core centers so the art department and sales team work across the board. No silos," Kathryn said as the waiter cleared the salad plates and refilled the green iced teas all the way around. It was a weekly lunch outing that Kathryn liked to do with Siobhan on Thursdays to get them both out of the office. Today, she had invited Adam along to discuss the budget particulars for the expansion. When lunch was finished, and the talk turned to business, Siobhan retrieved her iPad and began taking notes.

"I see that you are not a big fan of kale," Kathryn said, giving the side-eye to Adam's half-eaten entrée.

"Who really is, right?" he said, smiling. "If I were you, I'd be having this conversation over some good ole Texas barbecue, but that's just me."

Siobhan chimed in. "Oh, I don't think that Kathryn could keep that figure eating pork rinds."

Everyone laughed. *So he likes barbecue . . .* Siobhan was quick to note slyly in her meeting notes. Adam was as handsome as they came, and she didn't mind one bit being privy to some of his inner-workings outside of the office. It was good to know these things, she figured. One never knew. Besides, she could always delete it when she was ready to type up the notes. She was always looking out for her boss. Was the woman completely blind to the way that Adam Nichols looked at her? *Geez! Fashion moguls as brilliant as Kathryn could really be so clueless sometimes.* Anyone with eyes could see it.

"I agree with your vision one hundred percent," Adam said, leaning in and resting his massive, tan forearms on the edge of the white tablecloth, suddenly all-business. "It's moving from being an admired personality to providing trusted products and services. Think of the magazines less as printed product and more—an extension of *you*. Your brand: Kathryn Delacorte. This could continue to be a very lucrative opportunity if we pull all of our marketing capabilities together and educate the sales staff and team all across the offerings. It's really about selling the whole package."

"Exactly." Kathryn beamed.

Siobhan typed his words verbatim and then paused. Kathryn and Adam were staring at each other for a beat before she broke the silence. "Right. And maybe this would be a good time for me to suggest that getting Kathryn a publicist might be a good idea." Siobhan had been overrun with requests to manage Kathryn's speaking and appearance schedule, which was turning out to be the work of two assistants.

"I agree," Adam said. "It's definitely time."

Kathryn smiled and nodded. "It's settled, then."

"Great—I'll get you some names to consider," Siobhan said, tapping at her screen. "If we're done here, I'm going to get to this mountain of emails. Do you two mind if I just jump in a cab and head back to the office?"

Adam brightened. "Not to worry, I'll get Kathryn back in one piece."

Kathryn, who had been immersed in an email of her own, didn't hear the conversation and looked up to find Siobhan gone. "Did she leave without me?"

"She did. Can't find good help anywhere, eh?" Adam said, smiling. "Come with me. We can finish our meeting somewhere a bit sweeter."

He lead her up the street, and in a few short minutes they were in a retro-style ice cream parlor complete with pink countertops and chairs. "Now, don't tell me that you don't have time for a treat every now and then. What's your favorite flavor, Boss? They have sugar-free offerings, so you're safe."

Kathryn took pause. *How did he even know about her dietary restrictions?* She had to admit it. She could not remember the last time that she had an ice cream cone. "My favorite flavor? Well, it sure ain't vanilla," she said, tossing caution, and decorum, to the wind.

CHAPTER 54

★ ★ ★

SEPTEMBER 2014

THE GRAND BALLROOM AT THE Los Angeles JW Marriott was filled to capacity. Kathryn's new publicist, Geralyn Hall, who came highly recommended, had booked her in back-to-back keynote sessions, for the Women Who Lead conference in L.A. on the twenty-third, followed by the Women's Media Association in Phoenix on the twenty-fifth. It would mean missing that year's stint at Fashion Week in Paris, but Kyle and Mingon had it covered. That left Diann Spencer to stay back in Dallas and hold down the fort. It was an opportunity to really see what she was made of, Kathryn thought.

"With any luck, she will not do too much damage," Kathryn had said on the flight to LAX. She had decided to take Siobhan along for moral support, even though she could have traversed the bookings with ease. Siobhan definitely deserved a getaway with fancy hotel meals, room service, and watered-down lounge drinks.

The evening went like clockwork, although Geralyn was stuck deep in traffic on the 405 and missed the main event. Kathryn and Siobhan were served banquet fare and had to endure several lesser speeches and award presentations with an empty seat between them before it was Kathryn's turn to speak. The crowd was gracious and adoring. Luckily, Siobhan had arranged to have several boxes shipped to the hotel with issues of next month's *High Style*, to give out afterward to attendees, and was also able to snap several pictures of Kathryn during and after her appearance, to post online. It was blatantly obvious to Kathryn that she needed the kind of personalized assistance that only Siobhan could give.

Halfway through the meet-and-greet, just after Kathryn's speech, a demure young twenty-something with long dark hair and kind eyes approached the platform to speak to Kathryn. "Ms. Delacorte, I really enjoyed hearing you speak," the dark-haired girl said. "I was dragged here by a few of my colleagues, but was really impressed with what I heard tonight. Your take on inner beauty and on how success is every woman's birthright is truly inspirational. And your background—your life story—was so moving, especially how you did not let your setbacks in life define you."

"I'm glad that you enjoyed it," Kathryn said, bolstered that the risk of revealing some of her life struggles seemed to do some good. "Thank you for coming. Would you like an advance copy of next month's magazine?"

"I would. Thanks—and can I ask, do you have a media kit?"

Kathryn and Siobhan exchanged glances.

Just then, and quite on cue, Geralyn Hall appeared, flustered and panting. "I am not even going to tell you how heated I am that I missed it. Traffic was brutal!"

Kathryn's relieved but annoyed look said it all. She quickly introduced her tardy publicist to the young woman and smiled. "This is my publicist, Geralyn Hall. Geralyn, meet—"

"I'm Irene. I was just telling Ms. Delacorte how amazing her speech was."

"She is asking for a media kit," Siobhan said to Geralyn, then turning to the girl, "Do you think we could get a shot of you with Kathryn for our social media?"

The girl smiled. "Absolutely!" She leaned in close to Kathryn as Siobhan quickly snapped the shot.

Geralyn handed Irene a white folder embossed with Kathryn's name and a pristine issue of the magazine. "Here you go, honey. My card is inside. Just contact me if you think you might know anyone who would like to book Kathryn for an appearance."

"Thanks," the girl said, then handed Geralyn her own sleek black business card. "I will."

Irene looked over to where her friends were now calling for her as they were getting ready to leave the venue. "The crew is on the move," she said, shouldering her cross-body bag, into which she slipped the folder and magazine. "Oh—can you tag someone on that photo on Twitter?" she said to Siobhan. "It's *hashtag—BumpyFriedman@Global* all one word."

"You got it," Siobhan said, tapping onto the tiny screen. It's done!"

Geralyn blanched, then checked the name on the business card that Irene had handed her. She closed in behind Siobhan and Kathryn as they waved to the girl and her cohorts, about to more than make up for her late arrival. "Do you two even *know* who that girl was?"

"No. Should we?" Siobhan asked.

"Irene Friedman—the daughter of Global Network's Executive Producer, that's all. I'd say not bad for a day's work, Kathryn!"

Bumpy Friedman's phone went off just as he was stepping up to the tenth hole. He bristled and then softened immediately when she saw Irene's smiling face pop onto his phone screen. She was FaceTiming him from Los Angeles and looked so pretty in her studious glasses with her dark hair pulled up into a high ponytail. "Hi, baby girl—can't really talk. I'm stinking up the golf course right now with this game."

"Didn't mean to bother you, Dad. I wanted to pass along a lead for someone you might want to keep on file for the network. I think she'd make a great walk-on guest or person of interest for a documentary."

"Who is it?" Bumpy asked, waving off his turn.

"Kathryn Delacorte. She's an up-and-coming publisher out of Dallas. Google her. I also sent you a tweet—I snapped a photo with her at a luncheon where she spoke to a group of high-powered women. She's the real deal."

"Always looking out for me, you are," he said, wiping his forehead with his gloved hand. "Damn, it's hot as hell here in New York. You'd think we were playing in Tucson!"

"I'll send you her press kit. Make sure that you take a look."

"I will, sweetie." He trusted her instincts. "I'll have Lorraine file her in the 'keeper' pile. I gotta run—these guys I'm playing with mean business. Everything's business, though, right?"

"That's what you taught me," Irene said, a smiling blurry image bouncing on the tiny device.

"Gotta go—" Bumpy said. "Love you."

"Love you too, Dad!" He hit the red button with his pudgy thumb, and the screen went blank.

CHAPTER 55

★ ★ ★

DECEMBER 2014

THE HOLIDAYS BROUGHT A SLOWDOWN to the hustle that was the publishing business, leaving a skeleton crew the second to last week in the month, when everyone had left for their celebrations and the much-coveted three-week break that Kathryn had given a taxed and deserving staff. The January issue was out, lean but mean with plenty of pre-and post-party articles and pictorials to ring in the New Year.

Kathryn sat alone in her office, relishing the quiet calm of a job well done and another year of gains filling the coffers of Delacorte Publishing. Her thoughts quickly turned to deeper introspection when she pulled a red file folder from the top drawer in her desk that she kept locked. Even Siobhan did not have the combination. It was the Al Caffey file, and it contained a shuffle of grainy photographs of a purposeful Ellen Logan moving through her day, unaware of the surveillance being imposed on her private and seemingly wonderful life. *Why would I even consider ruining that?* Kathryn wondered. *For what gain?* She wondered secretly if she even deserved the right to ask the universe for this one thing that for so many years—and for good reason—she had denied herself.

"Still here?" Adam's voice broke through her reverie. He stood tan and lean in the doorway. Even from far across the room, she could feel his soothing presence, and the smell of his Tom Ford cologne sent a sweet and tantalizing mix of vanilla with top notes of saffron and nutmeg floating in the air.

"Just finishing up," Kathryn said. "Need to close out the books on a few things." Then she asked, "Why are you still here? I'm sure you have holiday plans to get to."

"On my way out. My father and I are heading to Tahoe this afternoon. There's a lodge there, and if we're lucky, there will be a lot of snow. He just loves a white Christmas. Not much of that stuff here in Texas."

Kathryn smiled. "Have a great time. See you in the new year."

"Right. See you in a few weeks," he said. "Happy holidays." He paused a moment and then slipped into the dark hall. She heard the elevator ding, the doors bump closed, and then once again, she was alone.

CHAPTER 56

★ ★ ★

GLOBAL NETWORK / NEW YORK CITY
MARCH 2015

BUMPY FRIEDMAN WAS ON A mission. He had less than a week in which to deliver. He was to announce the full lineup for the new talk show to the network, namely to his boss, Willard Conrad, whom he had promised a ratings-saving extravaganza the likes that the network had not seen in too many months to count.

The team was waiting in the conference room at seven a.m. with frenzied glances, blurry-eyed deer-in-the-headlights confusion, and panic-gripping lumps in their throats as Bumpy popped the tab on a warm Diet Coke to kick off the brainstorming session.

LeMaster leaned over and breathed coffee breath into Barry Paige's ear. "Bend over—grab your ankles—and kiss your ass goodbye."

It was a small cohort, just the main players. There was Thomas LeMaster, Director of Network Marketing. At six foot four, he was a towering executive with a square chin, close-cropped hair, and a baritone voice that got him some occasional voiceover work and the sporadic walk-on stint from time, giving him a good reason to keep paying the dues on his SAG card. He was as narcissistic as they come; never met a mirror that he didn't like; and had beady brown eyes that were in constant motion, darting around like two guppies in miniature fish bowls.

Barry Paige, to LeMaster's left, was one of the show producers. His assistant, Amelia, was seated across from the two. The young intern was suppressing a yawn as she opened a notepad to take the minutes. Barry's Converse gym shoe tapped rhythmically on the worn gray carpet as he swiped at his phone methodically. At age thirty-five, the redheaded ginger was already making a name for himself with his creative vision and keen sense of delivering to the market the type of talent that sold ads and drew audience share. The fact that he wore sneakers and tucked a neat ponytail beneath a baseball cap most days did little to discourage Bumpy's confidence in Barry's spot-on instincts. It was clear to anyone watching that Barry Paige was dead-set on doing everything he could to advance himself toward his goals to be the next Ron Howard.

"Here's what we've got," Bumpy said, knitting his pudgy fingers into a tight death grip atop a leather portfolio until they were white at the knuckles. He was just two months past the bypass surgery, and frankly, everyone wondered if his comeback could survive—along with the network's morning ratings. The answer lay in his concept for a decisively new and cutting-edge talk show that would feature four high-profile women of varying ages, who would each bring something unique and compelling to the eighteen to fifty-four female demographic in the eyes of the sponsors.

He placed the headshots for each candidate onto the mahogany conference table with flourish as he extracted each one from the portfolio. "We've got a famed psychologist and radio talk show host currently in syndication; a romance author, and a wild-child millennial actress—all of whom are in talks with us to seal the deal for the pilot show. That leaves the need for one more host."

With that, he reached into a paper bag he was carrying that held his six-pack of Diet Cokes and extracted a dog-eared back issue of *High Style* magazine and a one-page media bio on the smiling and elegant grand dame of publishing and fashion. "I am hoping that I kept this for a good reason," he said as he held up her press page and smiled. "I submit—our fourth and final potential acquisition—Ms. Kathryn Delacorte."

LeMaster and Barry Paige nodded. Delacorte was not a household name, but she was known in the industry for being ball-busting and promotionally savvy, as well as for having an uncompromising business sense and a sizable female following. Plus, at age forty-eight, she was an extraordinary beauty, which didn't hurt with the male viewership. She would more than do, if they would got lucky enough to get her on board.

"Are we talking to her people?" Barry asked, already searching her social media presence on Google.

"Not *exactly*," Bumpy said, looking squarely at Barry. "Not yet. That's going to be *your* sole job and purpose in life over the next forty-eight hours."

Barry looked up from his phone, a bit stunned.

"Go to Dallas and get us Kathryn Delacorte," Bumpy said with finality. "Or we'll all be back to producing game show segments in obscurity with washed-up celebrities on late-night cable—if we're lucky."

CHAPTER 57

★ ★ ★

DALLAS, TEXAS
MAY 2015

EW THINGS WERE MORE IMPORTANT to Kathryn than staying on top of the fashion trends, and nothing was more magical than Fashion Week in Paris. Unable to attend the previous year due to a run of speaking engagements, Kathryn had been forced to relegate the coveted task to her superstars, Kyle Dean and Mignon Perron, who were able to incorporate the time-honored tradition into a ten-page spread every year from their findings, photos, and inspiration gleaned from the advance viewing of the spring and fall collections at the show. She had already had plans to invite Adam along, thinking that he deserved to actually experience the lavish and culturally rich extravaganza, but she just was not sure how she would approach him about it. The opportunity came in one perfect instant when she literally bumped into him getting into the elevator at the end of a workday on her way into the parking garage. As soon as the elevator doors slammed shut and the two were alone with only the soft whir of the mechanisms whisking them to level G, Kathryn had started the conversation.

"The budgets look solid for the quarter," she'd said. "By the way, how is your dad doing?"

"He's recovering nicely from a knee replacement. He'll be off fishing expeditions for a while, but he's expected to bounce back in no time," Adam had said, and then added, "Do you think you'd like to maybe grab some real Texas fare sometime? Like barbecue? Or kale? Or barbecue kale? Whichever you prefer."

Kathryn paused and then thought better of it. "I don't know if that would be perceived well by the staff—you understand, right?" she'd said, glancing up at the digital letter G, illuminated above the door. The elevator settled with a thump, and the doors sprang open.

"Got it, Boss. I understand," he had said, allowing her to exit first. Together, they walked to their cars, which were parked one space apart.

"However," Kathryn had quickly added, "I was meaning to ask you if you would like to accompany me to the show in Paris this year. It would be good for you to see it first-hand."

He smiled, and took exactly one second to reply. "I—yes. I would be happy to go with you to fashion week in Paris."

"*Génial!* You can start brushing up on your French, then. I'll have Siobhan make the arrangements," Kathryn had said before sliding into her sporty blue Ferrari.

CHAPTER 58

★ ★ ★

PARIS, FRANCE

FOUR WEEKS HAD PASSED AND the day finally arrived. They were touching down at Charles de Gaulle airport after a pleasant flight that she was certain was Adam's first time flying first-class. He would be keeping an eye on expenses, no doubt, but she was more than happy to treat him to a trip he would never forget. Paris in the spring was mild and magnificent, and secretly, she couldn't wait to experience it with him. Fashion Week takes place in Carrousel du Louvre with one hundred shows in total spanning the city, ranging from the top fashion houses to the lesser-known names, where assistants, stylists, models—as well as a self-acclaimed "cool crowd" set—all descend on the French capital to see the next year's styles revealed ahead of the rest of the world.

It was a place where celebrities, fashion industry moguls, and anybody who was anybody would crowd the grounds outside the Louvre at the Louis Vuitton show, drawing gawkers, onlookers, and throngs of paparazzi hungry for a shot of anyone even resembling a Kardashian, or top recording artist who might be in attendance. The Paris show, attended twice annually, once in the spring and later in the fall, was serious work—with runway events and trade shows, as well as grand openings, promotional events, and lavish star-studded parties thrown by famous patrons and fashion houses. Along with New York, London, and Milan, the Paris show was the culmination of weeks and weeks of work by exhibiting designers to be taken in by editors and journalists who would be writing about it. *High Style* would be well represented with Mingon's creative vision and Kyle's natural writing panache, and there was little left for Kathryn to do but to step back, enjoy, and take it all in.

By comparison, the New York shows were more geared toward the trendy, mainstream, commercial offerings, such as T-shirts riddled with slogans and other message-inspired and athleisure-style clothing line that appealed to the masses and made political and moral statements. Paris, by contrast, offered a feast of sensory and avant garde fascinations that had a decidedly European slant, and whereby the styles spoke to a more selective and elite audience. In a less esoteric sense, it did serve to provide a keen forecast for what would be deemed "in" and "out" for the upcoming season in the high-end of men's fashion, haute couture, and ready-to-wear, which was the magazine's niche.

"This show draws designers from all over the world," Kathryn explained to Adam on the limo ride to the hotel, giving him a crash course about the tradition and its history. "Of course, the French have been exporting their style since the seventeenth century."

The hotel was twenty miles northeast of the city. The five-star, nineteenth-century structure was a work of art all on its own with a blend of old world flourishes along with contemporary comforts. Adam was speechless when they pulled up to the quaint two- story, stone exterior with ivory-colored brick architecture, green and white awnings, and intricate ironwork gates. Kathryn had an "in" with the manager and much preferred the obscurity of the lesser-known exclusivity of his establishment to the heavily booked hotels on the convention circuit. A doorman stood at attention at the entrance to the opulent lobby, giving one the feeling of having stepped back in time, or onto the set of an old foreign movie set. One fully expected the likes of Coco Chanel, F. Scott Fitzgerald, or Marcel Proust to be channeling through the chandeliers that hung in such stately defiance of time.

"It's magnificent," Adam half-whispered, causing Kathryn to smile, quite pleased that she was able to book what was, in her opinion, one of the finest offerings in a city overrun with tourists and aspiring hopefuls.

"That it is," she said, and then motioned to the bellman for a luggage cart. Kathryn had two large designer suitcases, a trunk, and one hatbox, and defied anyone to travel any lighter. The affair was worthy of needing to have the perfect wardrobe, as well as space to bring back some of the newest cutting-edge designs to test out back in Dallas, as well on her regular trips to New York and L.A. "Why don't you take care of the bags, and I'll get us checked in?" Kathryn said, hoping this would not make him feel slighted—as if she brought him along to be her errand boy, or to simply fetch her things. Kathryn was, if not anything else, far from helpless.

She returned a few minutes later with two key cards and handed one to Adam, announcing, "You will be on the lower floor here, and I will be just above you."

He smiled. "Thanks, that will be great."

She thought that he might be interested in coming and going at his will and figured that the lower floor would prove more convenient. All she could think about was a long, hot bath and perhaps a quick nap before venturing out to the festivities. "We can have an early dinner and then maybe take a look around, how does that sound?"

she asked.

"Perfect," Adam said. "I can meet you down here when you're ready. I'm feeling the need to read some Hemingway right now."

"Ha! Sounds good," Kathryn said. "See you in a couple of hours." She left him looking tired but excited in his dark denim jeans, cowboy boots, and rumpled linen shirt, standing in a place where it was quite likely princes and dignitaries, poets and dreamers had stood so many years ago.

CHAPTER 59
★ ★ ★

KATHRYN SLIPPED INTO THE LARGE ornate bathtub that was nonexistent to the rituals of a countess or woman of means in the Age of Enlightenment in Paris, who might have only fully bathed once a week. She thought of this fact with gratitude for being born in a time where advancement and privilege were a given, and unfortunately, for many, taken for granted. She thought how the topic might make for an interesting article and spread in one of the upcoming issues of *High* Style, a spin-off of sorts from Fashion Week, and made a mental note to discuss the idea with her staff writer, Stacy Cummings, when she returned to the States. It was nearly impossible for Kathryn to turn off her mind, as she was always thinking about one of her many magazines, an upcoming appearance, or problem that needed her attention. Taking an actual vacation of any kind was a thing of the past. She would just have to settle for the precious few moments that she could steal away here and there to sustain her. It was, quite certainly, the drive and duty that she felt to the magazine and to her staff—as well as her millions of readers.

The room was amazing. Each suite was posh and elegant with classic pastel-toned French décor, marble bathrooms, and a sitting room filled with artwork and antiques. Her particular suite had a terrace that overlooked a private garden with a view of Place Verdôme, a square located to the north of the Tuileries Gardens and east of the L'église de la Madeleine, a Roman Catholic church, built in the Neo-Classical style, which stood in testament to the glory of Napoleon's army. Kathryn knew this because instead of taking a much-needed nap, she scrolled through her iPad to learn more about the history and lore of her rich surroundings. She made a mental note of the cafes and bistros nearby, as well as the bars and nightclubs. While fashion was the theme of the day, she felt like a giddy tourist eager to explore the enchanting city. The hotel had two upscale restaurants, a quiet bar, and a spa complete with Chanel beauty treatments. On second thought, she imagined she might just stay put and never leave. Of course, that would be unfair to Adam, who was ready for his indoctrination into Fashion Week.

"You know, I was tempted to stay in that glorious boudoir all evening, order room service, and leave you to your book," Kathryn said, slipping into the deep leather corner booth where Adam was nursing a scotch, several chapters into his war novel.

"I'm a bit wiped out from the flight, too," he said.

"Any objection to staying here for a while? I think the team can get along without us at the Valentino reception," Kathryn said, reaching for her phone. "I will text Mignon and let her know we've arrived and will be taking a pass on the event."

"Sounds good," Adam said. "Did you want to call it a night, then? We can regroup in the morning before heading over to the Dior show."

"Actually, I'm famished. I'd love to enjoy a nice, quiet dinner here. Would you like to join me?" Kathryn said, hoping not to pressure him into feeling like he had to chaperone her. She was enjoying the company and wanted it to last a bit longer.

"I would love to, Boss," he said, motioning for the waiter. "Been smelling that prime cut wafting from the kitchen all night. I'm starving."

Kathryn smiled. "I promise, no kale tonight—oh, and please don't call me boss. It's Kathryn."

"Got it," he said.

"You know, there's an interesting little nightclub around the corner if you want to check it out afterward," she said. "It's all the rage with the locals."

"Madame Delacorte! he said with a boyish grin. "You just might be a bad influence on me, but I promise I will try to keep up with you."

She smiled. It was the city of lights, all right, and by her account, it was looking brighter by the minute.

CHAPTER 60

★ ★ ★

DALLAS, TEXAS

DIANN WAS POUTING, AS USUAL, over her latte and latest muffin order fiasco when the ditzy new temp accidentally sent a call to her line. She waited for Stephanie to get it, but then remembered that she had sent her down to printing for a fresh box of business cards.

Annoyed, she picked up the line, simply barking a curt, "*Yes?*"

The voice on the other end of the line seemed thrown. "Hello. Is this Ms. Delacorte's assistant?" It was a male voice with a New York City area code.

Diann leaned back in her chair so that she could see the edge of Siobhan's desk if she craned her head just right from outside her office door. Siobhan was nowhere in sight, which further annoyed Diann. *Everyone just abandons their duties, I suppose, when the Queen Bee is away!* she thought to herself. *Figures.*

She returned to the caller. "Who is this, please?" she asked, examining her muffin full of raisins. *What is so difficult about filling an order for a bran muffin with no raisins?*

she wondered. The muffin place had morons working for them. They always got her order wrong.

"This is Barry Paige from Global Studios. We're looking to get in contact with Ms. Delacorte. Is this Siobhan Cruz, her personal assistant?" the man said.

Diann thought for less than a second. "Yes—yes this is *Siobhan*. How may I help you, Mr. Paige, did you say?"

"We'd like to speak with Ms. Delacorte about a time-sensitive issue. Is she available for a conference call this afternoon?" he asked.

Diann knew full well that Kathryn had her hands full with the show activities in Paris and most likely would not stop to field potential bookings for her to appear at a function or award banquet. She felt it best to just pass on the request directly to her publicist, Geralyn Hall.

"Ms. Delacorte is out of the country, but I will be happy to refer your request to her publicist. "What is the best number to reach you?"

He gave her the number and five minutes later, curiosity got the best of her. She called Barry Paige back from another extension, this time posing as Geralyn Hall. She poured on a Southern accent, disguising her voice, and nearly fell off the chair when she heard the news that the network wanted Kathryn as the fourth and final host for a new morning talk show. It was a game changer for sure. If Kathryn took the job, there was only one way for Diann to go—right into Kathryn's shiny stilettos as Editor and Chief.

Diann hung up the phone and squealed with delight. Stephanie walked into her office to find Diann in a panic. "What time is it in Paris? Kathryn is flying back on Sunday, right? Then to Chicago? We have a lot to do to show her when she returns that this magazine stayed running like a top. C'mon! Let's get to it!"

Stephanie shuttered. Diann was on a bender. What else was new?

CHAPTER 61

★ ★ ★

PARIS, FRANCE

THE NEXT DAY FOUND KATHRYN and Adam further interested in stealing away from their smartphones, and the shows and exhibits, in exchange for the lightly attended tourist attractions that would otherwise command throngs of attendees. They hit every attraction over the next four days, making excuses that they were hitting the circuit with verve, seemingly missing their cohorts at every turn. Kathryn feigned a series of intercontinental conference calls, and Adam claimed to be holed up in his hotel with a stomach virus. Instead, the two traversed the city, enjoying a trip to the Eiffel Tower, the Arc de Triomphe, and the Catacombs, taking long, leisurely lunches in the bistros and cafes that were merely steps from their hotel.

The city of lights turned decidedly into something much more endearing to Kathryn, who found herself taken aback by the sheer joy and elation that she felt when she spent time with Adam. She could not ever remember feeling so safe and content as when she was walking beside him, or simply just sitting across from him, listening to him talk about his life; his family, his father, and his hopes for the future.

The last day before they were to return to the States, they talked in the hotel café until dawn and then hurried, each to their rooms, to pack for the limo waiting to take them to the airport. The only difference being that Kathryn would be taking a flight to Chicago for a meeting, and Adam would be returning alone to Dallas.

"I had a great time, Kathryn," Adam said as the two prepared to part toward their different airline gates.

"Me too," she said. For once in a very long time she had let herself come first. "I have at least fifty text messages from Diann Spencer, but I'm sure it's nothing that couldn't be handled when I get back," Kathryn said, smiling into Adam's soulful eyes. She had let someone in, and it felt scary and wonderful all at the same time. But, of course, there were boundaries, and no one knew that better than Kathryn. She had secrets and shreds of her life to retrieve, certain that once she was able to do so, she would regain a large part of herself that had been lost. She had made a life of protecting herself, and she was not about to change that now—for anyone. There was still work to be done.

He leaned in for a beat, and she was certain that he was going to kiss her. She turned and offered her cheek in an awkward collision of apologies.

"I'm—sorry, Kathryn," he sputtered. "My bad, totally. I am so sorry. I just—"

She waved it off and headed toward her gate, leaving him red-faced and fumbling.

"It's fine," she called in her wake. "See you back in Dallas in a couple of days."

She settled into her first-class seat, ordered a glass of

champagne, and powered off her phone to settle in for the long flight. She was certain that with things back home being as they were, and a knowing feeling that was quickly growing in her chest, that somehow, once again, things were about to change; and that she would somehow never be quite the same.

CHAPTER 62

★ ★ ★

FIRST THING MONDAY MORNING, DIANN knew that she had to cover her tracks. She would contact Geralyn Hall, Kathryn's publicist, and explain that there had been a mix-up with a message intended for her regarding Kathryn from Global Network. She hurried from the parking garage, up the elevator, and past Siobhan's desk before she could stop her.

Diann burst into her own office to find Geralyn Hall and a skinny man in a Global Network baseball cap sitting on the other side of her desk. Stephanie entered behind her with a tray of hot Starbucks.

Siobhan closed in on all of them and crossed her arms. "Diann, this is Barry Paige from Global Network, and you know Geralyn. They say they have an appointment with Kathryn. Did you know anything about this?"

Diann looked desperately at Geralyn, who nodded slowly. "Yes. Well, there did seem to be a bit of a *miscommunication* last week, I'm afraid, but we're good." Turning to Siobhan, Diann asked, "Has anyone spoken to Kathryn?"

"About what?" Kathryn said, appearing at the doorway. After having learned upon landing at O'Hare that the meeting in Chicago had been cancelled, she had decided to take the red-eye back. "Gosh, I go away for five days and all hell breaks loose! What's going on?"

Geralyn brightened. "Kathryn, welcome back. This is Mr. Barry Paige from Global Network." Then, turning to Siobhan, "Do you think we can get a conference room? Somewhere private we can talk?"

Diann stepped forward, and Geralyn waved her off. "Not you, dear." Then, turning to Stephanie, she added, "But we will take the lattes. Thanks."

CHAPTER 63

★ ★ ★

THE FOLLOWING WEEK KATHRYN FLEW to New York to meet with Bumpy Friedman. They met at a deli downtown near the TV station, and Kathryn was not surprised to see the same spirited twinkle in his eyes as she had seen in his daughter, Irene, who had come up to her after the benefit in Los Angeles to introduce herself.

"I follow my daughter's lead on most of my biggest decisions," Bumpy said, biting into a Kosher dill. "She has her mother's smarts. We both think that you will be perfect in the first chair."

"Well, I'm flattered that you think that I would be a fit for your new show. If I can talk about fashion, beauty, and self-esteem—you know, inspire women and people in general—then I think we should do the deal. I don't know of any larger platform I could hope for."

Bumpy nodded. He had high hopes for the show as well, and he knew that choosing the right talent was only part of the equation. It *had* to work as he had envisioned it, or it was over for him. He wanted more than anything to bring daytime television along into the twenty-first century and make his mark. It would be life-changing for all of them.

"We'll be setting up the promotional photo shoot after

the entire cast is signed on. We're hoping to have the contracts ready at the end of August, and then we'll arrange to do the photo shoot at the studio two weeks after that, just before we rollout the pilot. How does that sound?"

"It sounds like I will be needing a place to live here in New York sooner than I thought," Kathryn said.

"We have someone who can help you with that," Bumpy said through a mouthful of pastrami. "Big reality TV realtor. He hooks up all the celebrities. I'll get you his number."

He was far from conventional, that was for certain. So many thoughts had been whirring in Kathryn's head from the moment that she learned that the job was hers. Namely, how she would navigate between all of her worlds and responsibilities.

"I imagine it's a lot to take in," Bumpy said. "We are just so grateful to have your commitment. We'll do all we can to promote and support you. Please be sure to let me know if there is anything at anytime that you need—"

"Well," she cut him off indelicately, "there might be a couple of items that I would be interested in securing in order to feel more certain of signing."

He stopped chewing and pushed his plate aside. *Here it was. They all had their damn agendas.* Did he really think it would be so easy?

He scratched his balding head and felt the heartburn creep up in his chest. "And what might those two things be?" he asked.

"First of all, I'd like to use a photographer of my choice to take the promotional shots for the marketing of the show."

It took him about a millisecond to respond. "Done. What is the other thing?" Bumpy hedged, feeling that he had this broad and deal in the bag.

"I want to co-produce the show. My name on it—along

with yours—or no deal."

Within the hour, Kathryn was back at the airport ready to board a return flight back to Dallas. She had made the deal and couldn't have been happier. Before takeoff, she tapped away at the tiny screen on her smartphone to inform Siobhan of the good news—and to convey the following: See if we can book photographer Ellen Logan out of Houston for the photo shoot in New York on the 21st as well as for an exposé in the magazine right after that back at my ranch house.

Kathryn stared at the words for a moment. She knew what it would mean. Taking a deep breath, she hit *send*, hurling the message off into the ether. It was in motion.

CHAPTER 64

★ ★ ★

KATHRYN ARRIVED THAT EVENING AT Dallas/ Fort Worth International feeling too tired and excited to go anywhere but to her penthouse apartment to cozy up in bed with a glass of wine and the galley proofs of next month's issue. Instead, she received a phone call from Geralyn.

"I need to meet with you—pronto. It has to be tonight. I have a table for us at the Richard."

No amount of resistance mattered. Geralyn was insistent, and Kathryn was worried it had something to do with a scheduling conflict, perhaps even the contractual details involving the talk show. So, she told her driver to take her directly to the restaurant without first stopping by the office.

As soon as Kathryn walked in the door, she could see that it was a ruse. The entire restaurant had been closed to throw her a congratulatory party in her honor. Everyone was there—the entire staff, special clients, vendors, and even a few neighbors from her building. She was speechless.

Siobhan ran up to her with flowers and yanked off her coat. "Here, Kathryn—your adoring public awaits!"

A huge banner spanned the width of the restaurant with accolades and balloons bouncing everywhere emblazoned with "Congratulations" and "Way to Go!" in bright mylar lettering. There was a deejay, a full buffet spread, and an open bar. "Who approved this?" Kathryn half-joked. When she looked over and saw Adam standing at a distance, smiling, she knew she had her answer.

"You didn't have to do all of this," she said later, pulling him aside to thank him.

"Well, we couldn't send you off without a fanfare, could we?" Adam said, nursing a scotch and soda. It was bittersweet, all right. It was all happening so fast.

"When do you have to be out there?" Adam asked.

"In six weeks. Enough time to square things away here, I hope," Kathryn said. "God help us, Diann will be at the helm as acting Editor in Chief. I'll be counting on you to make sure that she won't drive Siobhan off."

Adam gave her a meaningful glance and began, "Kathryn, there is something that you need to know. I—"

Before he could finish his sentence, the crowd called for Kathryn to step up to the microphone in the deejay booth to say a few words. "SPEECH! SPEECH! SPEECH!" they chanted.

She broke away and stepped on stage, feeling truly humbled by the outpouring of love and well wishes from her staff. "I am not saying goodbye," she said, her voice tight with emotion. "It's just time for change; something we are all called to do. I assure you that the company will continue to grow and flourish just as it always has under the direction of some very smart, talented, and incredible people—each and every one of you. I will still be very involved." As she said this, she glanced down at Diann with a holding look. Diann raised her glass. Kathryn continued, "Thank you all for making our magazine what it is and what it will continue to mean to women everywhere moving forward."

The crowd broke into applause. She stepped down and searched the crowd for Adam to continue their conversation. But this time, it was she who could not find him anywhere.

The next morning, Adam's resignation was on her desk atop a printout of a press release by her publicist in the morning *Media Reporter*, which read: "*Upper management at Delacorte Publishing is bracing for a transition, as President–CEO, Kathryn Delacorte announced that she is stepping down to pursue a TV career with Global Network's new women's interest talk show,* The Gab*; a successor has not been named. How Delacorte manages transition to new management is critical. It will require a leader who will move Delacorte Publishing to the next level, toward a multi-media future—just like its owner. Look for a five-page exposé on the new talk show and its cast in the fall issue of* High Style.*"*

CHAPTER 65

★ ★ ★

TWO MONTHS LATER
HOUSTON, TEXAS

ELLIE STEPPED ONTO THE STAIRMASTER and draped her towel across the handgrips. The gym was filled with people—early morning die-hards like Ellie, who liked to get in a quick morning workout before they started their day. She had a work-related shoot in Brooklyn that Saturday, which was a favor for a friend who needed some publicity shots for her trendy new bakery café in Williamsburg. Ellie had decided to fly out early to enjoy two days of sightseeing in the city prior to the shoot.

She adjusted the incline on the exercise machine and fitted the earphones in place in order to hear the audio streaming on the console. She looked up. Every television high above the gym floor was tuned into a breaking news story that was just unfolding on the East Coast. Ellie stopped the machine and strained to get the details. The stoic blonde broadcaster reported: *An explosion has killed a family of five in Harrisburg, Pennsylvania. The device was a crude homemade pipe bomb believed to have been planted in the basement of a Harrisburg residence, just one hundred miles west*

*of Philadelphia. A full-fledged investigation is underway. Author-
ities strongly suspect this to be a hate crime and not an act of
terrorism. The condition of the suspect is yet unknown, but further
unconfirmed reports place the perpetrator on a vigilante rampage
targeting a local high school in Harrisburg . . .*

Ellie watched the macabre images outside of the suspect's home, an early eighteenth- century, multi-family
duplex with crooked eves and sagging siding, looming on
all ten screens. She knew every reporter and photojournalist in the country would be hot for a piece of the story,
which was quickly unfolding, and they would be scrambling at that very moment to get a flight out East.

Her heart quickened—she had booked extra time for
the trip and would have two full days before she would
be needed to photograph the bakery opening. She figured
that she could easily drive the three and a half hours to
Harrisburg from the city to work it in before heading back
for the photo shoot in Williamsburg by Saturday.

Within minutes she was on her cell phone with the
editor from *The Gazette*, an online news outlet with international reach that she did freelance work for from time to
time. "I want the Harrisburg story, Irv. I am heading there
this afternoon. I'll get you some great shots."

The flight was predictably overbooked and turbulent, but
Ellie managed to get from the plane at LaGuardia to the
car rental counter with her travel bag and cameras intact.
Experience taught her to check her clothes and tripod
equipment, but to carry on her valuable items—cameras,
film, and lenses—just in case. The last thing she needed
was to waste her two extra days in New York City waiting
for her replacement equipment to arrive should the airline
drop the ball. At all costs, the shoot would have to go on.

Ross would be returning on Sunday from Alaska, where
he was attending a Harbor Seal expedition. She hadn't seen

him in days and was looking forward to doing so after a relatively stress-free work-related weekend trip of her own in New York. They would have the boys the following weekend for visitation; so, alone time with her hubby was definitely top of list. It looked, however, like the universe had planned differently. She would text him later with the change in her itinerary.

Just as Ellie disembarked from the plane, further news of the tragedy in Harrisburg commanded all eyes onto the television screens throughout the terminal and onto smartphones as everyone's attention was fixed on the gruesome details unfolding. A full-fledged massacre was underway at Harrisburg High School. A bedraggled newscaster relayed the tragic litany of events: "*A rain of gunfire and the discovery of several more explosives have been the result of a SWAT team siege on the high school. Two people are known to be dead and several more injured in what appears to be a senseless act of rage.*"

Ellie could hardly believe her eyes. The tragedy was worsening by the minute. She hurried to claim her rental car, and once behind the wheel, punched in the coordinates to Harrisburg. Then, she phoned the spunky office assistant from *The Gazette* to arrange for a hotel room.

Unfortunately, the local Sheraton just outside of Philadelphia was as close as she could get. The resourceful office assistant, Megan, cleverly booked Ellie onto a room block as a convention attendee for an annual Sports-Recruiters convention being held at the hotel. Luckily, the reservation clerk never checked the attendee list for verification. As expected, throngs of network and independent news crews had already taken every hotel room in and around Harrisburg.

When she arrived, a cheese tray and a bottle of wine were waiting for her in the room, along with an NFL hat and a box of tiny basketball-shaped chocolates. A note on hotel stationary read: WELCOME RECRUITERS, TO THE CITY OF MOVERS AND PLAYERS!

The place was swarming with professionals from the college circuits, convening for their annual meeting, which Ellie gathered from the hoopla and signage posted near the registration desk, was being held in the Grand Ballroom and subsequent meeting rooms where some eight hundred fifty attendees filled several floors of the hotel for the workshops and seminars. She was about fifty miles from the site of the school shooting. It appeared that it was as close as she was going to get for the duration.

As the day progressed into night, more reporters descended on the tiny town to unpack the horrors of the calamity. They dissected it all—insufficient school security, weak gun laws, possible terrorist ties. The list went on and was the discussion of every major network vying for airtime and a new angle on the riveting tragedy as the officials continued to try to keep the microphones and cameras at bay.

Ellie was mentally preparing for the shots she hoped to get the next morning when the press would be given clearance to the site. She was half-listening to the television, feeling restless in the confines of the small hotel room.

Finally, she switched off the television, grabbed her camera, and headed out the door. She took the elevator down to the lobby, which was packed with badge-wearing conventioneers who made it hard to move. She hailed a valet for her rental car and made her way, with the help of Google maps, to the west side of town, where she found the mood to be a different kind of hectic.

She drove through what was once a booming Philadelphia business district, since replaced by low-rent housing and roadside chain motels that dotted the highway. She knew that numerous network camps were being set up with technicians and reporters filling the rooms, bars, and restaurants of the small town in order to be close to the action.

She spotted a road sign and suddenly felt hungry. She exited and slowed the Ford Escort to a crawl. There was a diner and several fast-food chains surrounded by a ghost town of foreclosed and failing storefronts.

The single freestanding restaurant was loaded with out-of-town media types who had the same aim in mind—to get the story. They were the curious and hungry in more ways than one.

She ordered a Chef's salad and an iced tea. Checking her phone, she calculated that Ross was most likely flying somewhere over the Atlantic by then. It would only be another three days before she would see him when she would be picking him up at LAX. She would be interested in hearing all about his trip after she was done showing him just how much she had missed him. Four weeks, she decided, was far too many days apart for any couple with a love as strong as theirs. She wondered how he was braving the coastal wilderness of ice glaciers and fjords with the team from the zoo. No doubt, he was having the time of his life working to bring back the Harbor Seals safely. It's what drove him. The thought of him doing what he loved most made her smile.

She overheard several crew members from a cable affiliate in the booth next to hers referring to a bar in one of the local hotels that was close by. After she ate, she started on foot in that direction and ended up at sports bar in the lobby of a Ramada. *A sports bar?* She shook her head at the irony. The public's appetite for news had, in many ways, become a spectator sport.

The small, cheesy sports bar was crammed with patrons, mostly more media crew and reporters. Every pool table, dartboard, pinball, and video machine was occupied. There was no space at the bar, and every television was tuned into the news of the moment—the Harrisburg shooting. A large rear projection screen was running the Jets game without the sound. A jukebox provided continuous servings of nameless rappers and The Stones. Everyone was busy drowning his or her senses in idle chatter and booze. She decided to snap a few shots capturing the journalists and camera crews in ready postures, glued to their laptops and smartphones, tapping away at tiny screens glowing in the bar light. *Click!* It was a sad social portrait of great proportions.

There would be several days of material to cover before the story faded from the public's interest; until the next big thing would happen and yank them from their beds, their families, and their pathetic lives, causing them to scramble to the next town or tragedy to do what they did best.

Ellie was once commissioned to fly to Michigan to photograph a fatal accident. A commuter train had derailed on its way from Canada to Detroit. She had turned down the offer because she knew that the newspaper would only pay for macabre—the most gruesome shots of the catastrophic crash. The commuter train had met with a freight hauling explosive chemicals. Thirty-three passengers perished in the calamity. Ellie had no desire to profit off of the misfortune of others. It wasn't what she did.

She ordered a light beer and struck up a conversation with a journalist named Rita from Chicago. The woman was a veteran staff-writer for *The Tribune*. She was clearly a pack-and-a-half-a day smoker, and had a know-it-all sense about her.

"Look," Rita gestured toward the television with her Bic lighter. "It's the radio shrink Doctor *Hannah*-something-or-other." She cackled in a huff of nicotine breath. "What's *she* doing there? Oh, I guess they're bringing in the reinforcements. I'm surprised that goddamn Dr. Phil is not holding court with the shooter's parents, for Christ's sake!"

Ellie stared with disbelief at the TV screen. "That's Dr. Hannah Courtland Murphy," she said, wondering to herself, What are the odds? Ellie was coincidentally booked to photograph Dr. Hannah and the cast of Global Network's-new woman talkfest, *The Gab*, just two weeks from then, in Manhattan. The well-known radio psychologist had an impressive and unwavering following of everyone from housewives to co-eds who tuned in to her network show weekly in search of tough love and sage advice. On screen, she looked haggard and disheveled; as if she had spent the past twenty-four hours wearing the same clothes.

"Jesus Christ!" Rita growled, draining the last drop from her bottomless glass of gin. "What's next? Oprah does open heart surgery? These celebrity-types are all alike. Chasing the publicity gravy train. Hell, if they just stand still long enough, it'll just goddamn hit them!"

"So, why are you here?" Ellie asked, hopeful that the crusty old newspaper maven would see the hypocrisy of her actions and eat her own words.

"Paycheck." She pulled out a cancer stick from her purse and waved it in front of Ellie's face and smiled through stained dentures. "And you? Why are you here, Tinker Bell?"

Ellie's answer was not one of life's greatest revelations, but it was the truth. "Actually, I don't know. I guess I just thought—maybe there was a bigger story here to tell."

Rita slipped her jacket on. She was dying to light up, and it was starting to spit rain outside.

"Yeah, we're all looking for that, *Tink*. Let me know when you find it."

CHAPTER 66

★ ★ ★

STEPHANIE ANDERSON HAD PHONED ELLIE a little over one month earlier to book her services. The two had attended classes at the University of Houston, where they might have crossed paths in the hallways on the way to their liberal arts degrees. Stephanie would have been three years behind Ellie Masters, but her sister, Carly, knew Ellie's roommate quite well and stayed in touch through the years. Just after her graduation, Stephanie worked for a concierge firm and had reconnected with Ellie via social media to arrange to purchase her services for a client interested in a photo spread for his shoebox city condo. The two had later collaborated on a shoot for the opening of a trendy Houston nightclub, when Stephanie had been working as a special events coordinator for a public relations company and Ellie was still photographing chipmunks in the zoo.

"You know Ellie Masters, right?" Siobhan had asked over yogurt cups in the lunchroom. She never forgot a fact, and Kathryn had brought up Ellie Masters's name on more than one occasion.

"Yes. My sister's friend and Ellie were roommates in college. I've booked her a few times. She's awesome with a camera lens."

"It seems that Kathryn is dead-set on having her photograph the promotional shots for the talk show in New York, as well as a private series of shots back at her ranch home for an exposé for the holiday issue. Can you see if she is available?"

"Sure," Stephanie said, secretly angling for a break from Diann and a free trip to New York. "I'd be happy to oversee the shoot at the TV studio—*if* you think that would be needed. You know how particular Kathryn is about the details."

Siobhan nodded. "I'll tell you what, get me Ellie Logan and you can manage the shoot—but only the one in New York. The ranch house is off-limits. Kathryn does not want anyone there but the photographer. You will need to be clear about that with Ellie Logan."

"Got it. Thanks, Siobhan," Stephanie said, scanning her phone for the number. It never hurt to position oneself to impress the boss. Her luck was turning.

"You have been requested by the grand dame herself," Stephanie said, imitating Kathryn's deep, sultry voice. "'I want the best, get me Ellie Logan!' Her *exact* words, I am told."

"Really?" Ellie smiled.

"Kathryn is my boss's boss, and I make it a point never to ignore the requests of the CEO. Plus, there's the kiss-up factor. I said that I could more than deliver Ellie Logan, folks—I can deliver her with bells on! I told Kathryn's assistant that I knew you personally, and she seemed extremely insistent that we *had* to get you to do the shoot. You gotta do this for me, Ellie. I'm counting on a promotion that this can help deliver."

"What's the job?"

"Kathryn Delacorte is about to make her television

debut along with three other celebrity-types on the cast of a new morning talk show called *The Gab*, just in time for fall sweeps. She insists on hiring you to photograph the network's promotional shots as well as an exposé for the magazine several days later at her ranch house in San Antonio. She wants a shoot of the entire cast, pronto—like in two weeks. What do you say?"

Ellie paused. In the mid-to-late-2000s, she had started taking on more commercial freelance projects where her unique perspective was used to create visuals for outdoor and magazine advertisements. Her work with live models was lucrative and impressive, although she loathed the industry and all it stood for, particularly its exploitation of women. Ellie Logan had little tolerance for ads in which women were overtly depicted as objects.

"The magazine is on point with women. I've seen it," Ellie said, considering the offer. There was something more substantive to it and the woman behind it, she thought. "Okay. Sure. I'm in. Have the information sent to me; any write-ups on the show, topics to be covered, set designs, whatever you've got. I'm thrilled to do it."

"Great—done! That's perfect. Kathryn will be so happy."

She'd heard it before, but it always was flattering when the CEO of a major magazine asked for you—by name, no less.

Little did Ellie know just how many times Kathryn had requested her work, anonymously, accounting for nearly half of the freelance calls Ellie received—all slated for one or more of Kathryn's publications or businesses.

"I'll send you the tickets and itinerary for both locations," Stephanie said. "See you in New York."

CHAPTER 67

★ ★ ★

PHILADELPHIA, PENNSYLVANIA
AUGUST 21, 2015

THE NEXT MORNING, ELLIE NOTICED that a new group of guests were filing from cars and cabs into the hotel, streaming into the lobby. Photographs were shamelessly documenting what appeared to be bereaved family members and friends who arrived on later flights and drove in from all corners of the state. Representatives from the school, grief ambassadors as they were called, were on hand. Very little order was maintained as floods of friends and relatives clamored for sleeping rooms at a facility that was already booked to capacity with conventioneers, news media, and paparazzi. The frustration and disorder only added to the sense of chaos and frenzy.

Ellie was swept up by the grief and desperation.

"Can you tell me what hospital they took the injured to?" a sullen grandfather asked as he twisted his hat in his hands.

A desk clerk directed him to an official holding a clipboard, who said to a quickly gathering crowd, "We can only furnish limited information about the shooting.

Please clear the way for the guests who are checking in."

A mother clutching a photograph slumped in her husband's arms as two younger children clung at her knees, crying. They were encircled by two sets of concerned elders, the children's grandparents, who had recently arrived from out of town. A female officer had just escorted them back from the local hospital and was helping the group back up to the holding room where families awaited more information. Fifty miles was not far enough away from the flash bulbs and fill lights of the media vigilantes who had been out scoping the hospitals and hotel lobbies for just such a scene.

One of the two, a little girl, had dropped her toy doll. At first, the despondent parents did not notice. Quickly, Ellie scooped up the doll and handed it to the child, who stood blinking, smoothing the doll's hair.

The father spun around to discover Ellie smiling down at his daughter. She was wearing her Nikon, which hung at her hip. "Leave us alone!" he bellowed. "Take your goddamn pictures of someone else!" With his large hand, he gave Ellie a shove and gathered his family in tightly as if he were holding a small umbrella in a storm and all of them were struggling to fit beneath it. "Just leave us alone!"

Ellie was incredulous. "No—wait. You don't understand." She removed the camera from her neck. "I wasn't going to take her picture . . . honestly. I wasn't. I swear it. Here—see?" She opened the back of the Nikon and extracted a roll of unused film that she had loaded earlier and handed it to him. "It's not of your family, but here, you can have it. I promise. I didn't take your daughter's photo."

She held out the cartridge to the bewildered man, who simply stared at it. It didn't matter. He was but a shattered shell. They had all come to see. To see what happened to a person at a time when the light in one's life—a child—was snuffed out. When a life was taken in an instant from the earth, never to be held, or touched, or gazed upon again. A time when a family of five was, with one horrifying phone call, suddenly and forever reduced to four.

A moment of compassion passed between her eyes and his. But not before an observer's shutter from somewhere in the crowd closed in on the poignant scene and snapped it for posterity. A clear shot of the man accepting Ellie's peace offering as his family stood by, stunned, frozen in time.

The second shot, taken moments later, captured Ellie bending over the little girl and her older brother to deliver words of comfort with the camera laying open and empty at her feet.

The photos appeared the next morning in *The New York Times* with the caption: THE REAL STORY IS THE ONE THAT DIDN'T GET TOLD. *Freelance photographer Ellen Logan put human compassion before exploiting a family's misery and is shown handing her film over to the father of a slain student from the Harrisburg school shooting as his wife and six- and eight-year-old children look on.*

CHAPTER 68

★ ★ ★

NEW YORK CITY
SEPTEMBER 2015

KATHRYN LINGERED OVER A STIFF glass of brandy in her new Upper East Side penthouse between Lexington and Third Avenues. It was a last-minute pick, seeing as how she would need somewhere to stay that was close to the television studio for weekly tapings of the talk show. She would still oversee the running of the magazine in Dallas, keeping a keen eye on Diann and the team. She would only be needed for the really big decisions and to give final approval on the magazine's galleys before they would go to press. Her people would handle most everything else. It would all work, along with weekend runs to her ranch house back in Texas, where she much preferred spending her time. The ranch home was her haven and strictly off-limits for business of any kind. Otherwise, computers, smartphones, and video conferencing would make working virtually from one end of the coast to the other, a viable solution.

A sworn recluse and self-proclaimed eccentric, Kathryn managed to stay out of the hostile path of nosy reporters and flash frenzied paparazzi. She had a cottage hideaway in Italy, as well as a villa in Greece just off the shore. These were the rewards from her cosmetic empire, publishing success, and newly emerging clothing line soon to be launched into mainstream specialty stores throughout the nation and in Europe—just in time for the exposure and notoriety that taking on the first chair on the debut talk show would deliver. The decision to have her lawyers draft an ironclad clause into her contract with Global Network, ensuring that they allow her to purchase rights to the show's pilot and first year run, would allow her to gain substantial creative input of the show. This was a critical factor, which hung in the balance up until the final hour, when the network's lawyers finally conceded.

She had wished that she could call Adam and tell him about the good news. She wished that she could tell him everything. Somehow, she believed that he might actually have understood.

Kathryn folded the inky newsprint neatly and studied the photo from the *Times* as if it were a work of art. Of all the pictures acquired throughout the past several years from detectives and private investigators taken of Ellie, this was by far the best.

The photo said it all in one shot: Ellie stooping to touch the cheek of Timothy Quinlin's little sister in the lobby of the hotel, moments after she had surrendered the unused film from her camera over to the distraught parents. Kathryn read the caption for the hundredth time and smiled. She was a precious angel, all right. An angel of mercy. Ellie was a good person. *No credit to me*, Kathryn thought with a pang.

How fortunate that the Masters had adopted Ellie as an infant. In spite of everything and all that had gone before, Kathryn was certain that it was the one thing she ever did that truly mattered, that counted for something. Her Ellie.

She studied the photo through eyes blurred with tears,

careful not to let them drip onto the newspaper. She drained the brandy from the glass and lingered over its soothing, searing descent down her throat. After so many years, the time had finally arrived. Katherine would be face-to-face with Ellie at the photo shoot slated for the next morning. She would need to summon every bit of strength not to reveal anything to anyone—especially Ellie. Not yet.

There was still the private shoot scheduled for the magazine exposé in three short days at the San Antonio ranch house, when she and Ellie would be alone. Once again, and as she had done so many years ago, Kathryn prayed that she was making the right decision.

CHAPTER 69

★ ★ ★

GLOBAL STUDIOS
NEW YORK CITY
SEPTEMBER 4, 2015

KATHRYN WALKED INTO THE TELEVISION studio on the day of the shoot already camera-ready. She was as stoic and beautiful as ever. Stephanie noticed her iconic azure eyes, taking it all in, before they landed squarely on Ellie. Kathryn looked directly at the beautiful photographer for a long while, and just stood there, smiling. Stephanie took this as an indication that Kathryn was pleased that she had been able to make the arrangements for Ellie's photography services, just as Kathryn had wanted.

Stephanie called to her, "Kathryn!"

But as she turned, she seemed disoriented and lost her balance. Luckily, Stephanie was close enough to catch her before she fell.

"Are you okay?" Stephanie gushed, grabbing her by the arm. "You almost took a tumble."

"I'm fine," Kathryn said, shaking it off. "I'm breaking in a new pair of Louboutins. Is everything ready to go?"

Stephanie checked her headset. "Uh, I'm so sorry. There

seems to be a *delay*," Stephanie said, turning down the volume on her two-way radio. "They are telling me that Casey Singer has not shown up yet, and we are ready to start shooting." Stephanie held her temples and struggled to keep calm. Diann would never let her forget it if, as the site coordinator, she botched this by not even being able to deliver the full cast for the shoot featuring their lionized boss. It was a bad reflection on both of them, not to mention Siobhan, who had given her full faith in Stephanie's ability to oversee the event.

"I'm going to get some water," Kathryn said reservedly. "I'm sure Casey will show."

Stephanie had organized every detail with flawless efficiency. There was a lavish continental breakfast with lox and bagels, pastries, assorted chopped fruit, and fresh- squeezed juices. Transportation had been arranged for each of the cast members from door to door, and hair and makeup artists were on hand to prepare and keep them primped throughout the session. Back at the magazine, they were holding the current issue from press for the completed network ad, which would appear on a two-page spread featured on the inside cover. It was Stephanie's further hope that if the publicity photos were as sensational as believed they would be, due to Ellie's inimitable magic, they would also have the billboard shots for the outdoor campaign. Stephanie had an eye for such things and looked the part in her sleek gray gabardine suit, Gap turtleneck shell, and round spectacles. But, if she was to impress Kathryn as the fashion executive she wanted to be, everything rode on this shoot being a success.

Stephanie looked over at Ellie, who was busy checking her camera equipment; fiddling with the fill lights and lenses. The large studio was eerily quiet without a live audience. The arena seats were dark in contrast to the closed stage set, which was fully illuminated in bright lights. The studio was otherwise empty of activity, except for a few assistants running around, adjusting light stands and taping down extension cords. A harried representative from the television station was off in a corner, fuming into his phone upstairs to corporate.

"You seem nervous," Ellie said. She had noticed that Stephanie was extremely jittery.

"No, I'm fine. It's all going to be fine, right?" Stephanie breathed unconvincingly, eyeing the studio door. Casey Singer, the youngest cast member, was unstable and far too unpredictable. *Why would Bumpy Friedman take a chance on such a wildcard?* she wondered. If the errant actress didn't show, they would have no choice but to cancel.

"You're sure you're okay?" Ellie pressed, testing the shutter of the new thirty-five millimeter. "Why don't I start with a few candid photos of them getting ready for the group shot?"

"Yes. That would be perfect," Stephanie said.

"It's going to be fine," Ellie said. "I can't wait to meet the ladies."

Just then, Kathryn walked up to Ellie and, smiling, extended her hand. "Hello. I'm Kathryn. Where would you like me?"

Ellie shook her hand. "Nice to meet you. Will you head to the stage for me, Ms. Delacorte? I want to get a shot of you in the first chair, looking off to the right," Ellie said.

Just then, as the two other hosts, Hannah Courtland Murphy and LaCosta Reed, paraded onto the stage, stepping into the bright lights, Stephanie's two-way radio squawked. She pressed the button on her headset, and a garbled voice confirmed, "*Casey Singer is in the building. Repeat: She's here.*"

Stephanie nodded her head, relieved. The cast was finally all in one place. "Cue the music," she said into her headset. "Let's get this party started!"

The four stiletto-clad women convened in hugs and high-fives on the set beneath a large fiberglass logo that read: *The Gab*. As the show's high-energy theme music kicked into full gear, streaming from the pulsating speakers throughout the studio, Ellie Logan snapped away, capturing every glorious shot.

CHAPTER 70

★ ★ ★

THREE DAYS LATER
SAN ANTONIO, TEXAS

THE MAGAZINE'S STAFF WRITER, STACY Cummings had been working for several weeks preparing the story that would be featured in the December issue of *High Style*. Kathryn had requested they use the private, scenic retreat of her ranch home to photograph the candid shots of her for the exposé.

It was nearly eleven and the house was empty. The hair and makeup crew had come and gone, and Kathryn had given the house staff the day off, explaining that she wanted the shoot to be natural and uninterrupted, like the conversation she was hoping to have with Ellie Logan.

A tray of hot tea and scones, along with a small gunmetal gray strongbox, was positioned on the coffee table. Inside the box was a weathered Bible, a rosary, and a holy medal of Saint Jude—treasures that had once belonged to Father Joe and that had been given to her by her grandmother. They were the only remaining relics of her past, along with the memories that all seemed to be flooding her mind with clarity at that very moment. Two Polaroids of Ellie as a newborn, taken at the hospital just minutes after Kathryn had brought her into the world, only to hand her over to the nameless, but blissful couple had been a later addition. And lastly, there was a note written to Ellie by Kathryn on the day she was born. It was still sealed, never having been opened, resting there in the bottom of the box.

Everything was there. Today, the only thing that mattered was securing a place, however remote, in her daughter's life. The only question being, was it possible? After so many years—and after the reaction she had at the photo shoot—she wondered, would she have the strength to go through with it? Was it even fair to Ellie to do so?

A sedan pulled up to the entrance and slowed to read the address on the gatepost. Then it pulled gingerly onto the stone-paved driveway. Kathryn's heart quickened as she watched her daughter get out of the car and approach the house.

- END -

ABOUT THE AUTHOR
★ ★ ★

JAMIE COLLINS WRITES LARGER THAN life women's fiction that is fun, sexy, and far from unforgettable. Her "Secrets and Stilettos" series is binge-worthy reading about the fast-track world of media and entertainment. As a former model/actress, she infuses her stories with Hollywood grit, sizzle, and heat reminiscent of the great women's fiction writers (Jackie Collins, Sidney Sheldon, and Olivia Goldsmith) of decades past on which she cut her writing chops reading and emulating their iconic styles. Collins brings a fresh, modern-day take on the throwback pocket novel tomes that defined an era of extravagance and excess in exchange for a world where women are more powerful, smart, and driven than ever. Collins' stilettos have been everywhere from nightclubs in Japan to the Playboy mansion, to dinner with a Sinatra. Her aim is to delight and entertain readers of women's fiction everywhere.

Check out Jamie Collins' website for more information about the books in her "Secrets and Stilettos" series at **www.jamiecollinsauthor.com**. Sign up to her mailing list to stay in the know and take the opportunity to join her **Stilettos Street Team** and become a part of the journey. There's nothing like a walk, in stilettos!

Follow Jamie Collins on Twitter, Facebook, and Instagram.

BOOKS BY JAMIE COLLINS